Also by Erle Stanley Gardner
Published by Ballantine Books:

The Case of the
Vagabond Virgin

Erle Stanley Gardner

BALLANTINE BOOKS • NEW YORK

First Ballantine Books Edition: April 1982
Second Printing: October 1983

PB 83-418

Cast of Characters

The Case of the
Vagabond Virgin

1

DELLA STREET, Perry Mason's confidential secretary, said, "John Addison is on the phone, Chief. He's so excited he's sputtering."

"John Racer Addison?"

"Yes. The department store man. He sounds as though he's about to explode into the telephone."

Mason nodded toward the telephone, said, "Tell Gertie to switch him over here," and picked up his desk telephone.

The click of the connection was followed by Addison's voice in a steady monotone, "Hello, hello. Hello, Mason? For God's sake, give me Mason! Put him on. This is a matter of the greatest importance. Get him on the line! Mason. Mason! Where the hell is Mason?"

The lawyer interrupted the monologue. "Good morning, Mr. Addison."

"Mason?"

"Yes."

"Thank heavens! Thought you'd never get on the line. Too many damn secretaries, telephone operators and what not! Too much of this damn, 'Put-your-party-on-the-line-business.' This thing's important. Can't wait around all day. Been trying to get you . . ."

"If it's that important," Mason said, "you'd better tell me what it is and make your complaint about the telephone service later."

"Mason, I want to ask you a question."

"Go right ahead."

"I don't want you to laugh at me."

"All right."

"And—dammit, I don't want you to think I've been associating with the wrong class of women. I haven't. This is a nice girl, a sweet little thing, pure and fresh . . ."

"What's the question?" Mason interrupted.

"Mason, can you put a virgin in jail as a vagrant?"

"Well," Mason said, smiling into the telephone, "that's something like the receipe for cooking the rabbit pie."

"No, no, I mean it. No kidding. Seriously speaking, they've got a sweet young girl in jail. Damnable outrage! Charged as a vagrant. What the hell's a vagrant? I thought the term only applied to . . ."

"In this state," Mason said, "the term vagrant is a catchall for everything the lawmakers couldn't list elsewhere. A Peeping Tom is a vagrant. A person who wanders about the streets at late or unusual hours of the night without any visible or lawful business is a vagrant. A person who lodges in a barn, shed, shop, outhouse, or other place without the permission of the owner is a vagrant. A person who . . ."

"Well, they've got this girl arrested as a vagrant and it's a damn outrage!" Addison said. "The idea of charging a nice girl with being a vagrant. It makes me sick. You know how to handle these things, Mason. Get her out. Go to it. Send me the bill."

"What's the girl's name?"

"Veronica Dale."

"Where is she now?"

"City jail."

"Know anything about her?"

"I know that she's no vagrant. She's a nice girl."

"Know what she looks like?"

"Certainly I know what she looks like. She's a nice, refined young woman, platinum blonde, hair like a halo, delicate, fragile-looking, smooth complexion, good figure —well, dammit, Mason, you know what I mean. Easy on the eyes. Rather plain, cheap clothes, but respectable. Definitely respectable! She was staying at the Rockaway Hotel and the police picked her up and threw her in as a vagrant. Damned outrage. I want her out!"

"May I use your name to—?"

"Good God, NO! Keep me out of it. Appear in the case as the lawyer. Just go down there and tell her . . . Well, just tell her you're her lawyer. That's all. Get the thing fixed up."

"How shall I fix it up?"

"Any way you want to. Only don't have her plead guilty. Put up bail. Demand a jury trial. Raise the devil with them, Mason. I know you don't monkey with small stuff, but make this big. Send me a bill, but get on the job fast. It takes speed in this case. Give it everything you've got. That's the law for you! Read the paper any morning and find four dozen assorted crimes committed during the night. Then the police go around picking on sweet young girls and making vagrants out of them. Dammit Mason, don't sit there talking when there's work to be done! Get down to the jail and get that girl out."

"I didn't want to interrupt you by hanging up, Mr. Addison," Mason said dryly.

"You're not interrupting me," Addison yelled. "I'm trying to get some action! I want somebody on the job. I want . . ."

"Exactly," Mason interrupted. "Good-by, Mr. Addison."

He dropped the receiver into place and grinned at Della Street. "I will now disrupt the morning's work, Della, to jump in a taxicab, dash down to the jail and enter the lists on behalf of a vagrant who is charged with being a . . . No, I mean a virgin who is charged with being a vagrant."

"Careful with your words," Della Street laughed. "The way you say it might make quite a difference."

"It might, at that," Mason agreed.

2

■

THE MATRON BROUGHT Veronica Dale into the visitor's room.

Mason regarded her curiously.

He saw a young woman who looked childish in her innocence, a platinum blonde with a poker face, wide blue eyes, thin, flawless skin and a good figure. Her thoughts, if any, were definitely not reflected in her face or eyes. The doll-like beauty would appeal to some men as unspoiled innocence, but a police officer on the prowl might well have mistaken her striking appearance for carefully planned man bait. One thing was certain, this girl would never be inconspicuous. She might have been anywhere from seventeen to twenty-five years of age.

"Hello," she said.

She was as artlessly friendly as a young puppy.

"Good morning," Mason said. "I'm Perry Mason, an attorney. I'm here to represent you."

"That's nice. How did you know I was here?"

"A friend told me."

"Your friend?" she asked.

"Perhaps *your* friend."

She shook her head. "I haven't any, not in this city," and then she added casually, "I haven't been here long enough."

"Well, I'm going to get you out of here. Can you tell me what happened?"

She said, "I was staying at the Rockaway Hotel. I went out to take a walk. I walked up the street for a while. Then I walked back. I didn't have anything in particular to do and then this man came up and wanted to know what I was doing, and I told him it was none of

12

his business. He pulled back his coat and showed me his badge and the first thing I knew I was being bustled into a car and they charged me with vagrancy."

"You must have been doing something," Mason said.

"I wasn't doing a thing."

Mason said, "According to the records, you were on the streets without visible means of support; you were apparently soliciting. The arresting officer said you told him you were simply walking the streets."

"Well, I wasn't going to tell him where I was staying and have him making a lot of trouble. It's none of his business. He wanted to know what I was doing and I told him I was walking. He wanted to know where I was staying and I told him I didn't have any place to stay, and he wanted to know how much money I had and I told him that was none of his business. And then he said I was doing something—well, something that I wasn't!"

Mason said, "Okay, I've put up bail in the sum of two hundred dollars for you and I'll enter a plea of not guilty. I don't think they'll do anything more about it. If you were staying at the Rockaway Hotel and have personal belongings there in the room, I don't think there'll be anything more to it."

"Well, I was staying there. I can prove it."

Mason said, "Okay. You're getting out on bail. I'll meet you outside." He signaled to the matron that the interview was over.

Harry Bend, the arresting officer, who was on night duty and who was losing time out of his day's sleep to appear as a witness against four or five arrests he had made the previous night, regarded Mason wearily.

"Hell, I don't know," he said irritably. "The dame was marching up and down the street and she didn't look like a professional, but . . . shucks, I was afraid she'd get herself in trouble somewhere and wind up in a vacant lot with one of her stockings tied around her neck. She gave me the eye. It may not have been a come-on, but it was an eye. I asked her what she was doing and she told me she wasn't doing anything. I asked her where she was staying, and she said she didn't have any place to stay. She didn't have any money. She didn't have any friends.

She was just walking around. I really didn't have anything on her, but there wasn't much else I could do."

"Soliciting?" Mason asked.

"She was looking them over. I didn't see her give any of them a come-on. I started questioning her mostly because she looked out of place. From her answers, I figured she was a good-looking kid who'd had trouble and decided to take what she thought was the easy way. I was afraid she'd wind up as a corpse."

"Well," Mason said, "she tells me she had a room at the Rockaway Hotel, that she'd just checked in, that she'd gone out to take a walk."

"Well, why the hell didn't she tell *me* that? I'd have given her a word of warning and that would have been all there was to it."

"She thought you were insulting, said you rubbed her the wrong way."

"So she went to spend the night in jail," Bend said. "Phooey! That doesn't make sense to me. I'll bet you five bucks she never was near the Rockaway Hotel. If she was, she'd been there a while and was hustling. Still, the Rockaway's a straight place. I don't get it."

Mason said, "I thought perhaps you'd take a ride up there with us."

"Why should I ride up there? I've got work to do. Let her tell it to the judge."

Mason said suavely, "If she *is* a respectable young woman who had a room at a hotel and was minding her own business and you picked her up on a vagrancy charge, it might be just as well if the matter never came to trial. After all, she's an attractive young girl and she has friends."

"Friends?"

"Yes."

"The hell she does!"

Mason said, "I'm here."

Bend suddenly regarded him with a puzzled appraisal. "Damned if you ain't!" he said with sudden incredulity in his voice. "Say, how did a high-priced lawyer like you come to be mixed into a case like this?"

Mason shrugged his shoulders.

14

Bend gave a low whistle, then after a moment said, "When do you want me to go?"

"I'm getting her out on bail," Mason said. "She should be here right away. I thought perhaps if you checked on the evidence with me, you'd be in a position to corroborate anything we might find."

"I'll check on it all right," Bend said grimly. "My other stuff has all gone over. All pleaded guilty. I'll just take a look at this, Mr. Perry Mason. And the more I think about it, the funnier it sounds."

"Come on," Mason said, "let's go."

They picked up Veronica Dale at the discharge room of the jail. She was signing a receipt for the manila envelope which contained her personal belongings as Mason and the officer entered. She looked up, smiled at Mason, saw the plain-clothes officer, regarded him for a moment with an expressionless countenance and then said, "Hello."

"Hello," Bend said and added inanely, "how are you feeling this morning?"

"Fine."

Bend said, "Mr. Mason tells me you were staying at the Rockaway Hotal."

"I've got a room there."

"Why didn't you tell me that?"

"It wasn't any of your business. I didn't like the way you acted."

"You'd have saved yourself a lot of trouble."

"I don't care. I didn't like your manner."

"Well, you certainly went to a lot of inconvenience to register the fact that you didn't like my approach."

She said, "It was a matter of principle. I try to like people. I couldn't like you, because you haven't any respect for womanhood."

Before Bend could recover from that one, Mason said, "Come on, Veronica. We're going to take a ride with Mr. Bend. Let's not insult him or try to pick a fight with him. After all, he was only trying to do his job."

"I don't like his job."

"Neither do I," Bend said bitterly, and then added,

"respect for womanhood! If you could see what I see, sister. . . . Hell!"

"Come on," Mason said. "His car is outside. We're going to take you to the hotel."

"Why?"

"I want Mr. Bend to see that you are registered there at the hotel and to see that your room actually was rented."

"All right," she said.

They left the jail. "You got a car here?" Bend asked Mason.

"No. I came in a taxi."

"Okay. We'll go up in the police car. How're you feeling, sister?"

"All right."

"Did you sleep?"

"Of course."

"Everything okay?"

"Yes."

"No hard feelings personally?"

"I don't like you, that's all. I have no hard feelings."

Bend look at her curiously. "I can't make you out. How old are you?"

"Just eighteen."

"The hell you are!"

She said nothing.

Mason said, "Come on, Bend, let's go."

Harry Bend drove the car to the Rockaway Hotel, slammed it angrily into the curb, climbed out of the door and pushed his way through the revolving door of the hotel. Mason, paying but scant regard to his client, was immediately behind the officer. Veronica Dale brought up the rear.

Bend marched up to the desk. "You got a Veronica Dale registered here?"

The clerk looked at him apprehensively. "Why? Is anything the matter? Is . . . ?"

"You got a Veronica Dale registered here?"

The clerk looked at the register and said, "Yes."

"What number?"

"309."

16

Bend jerked his thumb over his shoulder toward Veronica Dale. "Is this the party?"

"I don't know," the clerk said. "I came on duty at seven o'clock this morning. The room was rented after six o'clock last night. That's after I go off duty."

"You don't know whether this is the jane or not?"

"No."

Bend jerked one of the registration cards from the leather holder, turned it over so that the blank back of the card was uppermost, pulled the desk pen from the holder, and handed it to the young woman. "Write your name," he said.

She wrote "Veroncia Dale" in a firm, feminine hand.

Bend put the pen back in the container, said to the clerk, "Okay, let's take a look at her registration."

The clerk brought out the original registration card. The three men bent over the singatures, comparing them.

"There's no doubt but what they're the same," Mason said.

Bend said, "Say, look at this card, buddy. No address on it. Just the word 'transient.' How come? Do you let people register that way and get rooms?"

The clerk said, "Just a minute. There's a notation on the edge of this card."

He observed the penciled notation, then looked at a memo book said, "As it happens, this particular room was reserved by Mr. Putnam, the manager of the hotel. He telephoned instructions to have the room reserved for Veronica Dale and said that if she happened to have no baggage it was quite all right, that the room was to be reserved for her and . . ."

"When did this call come in?" Bend asked.

"About nine-thirty. That was about fifteen minutes before Miss Dale checked in."

"You got enough rooms so you can deal them out like that?" Bend asked suspiciously.

"When the manager says so," the clerk told him. "We always keep a couple in reserve for emergencies. This was an emergency room. Officially we were all filled up."

17

Bend turned to Veronica Dale. "Do you know this man, Putnam?" he asked.

She shook her head.

Bend said wearily to the clerk, "Give me a key. We're going up."

The clerk reached in the box and handed them the key to Room 309.

Veronica Dale walked over to the elevators with them, as calmly and naturally as though they were trusted friends of the family. Harry Bend snapped the floor number at the operator and the cage shot upward.

Bend stopped in the corridor just outside the elevator. His eyes were crafty. "Which way?" he asked Veronica Dale.

"Left," she answered with no hesitation.

They walked down the hall to the left. Near the end of the corridor they came to Room 309. Bend inserted the key and opened the door.

The room was fresh, the bed undisturbed. A small handbag stood on the baggage rack, apparently in the same position as it had been placed by a bellboy.

Bend calmly walked over, snapped back the catches on the handbag, opened it and looked at the meager assortment of feminine wearing apparel.

"This stuff yours?"

"Yes."

"You've got a driving license?"

"No. I don't drive."

"Social security number?"

"No."

"Any identification?"

"I have some cards."

"What are you going to do," Mason asked angrily, "arrest her all over again?"

"I'd like to," Bend said. "There's something cockeyed here."

"I fail to see it," Mason announced indignantly. "This young woman has a room in a local hotel. She has baggage. She goes out on the street looking for a place to eat and while she's trying to size up a suitable restau-

18

rant, you pounce on her, brow-beat her, and accuse her of soliciting. Naturally her feelings toward you are somewhat less than friendly and . . ."

"Oh, save it for the jury!" Bend said. "The hell with it."

"You going to suggest a dismissal?"

"You going to sue for false arrest?"

"Not the way the thing stands. You don't want to sue, do you, Veronica?"

"Of course not. It was a matter of principle with me, that's all."

Bend thought for a moment, then said, "Guess I'll dismiss."

"Okay," Mason said. "I'll take your word for it. I won't bother to do anything more about it. After the charge is dismissed, they can mail back the two hundred dollars I put up for bail."

Bend studied him dubiously for a moment, then said, "And I suppose someone's paying you a five hundred dollar fee."

Mason smiled and said nothing.

Bend grunted, turned on his heel and walked back down the corridor.

The girl walked over to the open traveling bag, snapped it shut and said, "These officers don't give a girl any privacy. You want to close the door?"

"I do *not*," Mason said, "and you don't want me to. You watch your step from now on. Whenever you have a man in the room, keep the door open."

"Why?"

"It's house rules."

"What difference does it make?"

"It might make a lot."

"I'm hungry."

"Didn't you have breakfast?"

"Just a little coffee and some mush. I could hardly eat the mush. Only gagged a spoonful or two down."

"You got any money?"

"A little."

"How much?"

"I think around a dollar and twelve cents."

Mason said, "Do you know a man by the name of . . ."

"Yes?" she asked as Mason broke off.

"Nothing," Mason said.

He opened his wallet, took out two twenties and a ten and handed it to her.

"What's this for?" she asked.

Mason said, "Don't bother about it. I'll put it on my bill as expenses."

"You mean that's for me?"

"Yes."

Her gratitude was childlike in its simplicity. She came toward him, put her hands on his arm, looked up at him with round innocent eyes. She puckered inviting lips.

"But *why,*" she said softly, "should *you* do this for me?"

Mason said, "I'm damned if I know," gently disengaged her hand and walked out of the room.

From a telephone booth in the lobby he called the number of the big department store on Broadway and asked for John Racer Addison.

The feminine voice on the other end of the telephone said, "I'll give you Mr. Addison's office." The connection clicked, and another feminine voice said, "Mr. Addison's office."

"Mr. Perry Mason," the lawyer said. "I want to talk with Mr. Addison."

"Just a moment, please. I'll connect you with Mr. Addison's secretary."

A few moments later a third feminine voice came over the line. "Put your party on, please."

"I'm on," Mason said. "I'm Perry Mason. I want to talk with Mr. Addison."

"Is this Mr. Mason?"

"Yes."

"Mr. *Perry* Mason?"

"Yes."

"You're on the line?"

"Exactly," Mason said.

"Just a moment. I'll get Mr. Addison."

A few seconds later Addison's voice came booming over the wire. "Hello, Mason. Where are you?"

"I'm in a booth at the Rockaway Hotel. I've been thinking over your complaint about not being able to get me on the telephone unless you go through a lot of red tape . . ."

"Yes, yes. Where's the girl? What happened? Where's—?"

"She's upstairs in her room here at the hotel," Mason said. "Room 309."

"Yes, yes, I know."

"Technically she's out on bail," Mason said, "but I have the assurance of the arresting officer that the complaint will be withdrawn and the case dismissed. Anything else?"

"No, no. That's fine! That's swell, Mason! That's good work. Very good work. Send me a bill. I knew I could depend on you! That's the sort of service I like, Mason."

"Under the circumstances," Mason said, "the bill will perhaps seem out of proportion to the importance . . ."

"No it won't! No it won't. Send me a bill. I'll send you a check. I'm glad you got her out."

"As a matter of curiosity," Mason said, "how long have you known Veronica Dale?"

"I don't know her," Addison said testily. "I've just met her. I don't want my name connected with it at all. I intended to tell you not to let her know who was hiring you, but you hung up on me. You . . ."

"I didn't let her know," Mason said. "Your name hasn't been mentioned. You did tell me not to let her know, and I didn't hang up on you."

"That's fine. That's fine. That's perfectly fine, Mason! Send me a bill."

"I will," Mason promised. "And here's something you can be thinking over. Either that girl is pretty dumb, or she tried hard to get herself arrested."

"What do you mean, Mason?"

"I'm not certain I know," the lawyer answered, "but I'm just telling you for what it's worth—either she's dumb or she tried pretty hard to get herself arrested."

21

"Bosh!" Addison snorted. "She's not dumb, she's naive."

"Perhaps you're the one who's naive," Mason warned and hung up.

3
■

                    DELLA STREET SLIPPED unobtrusively into Mason's private office.

The lawyer looked up from his work.

"Mrs. Laura Mae Dale to see you."

"What about?" Mason asked.

Della Street smiled. "She says it's highly personal and confidential."

"Well, tell her to give you an idea of what it's about if she wants to see me," Mason said irritably, "and then make an appointment for . . ."

"Mrs. Laura Mae Dale," Della Street said archly, "is Veronica's mother."

"Veronica?" Mason said, frowning, striving to recall the name. "Veronica. She . . . Oh, yes, the incarcerated virgin."

"Exactly."

A grin spread over Mason's face. "Do you know, Della, I rather thought there might be a sequel to that case. Did we send Addison a bill?"

"Yes, five hundred dollars. The statement went out this morning. Addison's secretary rang up and asked for an immediate bill."

"What does Mrs. Dale look like?" Mason asked.

"Rather capable. She's about forty-five years old and seems to have a lot of poise. She's plainly dressed but they're good clothes and she wears them well."

Mason said, "Bring her in, by all means, Della. Let's see what she wants."

Mrs. Laura Mae Dale, escorted into Mason's private office by Della Street, moved with swift efficiency. She might have been accustomed to offices. She certainly was accustomed to meeting people.

"How do you do, Mr. Mason? I've heard so much about you. And you were *so* nice to my daughter."

She glided across the office to shake Mason's hand.

Mason sized her up.

She weighed perhaps a hundred and thirty pounds and wore her simple clothes with an air of calm assurance. She might have been nervous but she had quite evidently learned self-control and poise. She seemed to know exactly what she intended to do and how she intended to do it.

"Sit down," Mason invited.

"Thank you. I want to express my appreciation for what you did for Veronica."

"Nothing at all," Mason assured her.

"It certainly *was* something. It was splendid! To think that a big lawyer like you would drop your business to befriend an innocent young girl. How did she happen to call on *you*, Mr. Mason?"

Mason said, "That's a matter I don't feel free to discuss. So any surmises you care to make must necessarily be met with a simple 'No comment.' "

"You don't have to be cautious with me, Mr. Mason."

"No comment," Mason said.

Her smile was gracious. "Veronica is such a nice girl, Mr. Mason, but *terribly* impulsive."

The lawyer nodded.

"She wanted to start out for herself, and she started hitchhiking. Of course, *I* didn't have any idea she was leaving. She knew I'd put my foot down. She left me a note, just saying that she was going out to make her own way in the world and that she'd get in touch with me when she became established."

"And you followed her here?" Mason asked.

"That's right."

"How did you know she was here?"

Mrs. Dale smiled. "Children are *so* simple. Even when they think they're being inscrutable they're like open books. Veronica had been talking about coming here for a couple of months. Then, all of a sudden, she quit talking about it. Heavens, the child was as transparent as window glass."

"When did you get here, Mrs. Dale?"

She smiled indulgently. "Not until the morning after Veronica arrived. Veronica hitchhiked and so did I. But she made better time than I did."

"How did you find out what had happened? In other words, why did you come to me?"

She said, smiling, "I made a round of the hotels, trying to find out where Veronica was registered. I tried the cheaper ones first. I had a hotel directory with rates and all that information. Finally I found the right hotel, the Rockaway. Of course, Mr. Mason, I didn't want Veronica to know I was following her. She would have been furious, but, after all, she's my only chick, and I wanted to make certain she was all right."

Mason nodded.

"So, I rang her room," Mrs. Dale said. "I just wanted to hear her voice on the line and then I would have hung up, but she didn't answer. So then I got in touch with one of the chambermaids and a little bribery did a lot. She told me she thought the girl had been in trouble, that she'd returned to the hotel with an officer and with Mr. Mason, the famous lawyer. You really *are* famous, Mr. Mason. The chambermaid recognized you from your pictures. Well, of course, with that as a clue I found out all about her. I felt terribly about it, Mr. Mason, but there's no use worrying about water that's gone under the bridge. Never cry over spilled milk, that's my motto. I have a philosophy of living my life from day to day. I've tried to teach Veronica to be the same way."

"How old is she?" Mason asked.

"That girl's barely eighteen, but you wouldn't believe it."

"Eighteen is rather young."

"It certainly is, but Veronica is a nice girl, a level-headed girl, and you can trust her *that* way."

24

Mason said, "She looked older than eighteen to me."

"Doesn't she?" Mrs. Dale beamed. "But that's all she is, just barely eighteen."

"You're going to talk with her?" Mason asked.

"Heavens, no! I wouldn't let her know I was here for anything on earth. I just followed along to keep an eye on her and see that she didn't get into any trouble. I thought she was a bit young to go out by herself in the world, but if she could make it all right, I wanted to—well, I didn't want to do anything that would interfere with her career or her independence."

Mason's nod was vague encouragement to go on.

"You see, Mr. Mason, I think that's the way people learn. That's the way I learned, anyway. I started out for myself, only I *do* wish I'd had a mother to keep an eye on me and help me . . . Well, that's water under the bridge. Never cry about spilled milk. Sufficient for the day is the evil thereof and all that stuff. Don't you think so, Mr. Mason?"

Again the lawyer nodded.

"Well, it looks very much to me as though Veronica can make her own way now. She's landed a job in a department store—thirty-one dollars a week."

"I see you have pretty accurate information," Mason said.

"Heavens, yes. I've been keeping tabs on her in a roundabout way. She is a peculiar girl. She's friendly like a puppy. She'll talk to people who are friendly. Take a chambermaid for instance. She'll tell everything she knows to a friendly chambermaid. But that officer, the way he approached her—why, Mr. Mason, she wouldn't have told him a thing even if he'd tortured her."

"You're going to stay here?" Mason asked.

"Well, I have some business of my own, a little restaurant that I have to run, just a small town in Indiana, a place you'd never have heard of. Now that I know Veronica is all right, I'll go back, but I want to pay your bill, Mr. Mason. I can't begin to thank you."

Mason gave the subject a frowning concentration for a moment, then said, "Well, if you really want to pay me, you can give me fifty dollars to square things up."

"Nonsense, Mr. Mason. You put up bail money. You're a high-priced lawyer. You . . ."

"That's all right. I'm going to get the bail back. They've dismissed the case."

"But, Mr. Mason, it's absurd to think that you could do anything like that for fifty dollars. Five hundred dollars would be more like it."

"No," Mason said, "fifty dollars will be all right under the circumstances."

Mrs. Dale opened her purse, took out a single blank check and a fountain pen. "May I have something to write on?"

Della Street said, "Right this way," and seated Mrs. Dale at her secretarial desk.

Mrs. Dale filled in the bank with pen and ink, the Second Mechanics' National of Indianapolis, made a check payable to Perry Mason in the amount of one hundred and fifty dollars and then having signed it in a firm hand, wrote on the back, "In full payment for services rendered in the case of my daughter Veronica Dale."

"There," she said, blotting the check. "I think *that* will do it. That's more like it. My conscience wouldn't let me settle for any fifty dollar fee. Fifty dollars to Perry Mason! Bosh!"

She cocked her head on one side, surveying the check, then nodded and passed it over to Della Street.

Della Street wordlessly handed the check over to Perry Mason.

"And may I have a receipt?" Mrs. Dale asked.

"The check will be sufficient receipt the way you've made it out," Mason said.

"But I think it's more businesslike to have a receipt. I would really prefer . . ."

Mason said to Della Street, "Make out a receipt, Della. Show that we have received a check drawn on the Second Mechanics' National in the sum of one hundred and fifty dollars, that when this check is *paid* it will constitute payment in full for services rendered Veronica Dale to date."

Della Street nodded, placed duplicate receipt blanks

in the typewriter and had just started to type when the phone on her desk rang.

She picked up, said, "Hello," listened for a few moments, frowned, glanced dubiously at Perry Mason, then at Mrs. Dale. She said into the telephone, "It's impossible right at the moment. We'll call you back in a few moments . . . Yes, a very short time."

She hung up, scribbled a note, then went on and finished typing the receipt.

When she handed Mason the receipt, the note on top of the receipt read, "Addison phoned that he has to see you *right* away. He seems terribly upset."

Mason nodded, crumpled the note, tossed it into the wastebasket, signed the receipt and passed the paper over to Mrs. Dale. "I think you'll find this is in order," he said, "and I'm afraid I'll have to ask you to excuse me. I'm terribly busy and have to call a client."

"Oh, I understand," she said, getting to her feet. "And, thank you *so* much, Mr. Mason."

"You'd better leave your address with . . ."

"Oh, but I did that already. I gave it to your receptionist at the switchboard."

"Okay, thanks," Mason said, getting to his feet.

"And you won't mention my visit to anyone?"

"Not to Veronica?"

"Heavens, no. I don't want that girl to know I'm anywhere in the city. If she thought—well, you know, she'd think I was spying on her. She's very high-strung."

"Suppose," Mason said, "Veronica should come in and want to pay me?"

Mrs. Dale thought that over for a moment, then said, "Just tell her that the fee has been paid by a friend, Mr. Mason. You don't need to say any more than that, simply that it was paid by a friend. And now, Mr. Mason, I simply *mustn't* take any more of your time."

She bowed, nodded smilingly to Della Street, and sailed out of the office.

Mason said, "She certainly dug up a lot of information in a short time, Della. Paul Drake should have her working as a detective."

"I suppose she really pumped that chambermaid," Della Street said. "Shall I get John Addison on the phone?"

Mason nodded.

Della Street rushed the call through, then said, "Here he is, Mr. Mason."

Mason picked up the phone, said, "You calling me, Addison?"

"Yes, yes. I have to see you right away. At once!"

"Can you tell me what it's about?"

"Not over the phone. Not when I'm talking from the office. Dammit, no. I want to see you. I don't want to have to wait in your office. I want to come over and dash right in."

"Come on and dash," Mason invited. "Incidentally, there has just been an interesting development in connection with the case of your friend, Veronica . . ."

"Dammit, Mason," Addison shouted over the phone, "don't keep referring to her as my friend!"

"Isn't she?"

"No," Addison shouted. "I'm coming up. I want to see you when I get there!"

And Addison slammed up the receiver at his end without so much as waiting to say good-by.

4

GERTIE, the good-natured receptionist, tiptoed into Perry Mason's private office.

"Gosh, Mr. Mason," she said in an awed whisper, "Mr. Addison is out there and he's fit to be tied."

Mason grinned. "He's accustomed to having his own way about ninety-nine per cent of the time. Tell him to sit down."

"He won't sit down, Mr. Mason. He paces the floor and glares. He told me to go tell you he was there and wanted to see you right away."

Mason said, "Keep him waiting a couple of minutes,

just for the principle of the thing, and then send him in."

John Racer Addison presented an incongruous appearance as he entered the room three minutes later.

Quite evidently a man accustomed to conducting himself with a bearing of authoritative dignity, he was now so upset that his careful measured stride had given place to quick, short, waddling steps as he hurried toward Mason.

As Gertie expressed it afterward in a tête-à-tête with Della Street, "He reminded me of a goose trying to go some place in a hurry and not really getting anywhere, just wagging his tail feathers faster than usual."

Addison was a chunky, thick-chested individual who paid careful attention to his clothes. Having studied how to make people come to him, the big department store owner was in uncharted waters now that it became necessary for him to make the approach.

"Hello, Addison," Mason said, walking around the desk to extend his hand.

Addison all but brushed the greeting aside with a perfunctory handshake. "Mason, I'm in the devil of a mess—the very devil of a mess!"

"Sit down," Mason said. "Let's have it."

Addison glared at Della Street.

"You know Miss Street, my secretary," Mason said, "She sits in on all my conferences, makes notes and keeps the facts straight. You can trust her absolutely."

"I don't want to trust anyone," Addison said. "I've done too much of that already."

Mason merely smiled and sat behind his desk, waiting for Addison to go on.

The silent tension was too much for the department store owner.

"Oh, all right," he said, "have it your own way. Dammit, everyone seems to be having his own way these days."

Della Street held an unobtrusive pencil over her open notebook.

"Just what seems to be the trouble?" Mason asked.

"Mason, I'm being blackmailed."

"By whom? For how much? And over what?"

"A man I've never heard of before, chap by the name of Dundas—George W. Dundas."

Mason smiled and said, "George W., eh? I presume Mr. Dundas' fond mother christened him George Washington, hoping that he would turn out to be another Father of his Country, in place of which he turns out to be a blackmailer."

"As a matter of fact," Addison said, "I believe his middle name is Whittley. The man writes, I believe, a newspaper column under the by-line of George Whittley Dundas, a gossip column that appears, as I understand it, in one of the tabloids. I have a specimen column here which I've cut out for you."

Addison's well-manicured hand nervously jerked a wallet from the inside of his vest pocket and extracted a folded section of newspaper.

"Oh yes," Mason said, his eyes glancing down the column. "One of these gossip things making its success by innuendoes." He selected a passage at random and read, "What young married woman has recently been trotting around the night spots with a 'friend of the family?' And does hubby realize that a Reno lawyer has already been consulted?"

Mason looked up and said, "This stuff makes nice reading for persons of a certain type of mind. You can't tell whether the stuff is true or not. If you happen to know someone who's a target for gossip it's all right, but this 'young married woman,' whose name is discreetly not mentioned, may well be only a figment of the imagination of George Whittley Dundas. What does Dundas want with you?"

"I'm not dealing directly with Dundas," Addison said, "but with a man by the name of Eric Hansell who says he's leg-man for Dundas and gets most of the facts Dundas uses in his column."

Mason said, "That looks like a sweet blackmailing setup. If you come right down to it, you really haven't anything on Dundas. He can repudiate Hansell at any time."

"I suppose so, I suppose so," Addison said nervously. "I'm not interested in the mechanics of the thing. As far as I'm concerned, it's blackmail pure and simple."

"Suppose you tell me about it."

Addison crossed his left leg over his right knee, shifted his position, then nervously uncrossed his legs, then recrossed them, with the right leg over the left knee. "Dammit," he said, "I don't know how to start."

"Begin with the time you met this virgin," Mason said.

Addison was visibly startled. "Eh? What's that?"

"You heard me."

"How did you know she had anything to do with it?"

Mason merely smiled.

"Well," Addison said, "I suppose it's as good a place to begin as any other. It was about nine o'clock Tuesday night. I saw this young woman, with a light suitcase, standing by the side of the road. She wasn't using her thumb, but her attitude said very plainly that she was looking for a ride."

"You stopped?"

"At first I didn't. I assumed she would be some hardened old battle-ax, and I definitely didn't want to have anything to do with her. I drove by, but I glanced at her as I went by, and saw she was a young, sweet-looking girl. I simply couldn't leave her there where some unprincipled, irresponsible person might have picked her up and taken advantage of her. I stopped the car and backed up."

"She was properly grateful?"

"She was very sweet," Addison said.

"Go on," Mason commented dryly.

"Naturally," Addison said, "in picking up a young, unsophisticated, fresh, unspoiled woman of this type, one engages in conversation."

"All right, let's have the facts."

"At first there was a certain constraint," Addison said. "She was sizing me up. Her manner was somewhat diffident and cautious, a little uneasy. But I soon put her at her ease and convinced her she was riding with a man whose interest in her was purely a fatherly interest."

"Purely," Mason repeated tonelessly.

"Eh, what's that?"

"Go on."

"She was soon confiding in me freely, telling me her

31

story. She had a good mother, and she was fond of her mother. But the child was simply bored stiff with the small town where her mother lived. And it looked as though the girl never would get out of that deadly dull small-town environment."

"What sort of home life?" Mason asked.

"No home life at all. The father is dead. The mother runs a small restaurant lunch counter, some place about fifty miles from Indianapolis. It's too far to commute to see shows, yet near enough so most of the business flows into the big city, leaving this little town pretty static, or so I gathered from her conversation. She talked freely enough, once she got started. The child had to wait tables, wash dishes and help out. She found it a dreary monotony of small-town drudgery. All the really interesting young men have gone to the larger cities where there is more opportunity. Those who are left have no romance, no soul, no fire."

"She evidently made quite an impression on you."

"What makes you say that?" Addison snapped angrily.

"Because of the way you remember her words—no soul, no fire."

Addison glared.

"How old?" Mason asked.

"Eighteen."

"You sure?"

"Hell, no! How can I be *sure*. Am I supposed to have been there when she was born or . . ."

"See her driving license?"

"No. Hang it, Mason, I can't tell the age of a girl like that. Anywhere between sixteen and twenty-five she'd have me fooled."

"All right," Mason said, "what happened with you and Veronica Dale?"

"Well, she told me very frankly that she had decided to go out in the world and seek her fortune, try and get a job somewhere and be independent. Then she was going to write to her mother and tell her mother where she was."

"Did she give you her mother's name at that time?"

"No, I didn't find out too much about the details there. You see, it was a short ride, only twenty miles, and I was more concerned with what she intended to do in the future, that is, what her plans were and where she intended to stay."

"She told you?"

"She admitted that she was rather short of actual cash and that she didn't have any particular plan. She was a young woman who felt self-reliant and in place of shunning the experiences of life, she seemed only too anxious to wade out and meet them halfway. It was—hang it, Mason, it was shocking to me. It frightened me. I've done so much planning in my life and worked so hard to get a feeling of established security that it was a shock to me to find this young girl looking forward to spending a night in a strange city where she knew no one, with hardly adequate funds to furnish her with a little food, let alone shelter."

"So you gave her money?"

"The problem was not that simple," Addison said. "There was the question of getting a room in any decent hotel. As you probably realize, Mason, it isn't simply a matter nowadays of walking into a hotel and getting a room. In the first place, hotels are rather unwilling to accept unescorted women when they don't know something about the guest's background. Then again, with all the willingness in the world, where reservations haven't been made for days, sometimes weeks, in advance, it's virtually impossible to secure decent accommodations."

"So what did you do?"

"So I stopped at one of the outlying service stations, made a call to a friend of mine, the manager of the Rockaway Hotel. I told him that I was having this young woman, Veronica Dale, inquire at his hotel for a room. I wanted him to be certain that a room was available, and he assured me that he would see to it she had proper accommodations. I told him, of course, that I would vouch for her."

"So then what did you do?"

"Then I returned to the automobile, drove the girl to the Rockaway Hotel and told her to go in and get herself a room. I stayed there, parked in front of the hotel until I saw that she had registered, and actually had a room. You know, Mason, in most of these hotels they keep one or two rooms, no matter how crowded they may be, for emergencies—in case there have been duplicate reservations, where the hotel might be liable for damages, or where some very influential customer comes in unexpectedly—any of the hundred and one emergencies that may show up."

"Then what?" Mason asked.

"Then I drove home, completely satisfied that I had done everything I could."

"You learned she'd been arrested for vagrancy?"

"I did."

"How?"

"The matron at the jail called me, said Veronica wished to have me notified, that she wouldn't let the call be put through the night before because she didn't want to bother me. Can you imagine that? A sweet, pure young thing spending a night in jail, simply because she . . ."

"How did she know who you were? Did you give this girl your card?"

"To be frank with you, Mason, I didn't. I felt ashamed of myself, but nevertheless there are certain precautions which a man in my position has to take. However, I presume she satisfied a perfectly natural curiosity. While I was telephoning from the service station, she must have read the registration slip that was on the steering post of the automobile and remembered my name and address. So she had the matron phone me."

"What time did you get this call telling you she was under arrest for vagrancy?"

"Just before I called you."

"All right," Mason said, "that apparently brings us up to date on that. I take it you haven't seen her since I arranged her release."

"Oh, but I have," Addison said. "I gave her a job. I called her up at the Rockaway and suggested she interview the personnel manager at the store."

"When did you do that?" Mason asked.

"I did that shortly after she was released from jail. You telephoned me from the lobby of the Rockaway Hotel, I believe, telling me that everything was fixed up and that the girl was in her room, so I telephoned back shortly after I received your call."

"You didn't tell me about that."

"I haven't talked with you since."

"I mean, you didn't tell me you were going to do it."

"Dammit, Mason, do I have to tell you every time I turn around?"

"It's sometimes advisable to tell your lawyer things."

"Hang it, Mason, you act as though this girl were poison or something!"

"You seem to have some trouble getting her *out* of your life."

"Don't talk like that. I tell you the girl's a pure, sweet, lovable child."

"Any blackmailing, I take it, is purely coincidental," Mason said.

"You're damn right it's coincidental," Addison rasped. "Wait until I tell you how it happened."

"That," Mason announced, "is what I'm waiting for."

"Well," Addison said, "when Veronica Dale called on me, I gave her a frank, fatherly talk. I told her that she couldn't expect to go drifting around the country, particularly at night, without having embarrassing experiences. I told her I didn't want to alarm her unnecessarily, but I called her attention to some of these sex murders that have been taking place around the country, and then I sent her down to see the head of my personnel department."

"And gave her a job?"

"I suppose she was put to work. The fact that she came to the personnel department with a card from me should assure her of a job. I naturally assumed it had. I didn't even bother to check up on it."

"So, as far as you know, she's working for you in your store right now."

"I would say so, yes."

"All right, what about Dundas?"

"Well, this man, Eric Hansell, called me up and said

he wanted to interview me in connection with a newspaper story, 'a little character sketch for one of the columnists,' was the way he expressed it. Well, you know, Mr. Mason, a man in my position cannot afford to offend the Press. I am not averse to publicity. I never have been."

"No," Mason said dryly.

"Well," Addison said, "the interview was entirely different from anything I had anticipated. Mr. Hansell turned out to be a red-headed, flippant young man of a type one is more accustomed to associate with race horse touts than with reputable newspaper people. I found him very disgusting and very impudent. He asked me a few questions about my life, my partner and my business affairs—impertinent, personal questions, asked with an air of arrogant impudence. And then when I was on the point of throwing him out, he wanted to know about my relationship with Veronica Dale.

"The thing absolutely flabbergasted me, Mason. This man seemed to have gone out of his way to get a lot of facts. He evidently knew that I had telephoned the manager of the Rockaway Hotel and went on to tell me that George Dundas was going to publish something about me in the gossip column and wanted to know if there was any truth to the rumor that I was intending to marry Veronica Dale, a young woman who had been established in a downtown hotel through my connections, and arrested for vagrancy that same night.

"I'm afraid I lost my temper, Mason. I shouted at him. I told him to get the hell out of there, and he merely scraped a match on the under side of my desk, lit a cigarette, looked at me patronizingly and said, 'Okay, Fatso, we'll run the story . . .' Imagine, Mason, in my own office, this young, insolent whippersnapper referred to *me* as *Fatso!*"

"A certain lack of respect," Mason said, carefully refraining from glancing at Della Street.

"Lack of respect!" Addison exclaimed. "It was the height of insolence!"

"So you threw him out?"

"Well," Addison said, "the situation became somewhat complicated. If Dundas should publish anything like that . . ."

"You'd sue the newspaper for libel," Mason said.

"But, Mason, there are certain damnable facts—that is, the facts themselves are innocent enough, but it's easy to see how they could be distorted. As Hansell pointed out, they could marshal a certain set of facts. I *had* brought Veronica Dale to town. I *had* telephoned the manager of a hotel, insisting that the young woman be given a room, stating that I would vouch for her. She *had* been arrested for vagrancy. I *had* hired my personal attorney to get her out on bail and see that the case was dismissed. Then I *had* given her employment in my store. I naturally wouldn't like to see those things in print. You can understand my position. It's innocent enough, but—well, there are those who would cock a cynical eyebrow at the whole thing. The sequence is unfortunate."

"It is, indeed," Mason commented.

"So," Addison said, "something has to be done, and done right away."

"How much does Eric Hansell want?"

"He didn't say. He's smart enough, all right. Money was never mentioned at all. Hansell merely said that he was getting facts for Dundas' column. That he did the leg-work for George Whittley Dundas; that he had this bunch of facts and he wanted to verify them. He wanted an interview with me. He wanted me to state definitely whether or not certain things were true."

"And what did you state?"

"I told him that any insinuation that my interest in Veronica Dale was other than an impersonal, fatherly interest was the height of absurdity. And then when he asked me either to confirm or deny certain facts, I saw that I was getting into rather hot water. I told him that I had no further time to give him, and kicked him out of the office."

"Then what?" Mason asked, "You telephoned me immediately?"

"No, Mason, I didn't."

"Why not?"

"I didn't know just what to do," Addison said. "I paced the floor there in the office for—dammit, I don't know, it may have been an hour. I hated to come to you with this thing more than I ever hated to do anything in my life. I feel as though you're sitting back there laughing at me. You have that smug attitude of—dammit, Mason, I tell you you'd have done the same thing under similar circumstances. You know you would!"

"Your interview with Hansell took place when?"

"I would say about an hour and a half ago."

"He left a card?" Mason asked.

"No, he gave me a telephone number. Of course, Mason, the damn thing is blackmail, but it's handled so cleverly you can't prove it's blackmail. Here's the number."

Mason took the folded paper Addison fished from his pocket, turned it over and over in his fingers. "Of course," he said, "since this is plain blackmail, Hansell probably isn't any pure white lily. He knows his way around and he's done this stuff before. He probably has a criminal record."

"But," Addison said, *"my* hands are tied, Mason. There's nothing I can do. I can't afford to get into any controversy. The facts could be distorted by my business rivals and—hang it, the thing would be terrible. My partner, for instance, would simply hit the ceiling."

"Your partner?"

"Edgar Z. Ferrell."

"Where is he now?"

"Fortunately, he's on his vacation. Ferrell is the conservative member of the firm. He's—well, he's definitely not broad or liberal."

"Something of a stick?" Mason asked.

"I wouldn't care to be quoted."

"No one's going to quote you. You're talking to your lawyer."

"Something of a stick," Addison said with feeling. "The damn fool's a stump! An old-fashioned, deeply rooted, decayed stump, full of worms, with ants crawling all over the bark, and bird droppings on the top. As far as the business is concerned, I've been carrying him on my back for five years. The man hasn't had a constructive idea or a decent suggestion in all that time.

"He's had training as an accountant and he spends his time puttering around with the books, making graphs, sticking his nose into accounts, auditing first this, then that, making a plain damn nuisance of himself.

"In a business like ours, a man can't waste too much time in analyzing. It's fine to know what departments have made the most money, but, after all, that stuff is post-mortem. An executive should be on the firing line, getting ideas, not dissecting the accounting corpses of last year's mistakes."

Mason smiled. "I take it that your partner, from time to time, submits figures, statements and graphs, showing where your ideas have lost money?"

Addison's face reddened. "He pounces on every mistake like a hawk on a sitting duck. He never takes any responsibility himself. Oh, hang it, what's the use? The man's a sponge, a parasite, a thorn in the flesh, but I've had too much from him. I simply couldn't stand to have him read some juicy item in a scandal column and come into my office holding the clipping in his hand and going 'tut-tut.' I'll pay. I'll have to pay."

"How did he acquire an interest in the business?"

"He inherited his father's stock. At the time, I should have bought him out, but I felt that I needed a younger man in the business. Because he was younger in years, I thought naturally he would have more flexibility, more receptivity, more energy, more initiative, more adaptability."

"And in place of that?"

"He had nothing. A hidebound, narrow-minded, bigoted stick-in-the-mud!"

"Why don't you buy him out now?"

"Unfortunately," Addison said, "the business has prospered. It's continued to prosper. You know what happened during the past few years, Mason. People have gone crazy. They'll pay any price for any sort of merchandising tripe. I shudder to think of what's going to happen when the inevitable reaction comes, but right now our shelves are stocked with merchandise that is low on quality and long on price, and people are buying it hand over fist. Price means nothing any more. If people want something, they want it, and that's that. The price perspective has been warped beyond all belief, Mason."

"Ferrell is married?"

"Oh, yes."

"His wife with him on his vacation?"

"No, Mr. Mason, she isn't. He had to go to the Northwest on a business trip and he took along his fishing tackle. He decided to take a trout fishing trip while he was up there. That's one thing he likes. He's enthusiastic about fishing."

"Go by auto or train?"

"By auto. And he certainly was loaded. Took out the back seat so he could pile in more camp stuff, bed rolls, tent and what not. Right now he's somewhere between Las Vegas and Reno, I believe. He'll be back in two weeks, the date of the annual stockholders' meeting. I have just that much time to get this whole thing cleaned up—just two weeks. If he got any inkling of this he'd raise the devil. I'm hoping to work things around in such shape that I can buy him out. Frankly, Mason, I have a fund set aside for that purpose and the moment the industrial reaction sets in, the moment the pendulum swings the other way, so that it looks as though we're facing a steadily declining sales volume, I'm *going* to buy Ferrell out. There are indications that make me think I won't have long to wait. This is March. I think by July I can make the deal."

"Well," Mason said, "I think the thing to do is turn a private detective agency loose on Hansell, see if we can find out something and . . ."

"Don't do it," Addison said. "The plain, simple facts of the case are absolutely suicidal, Mason. I can't afford to let these fellows bring any of this stuff out. We're going to have to pay off."

Mason drummed with his finger tips on the edge of his desk. "You've told me *all* the facts?"

"Yes."

"Did you do any necking with this Dale girl?"

"Why, Mr. Mason!"

"Did you?"

"No."

"Now, look, Mason said, "you're talking to your law-yer. Did you touch her at all—kiss her good-by or any-thing of that sort?"

"Well," Addison said, "there was no necking, as you describe the word, a word, incidentally, that is highly of-fensive to me. She *did* kiss me good-by, but it was just a kiss of gratitude, the simple, childlike gesture of an un-spoiled, inexperienced young woman."

"I know," Mason said, "and then she contrives to get herself arrested for vagrancy."

"Don't talk that way," Addison said. "Hang it, Ma-son, are you aware of the necessary implication in what you say?"

"Certainly."

"You mean this young woman contrived to get herself arrested?"

Mason said, "Addison, speaking as your lawyer, let me tell you something of the facts of life. You pick up a young woman, a girl who says she's eighteen. The girl goes to a hotel. You get a room for her in the hotel. She is arrested for vagrancy. You telephone me to get her out. I do so. Her mother shows up. Her mother says she is just eighteen. She . . ."

"Her mother?" Addison interrupted. "That's impossi-ble. Her mother is two thousand miles away."

"Her mother was in the office just a few minutes ago," Mason said.

"What did she want?"

"She wanted to thank me for what I'd done for Veron-ica, and she wanted to pay my fee. So I charged her a hundred and fifty dollars, she left her check and I gave her a receipt showing that the check *when paid* would cover my services. You can pay me with a personal check now, and when you get back to your office, you can tear up the bill I sent you for five hundred dollars. Then if anyone ever says anything about my bill, I'll simply say the mother paid me a hundred and fifty bucks and have the bank records and the carbon copy of my re-

41

ceipt to prove it. When the check clears, I'll pay you the hundred and fifty in cash. In that way no one can ever prove you paid me a penny on Veronica's case."

"Well, that does change things. . . . But it still doesn't let me out, Mason. I'm going to pay. I'll have to pay. This damn partner of mine—and there are minority stockholders—and the meeting just two weeks off. . . . No, Mason, I've *got* to pay. Keep it as low as possible, but pay. Get rid of these leeches. Keep it out of the damn column."

Mason said wearily, "I don't suppose there's any use arguing with you. Forget it. Just leave the matter in my hands."

"But look here, Mason, I want to pay. I can't afford to have my name mentioned and . . ."

"What happens when you pay the blackmailer?" Mason asked.

"How should I know? I never paid one."

"So I gather."

"What do you mean?"

"The blackmailer takes the money and spends it, and then he comes back for more. The way you make your big mistake with a blackmailer is paying him the first time. Once you've done that, he really has you hooked. Sooner or later you have to do something to protect yourself. When you do, and it comes out in evidence that you've been paying the blackmailer to keep quiet, you could protest your innocence until the cows come home. It doesn't do any good. The time to have a showdown with a blackmailer is when he first puts the bite on you."

"Mason, I tell you I can't do it! I . . ."

Mason said, "All right. Leave the thing in my hands. I'll take care of it for you."

"But I want to pay."

"No," Mason said, "you *don't* want to pay. What you want to be sure of is that your name doesn't get put in a gossip column in connection with an affair with an eighteen-year-old juvenile delinquent. That's what you really want."

"Juvenile delinquent, my foot!" Addison said.

"Let it go," Mason told him. "We won't argue about it. Where do you do your banking?"

"At the Farmers and Mechanics Second National."

"All right," Mason said, "you owe me a fee for taking care of that vagrancy matter, five hundred dollars. As I said, I've sent you a bill."

"Well," Addison said testily, "add it to your bill in connection with this. That's only going to be a drop in the bucket to what you'll charge me on this thing."

Mason said, "I want a check now. Tear the bill up when you get back to your office."

Addison flushed.

"Hang it," Mason said irritably, "use your head. I don't want that bill and that check to go through your bookkeeping department. Della, hand me a pad of blank checks on the Farmers and Mechanics Second National."

Della Street opened a drawer in the big table where she kept checks on all of the banks and handed Mason the oblong yellow pad.

Mason slid it over to Addison. "Make a check," he said, "for five hundred dollars."

Addison made the check.

"All right," Mason said. "Now we can forget about that vagrancy matter. I'll handle this other thing and send you the bill. There's no reason why that can't go through regular channels. Don't talk with Hansell. If *anyone* asks if you know Hansell, tell him you can't recall the name. In case Hansell should call again, tell him you're busy. Don't let him get you on the phone."

"But I can't afford to adopt that attitude, Mason. After all, the man has too much on me in the line of facts. I . . ."

"Tell him you're busy," Mason repeated. "I'll handle everything. Now go on back to your department store, tear up my bill for services on the vagrancy case when you get it and then forget about it."

Addison heaved a sigh of relief. "I get you now, Mason. Dammit, you're clever! Pay them what you have to pay them, but don't go beyond ten thousand dollars without consulting me—oh, hang it, don't go any higher than

43

you have to! But pay him whatever he needs. I suppose I'm hooked, and hooked good and proper. After all, a man in my position has to make allowances."

Mason said, "You pay him ten thousand dollars now, and you'll be paying someone else ten thousand dollars within thirty days, and they'll ten-thousand-dollar-you to death for the rest of your life. You can't pay a blackmailer. You should know that, Addison."

"Dammit, Mason, I've *got* to pay him."

"Leave Hansell to me."

"You'll pay him?"

"I may. If I do I'll handle it so we don't have ever to pay him again."

Addison heaved himself up out of the big chair. "All right, that's why I have you as my lawyer. You're all right. You'll soak me, damn you, but go ahead. Goodby."

Mason turned to Della Street as soon as Addison had left the office. "Della, put on your gloves, will you?"

"My gloves?"

"That's right."

Della Street opened a desk drawer, took out a pair of light leather gloves, put them on her hands.

Mason walked over to the coat closet, took a pair of gloves from his overcoat pocket, put them on and said, "Now I want that pad of checks on the Farmers and Mechanics Second National."

Della Street handed him the pad of checks. Mason pulled back the pad so that he could extract one from the center. "I guess this won't have any fingerprints on it," he said.

Della watched with a puzzled frown while Mason walked over to the window, placed the check for five hundred dollars John Racer Addison had given him against the pane of glass, then, superimposing the other check over it, with a sharply pointed pencil carefully traced the signature.

He returned to his desk, opened a desk drawer, took out a bottle of India ink and, with a steel pen, carefully traced a black ink signature over the penciled lines.

"How does it look, Della?"

She examined it carefully and shook her head. "Not too good."

"What's wrong with it?"

She said, "There's a certain little tremor in the lines. Addison's signature is a dashing, sprawling signature that's made at high speed. When you traced this you did it very slowly and there's a stiff, wooden appearance about it, and here and there are little tremors which are apparent—hang it, Chief, I don't like to be critical, but it's not a good forgery, if that's what you're intending."

Mason grinned, and said, "That's fine. You'll also notice, Della, that if you look carefully, on the second *d* I've missed the loop a little bit, and even without a magnifying glass you could see the line of the pencil just inside the ink line on the curve."

"So you can," Della Street said.

"All right," Mason said, handing her the check, "be careful you don't touch this except with gloves. Go down to one of the stores selling typewriters, ask to try out one of the new model typewriters, keep stalling around until the clerk goes to wait on someone else, then slip this check into the machine, make it in favor of Eric Hansell in the sum of two thousand dollars, then bring it back. Be certain there isn't a fingerprint on it."

Della Street's eyes widened as she looked at Mason's face, now suddenly granite-hard.

"You mean . . . ?"

"I mean," Mason said, "that you do exactly as I tell you without knowing anything whatever about the reasons for doing what I'm telling you."

She let that soak in for a moment. "You mean in case anything should happen you don't want me to . . ."

"I mean I want you to do exactly as you're told and know just that and nothing else."

She said, "Isn't that rather dangerous, Chief?"

"For whom?"

"For both of us."

"Not for you," Mason said. "You're my secretary. Go down and make out the check to Eric Hansell for two thousand dollars. Incidentally, Della, when Mr. Hansell calls on me this afternoon, you can step out of the office. My conversation with Mr. Hansell will be confidential."

She studied him for a moment, then picked up the check and wordlessly left the office.

When she had gone, Mason picked up the telephone and said to Gertie at the switchboard, "Get me the Drake Detective Agency, Gertie. I want to talk with Paul Drake."

When he had Paul Drake on the line, Mason said, "Ring up every bank in town, Paul. Tell them who you are. Here's a tip you can pass on: A rather clever, personable young man is presenting checks payable to himself in substantial amounts. These checks apparently are drawn by men of considerable prominence who have large accounts. The man can identify himself as the payee. The checks are forged. The signatures are usually traced in pencil from genuine signatures and then covered with India ink.

"You can point out to the banks that India ink is used because it effectively covers the pencil marks of the tracing. Therefore, they should be suspicious of any checks presented with India ink signatures, and make a careful investigation for possible forgeries."

"Thanks," Drake said. "That's a hot tip. I'm tickled to death to be able to do things like that for the banks. They remember it."

"Okay," Mason said, "get busy," and hung up the phone.

Mason picked up the phone number Eric Hansell had left with John Racer Addison. It was Westmore 6-9832.

He picked up the telephone, said to Gertie, "Get me Westmore six nine eight three two, Gertie. I want to talk with Mr. Hansell at that number."

5

MASON, wearing his topcoat, hat
and gloves, paused in the outer office to bend over Gertie
at the switchboard.

"I'm going down to Paul Drake's office," he said.
"I'm expecting Eric Hansell to come in in a few minutes. When he arrives, notify Della. She'll take him into
my private office. *After* he has entered my private office,
call me in Drake's office. Got that straight?"

"Straight," she said.

"Okay," Mason told her, "be a good girl."

"How good?" she asked, smiling.

"Good as you can," Mason told her, starting for the
door.

She pouted and said, "Now we're right back where
we started."

Mason left the office, walked down the corridor to the
office of the Drake Detective Agency, opened the door,
walked in and said to the girl at the switchboard,
"Where's Paul?"

"In his office."

"Alone?"

"Yes."

"Tell him I'm coming in," Mason said, and, opening
the latched gate at the end of the partition, walked past
a veritable rabbit warren of offices, to tap on the door
marked MANAGER PRIVATE.

"Come on in, Perry," Drake called.

Mason entered the office.

Paul Drake looked up from some reports he was
studying. He was almost as tall as Perry Mason, but built
in a loose-jointed, disconnected manner which made his
motions seem awkward and angular.

"What's on your mind?" he asked.

Mason said, "I'm slipping a fast one over on a chiseler."

"Need any help?"

Mason said, "I am hiding out for about ten minutes, Paul. Go ahead with your work."

"No, this is swell. I'll talk with you. After all, you're a customer."

"Have been," Mason said, grinning.

"Anything for me in this case?"

"Probably, before it gets done."

"What's cooking?"

"Blackmail."

"Can't we . . ."

Mason interrupted by a shake of his head. "None of the usual stuff, Paul. In the first place, there isn't time and in the second place, the client won't stand for it. But I think it's going to ripen into something that you can use before it gets done. How's business?"

"Pretty good."

"Got all the operatives you want?"

"I have now. There was quite a shortage of good men for a while, but now I've got a swell staff."

"You rang up the banks?"

"Sure. Where did you get the tip on that, Perry?"

"Oh, something I picked up."

"None of the banks here had heard of it. The fellow must have moved in from out of town."

"That's right."

"You're playing 'em close to your chest this time, aren't you?"

Mason grinned.

The phone rang.

Drake picked up the receiver, said, "Hello. Yes, he's here. He . . . okay, I'll tell him."

He dropped the receiver back into place and said, "Gertie says to tell you your party is all fixed up."

Mason got up. "Okay, Paul. Thanks. Here I go."

"You're meeting this blackmailer?"

Mason nodded.

"You'd better have a witness, Perry."

48

Mason grinned, and said, "This time a witness is the *last* thing I want."

"Bad as that?" Drake asked.

"Worse," Mason told him, and left Drake's office, to walk down the hall.

He entered through the reception room of his own office, nodded to Gertie at the switchboard, then went bustling on into the private office.

Della Street had followed instructions to the letter. Eric Hansell was seated in a big overstuffed client's chair. His hat, with the brim up, was on the corner of Mason's desk. As Mason entered the room, she was saying, "Mr. Mason will be right in. He had to step out for a moment and . . . oh, here he is now."

Mason nodded to Della, looked inquiringly over at the client's chair. "Eric Hansell?" he asked.

"Right," Hansell said without getting up.

Mason slipped the two thousand dollar check out of his pocket. He walked between the desk and Hansell, turned his back to the blackmailer. His gloved hands carefully placed the check for two thousand dollars on the inside of the hat, then Mason was taking his coat off, taking off his gloves. He placed the gloves in the coat pocket, walked over to the coat closet, hung up the coat, placed his hat on the shelf, straightened out his coat, turned to Hansell and said, "I understand you have something to say to me."

Hansell sized Mason up with green, impudent eyes, then looked across at Della Street. He took a long, deliberate drag at the cigarette he was holding in thin, nicotine-stained fingers and said, "Not now."

"That's all, Della," Mason said.

Della Street glided from the office.

Mason went over and sat down in the swivel chair behind the desk.

Hansell's appraisal was slow, steady, insolent.

"What do you want?" Mason asked.

"Nothing."

"You called on a client of mine."

"Did I?"

"You know you did."

"I get around a lot. I call on lots of people. I don't ask 'em who their doctor is or who their lawyer is. I don't give a damn."

"All right," Mason said, his face cold and granite-hard, "you called on one of my clients."

"So what?"

"So I called you."

"For what purpose?"

"No purpose."

"I didn't come here to play ring-around-the-rosy."

"How about button-button-who's-got-the-button?"

"I'd rather play showdown."

"What are you holding?" Mason asked.

"You know. Four aces. And if you've got this joint wired for sound, it'll be just too bad for . . ."

"It isn't wired."

"A lot of you lawyers get half smart."

"The place isn't wired."

"Okay. If it is, you'll be sorry. Your client will fire you."

"You're associated with George Whittley Dundas?"

"I work for him."

"Salary?"

"Never mind about my arrangements. They're satisfactory. I get the compensation I want and Dundas gets the facts—the ones I choose to present to him."

"And the ones you don't choose to present?"

"They're lost in a deep well of silence."

"When you give the facts to Dundas, he publishes them, is that right?"

"That's right."

"When you don't give them to Dundas, they don't get published."

"Right."

"What influences you in making your decision?"

"Various things."

"Money?"

"What do *you* think?"

"I'm asking."

"I'm not answering."

50

Mason said, "We're not going to get anywhere this way."

"Be your age," Hansell said. "You didn't study law in a seminary, did you?"

"How much?"

Hansell shook his head and said, "Phooey."

"After all," Mason said, "we have to have something to put our sights on."

"Do your Christmas shopping early," Hansell told him.

"How early?"

"That's up to you."

Mason said, "I presume you have your facts straight?"

"I always have my facts straight. Your client went overboard for a cutie he picked up on a hitchhike. He used his influence to get her placed in a friendly hotel. He knew the manager. He could call on her there but he didn't. The trick got picked up for vagrancy. Addison's high-priced lawyer came running to the rescue. Nice story: 'What big shot got a cutie a room, only to have the trick get picked up for vagrancy before Sugar Daddy could reach for the gravy? What made Perry Mason, the high-priced lawyer, rush to jail to bail Miss Innocence out? It would break my heart not to turn a story like that over to Dundas."

"Your heart's been broken before?"

"Life's full of disappointments."

Mason said, "Okay, I'll get in touch with you."

"Hell, you're in touch with me now."

"I said I'd get in touch with you later."

Hansell's face flushed. "I'm not accustomed to traipsing around to people's offices. Next time *you* can come to *me!*"

He heaved himself up out of the chair, snapped his cigarette butt insolently in the direction of Mason's wastebasket, missed it by an inch or two and let the butt continue to smolder on the floor. "You have my address," he said. "When you want to see me, telephone and make an appointment and come to me—and if your client is smart that'll be before seven o'clock tonight. Dundas has a deadline of ten o'clock and he'd want to have time really to do justice to *this* story."

"Would he pay more than Addison?"

"How much would Addison pay?"

"How much would Dundas pay?"

Hansell said to Mason, his voice sharp with anger and disappointment, "Don't get me wrong. Dundas publishes stuff I give him because that stuff is good. He keeps me on his payroll because I hand him enough good stuff to make it worth his while to pay me. That means that I have to pass in a lot of good hot material, a hell of a lot of it."

"Well?" Mason asked.

"If I didn't have Dundas, I wouldn't have any avenue of publicity," Hansell said. "For the love of Mike, do I have to draw you diagrams? Cripes! For an attorney you're the greenest . . ."

He picked up his hat, suddenly stopped in a posture of frozen interest.

After a moment he picked the check out of the hat, looked at it, then looked at Mason. "I'll be damned!" he said.

Mason said nothing.

Hansell looked at the check once more, then walked across to where he had flipped the cigarette butt, picked it up, ground it out and deposited the butt in the ash tray on Mason's desk. "I missed your wastebasket," he said.

Mason said nothing.

"I'm sorry," Hansell told him.

"That's all right."

"You know, in this business, Mason, we meet all sorts of people."

Mason nodded.

"But," Hansell went on, "we don't like checks."

"We don't like blackmailers."

"Okay," Hansell said, a twisted smile distorting his face, showing yellowed teeth, "get nasty if you want to. It's your party. You're paying for it—and remember, if there's any funny stuff about this or if you've got this office wired, you're the one that's going to be sorry. I'm a legitimate news man. I stumbled onto a scandal about John Racer Addison. I went to him to try and get it confirmed. You're trying to bribe me not to publish it. I'm only taking the check because it'll show the facts are right."

Mason said nothing.

"A nice little cutie!" Hansell went on. "Old fatherly John Racer Addison was putting her in hotel rooms, getting her out when she was arrested on a charge of vagrancy. Dear old Daddy Addison—now then, damn it, if you've got the place wired for sound, you can put the whole record on.

"And I'll tell you something else. The stuff is all in an envelope, ready to go to Dundas. If anything happens to me, the envelope will be in the mail in time to make the deadline. Dundas would give his eyeteeth to publish an item like that, naming names."

Mason said wearily, "I told you the place isn't wired."

"Well, if it is, it'll make a good story."

Mason yawned.

"Damn it, we don't like checks," Hansell said after a while.

Mason said, "I know. You told me that before. You'd like the money in small bills. You'd put 'em in your pocket and walk out. Then next month you'd be back with the same story and again and again and again. The way it is now, in order to get that two grand, you put your John Hancock on the back of the check and shove it through the bank. If you come back with a repeat, things are going to be tough."

Hansell sneered. "So you think you're smart. You give a check. Hell, that ain't smart, for my money it's dumb."

Mason yawned.

"Hell, I'm not going to even be diplomatic about it. I'm in the saddle. Your client wouldn't pay me because he thought I'd be back. He sent for you because he thought you'd be smart enough to figure out some way so I couldn't come back for more. *He'd* have paid five grand. You told him how smart you were and to make a *check*

53

for two grand. All right, you're supposed to be smart. Now let's see how smart you are."

Hansell folded the check, slipped it down in his vest pocket, said, "Okay, wise guy. Let's see you earn your fee."

Mason yawned again.

Hansell pulled his hat down on his head at a jaunty angle.

"You can go out through that door," Mason told him.

Hansell walked over to the exit door, pulled it open, paused in the doorway, turned back to regard Mason with his impudent, twisted smile.

"Wise guy!" he said sarcastically, and walked out.

The door clicked shut behind him.

6

■

IT WAS SHORTLY before closing time when the telephone on Della Street's desk rang. She picked up the receiver, said, "Just a moment, Gertie," turned to Mason and said, "John Racer Addison again."

"On the line?" Mason asked.

"In the office."

Mason frowned, said, "Okay, Della. Bring him in."

Della Street said, "I'll be right out, Gertie," hung up the telephone and went out to escort Addison into the private office.

"Hello, Addison," Mason said. "I'm expecting developments in that matter about which you consulted me. However, there's nothing I want to discuss with you. The situation is . . ."

"No, no," Addison said. "It's not that."

"Sit down," Mason invited.

"I can't sit down," Addison said, waddling back and forth across the office with short, nervous strides, pacing frenziedly. His hands were clasped and he started cracking his knuckles, one at a time.

Della Street indicated with a little grimace that her teeth were on edge, but Addison continued popping his knuckles as he walked.

"What is it?" Mason asked.

"All hell's broke loose," Addison said.

"Your little virgin again?" Mason asked.

"My virgin?"

"The vagabond virgin."

"Oh," Addison said, as though he had entirely forgotten about that. "What did you do with that?"

"All fixed up, I think," Mason told him. "Remember if anyone should ask you if you know Eric Hansell, you can't recall the name, and you're very sure you've *never* had any business dealings with him."

"Of course, of course," Addison said impatiently. "My God, Mason, I turned that matter over to you. I expect you to handle it. Charge me whatever it's worth, but get me out of it. I'll go to ten thousand—dammit, I'll go anywhere I have to. Don't bring that up now. I've got enough to worry me!"

"I take it," Mason said, "this is something new."

"Something new," Addison said, looking almost angrily at Della Street.

"It's all right," Mason told him. "Della stays here. Now quit beating around the bush. What's the trouble?"

"My partner, Edgar Z. Ferrell, I told you about him."

"That's right, on vacation in the Northwest, handling a business deal up there and then going fishing."

Addison said, "Mason, what I'm going to tell you has to be absolutely confidential."

"You've never had any leaks so far, have you?" Mason asked.

"This is something different. This is a mess!"

"Go ahead."

Addison said, "Ferrell is a peculiar chap. He's married to a very attractive woman. What Lorraine Ferrell ever saw in Edgar is more than I know. She's a pippin,

55

a swell-looker, a smart, witty woman with lots of *oomph*."

"I take it," Mason said, "that your partner, Ferrell, does not have *oomph?*"

"He's a stick, a stump, a drip, a droop. My God, he's dumb!"

"Go on."

"I'll have to tell you about this from the beginning," Addison said.

"You'd better start," Mason told him. "We've wasted enough time beating around the bush."

"About three weeks ago," Addison said, "I had a chance to buy some property for a country estate. It was about twenty miles out. The place was run down. Originally there had been three hundred acres in it. Then it had been split up until finally there was only a twelve-acre piece left, and the old ranch house."

"Go on," Mason said as Addison paused. "And you'd better sit down while you're talking. I can hear you better."

Addison hesitated a moment, then waddled over to the client's chair and plunked himself down in the cushions.

It was a deep, comfortable chair, Mason's idea being that a client who was completely relaxed physically would be more apt to tell his entire story than one who was seated in a hard, uncomfortable chair.

"Go on," Mason said impatiently.

"Well, I looked the place over. Ferrell was with me. It was a nice property if you had any use for it. I didn't have any use for it. I couldn't see it as a business speculation because the house was too big to leave all by itself and I didn't want to put in a caretaker. It was a rambling, old-fashioned, two-story ranch house. Lots of room in it and lots of room around it. There was a barn and a garage, and the place was ideally located, so far as privacy was concerned, a little winding stream bed with brush, a lot of big oaks around the place and level ground back of the farm, plenty of water for all ordinary purposes and this rambling, old-fashioned frame house that could be picked up fairly cheap."

"You bought it?" Mason asked.

"I turned it down," Addison said.

"Then what happened?" Mason asked.

"Then two days later Ferrell secretly bought the property himself."

"Without telling you?"

"Without telling me a word about it. I only happened to find out about it last Tuesday, and then by accident."

"Of course," Mason said, "since you didn't want the place, it's all right. But if you had been acting a little cool about it so as to get the price down, with the intention of making a counter offer, Ferrell's action was rather unusual for a partner. He didn't discuss the matter with you—ask you if it would be all right if he made an offer?"

"Not Ferrell!" Addison said. "That one deal shows you the kind of a duck he is."

"What did he want the place for?" Mason asked.

"Now there," Addison said, "you've got me."

"What do you think?" Mason asked.

"What do *you* think?"

Mason said, "What I think doesn't coincide with your sketch of Lorraine Ferrell, and your comments on Edgar Ferrell's character."

"Well," Addison said, "I'm telling you what I know. Perhaps there's a lot I don't know."

"I take it," Mason said, "you didn't come to consult me about your partner's country estate."

"I wanted to explain to you how it happened I went out there."

"When?"

"That night I picked up Veronica on the road—Tuesday."

"Oh," Mason said.

"Why do you say, 'Oh' in that tone of voice?" Addison asked indignantly.

"I'm damned if I know," Mason told him. "Go on with your story."

"Well, there's no reason for it," Addison snapped. "You're putting two and two together and making twelve. You're getting your cart so far in front of the horse . . ."

"Just give me the facts," Mason said, "and after I have the whole picture I'll try and fit it into a frame."

"Well," Addison said, "it's like this, Mason. I went out and looked at that property, I guess around three weeks ago. As I told you, I didn't want it. Didn't see any reason why I should take it. Tuesday afternoon the real-estate dealer who had offered me that property rang me up and asked me if I wanted to look at something else. We talked a bit over the phone, and he asked me how my partner liked the property he'd bought. I didn't know what he was talking about. He explained, and it turned out Ferrell had bought this property."

Mason nodded.

"Now, then," Addison went on, "the real-estate agent said that Ferrell had been in a terrible hurry to get the deal in escrow and get possession of the property."

"I see nothing particularly unusual about that," Mason said.

"Wait a minute. Remember this conversation was Tuesday. The dealer then went on to tell me that Ferrell had told him that he had to be in possession of the property by Tuesday because he was going to be out there for two or three weeks starting Tuesday noon."

Mason frowned.

"Well," Addison said, "I kept thinking the thing over. I began to wonder if Ferrell was perhaps trying to pull over a fast one on me or on his wife, and I decided to drive out Tuesday night and find out."

"And what did you do?"

"Got in my car, drove out to the place."

"What did you find?"

"Nothing, no indication that there was anyone on the place, although one thing struck me as a little peculiar."

"What's that?"

"Someone had been out there—you remember it had rained—let's see, I guess it was Monday night and there was a place over by the side of the house where the ground was soft enough to show automobile tracks. You

58

could see that one or two automobiles had been in there quite recently."

"Anything else?"

"No, the thing bothered me, that's all. I finally came to the conclusion that Ferrell had bought the place as an investment, had someone on the string with whom he thought he could make a deal, that he'd taken this person out, showed him the property, the person had liked it, and Ferrell had agreed to assign him his rights in the escrow."

"That sounds like a logical conclusion," Mason said.

"It sounded like it at the time, all right. It was an explanation that occurred to me and I was satisfied with it. I felt that Ferrell had been going away on his vacation Tuesday noon. Therefore, he wanted to conclude the deal on Tuesday with his own prospect. So he'd left the store shortly before lunch on Tuesday and taken the prospect out there and showed him the place Tuesday afternoon, taken the man's check, given him a receipt and gone on, on his vacation."

"Well, why not?" Mason asked.

Addison took a telegram from his pocket. "And here," he said, "is a telegram that was sent night letter Wednesday night, that certainly tends to bear out that supposition."

Addison handed the wire over to Mason.

Mason took the wire but for the moment didn't read it. He said instead, "What's all this build-up about, Addison? You evidently have received other information which makes you think this explanation was incorrect."

Addison nodded, said, "Read the wire."

Mason unfolded the telegram and read:

ARRIVED LAS VEGAS SAFELY. EXPECT REACH RENO TOMORROW NIGHT. ALTURAS DAY AFTER. WILL CALL FOR TELEGRAMS CARE WESTERN UNION BUT DON'T WIRE UNLESS SOMETHING IMPORTANT. AM TRAVELING IN EASY STAGES THOROUGHLY ENJOYING MYSELF. REGARDS.

Mason folded the wire, said, "What's getting you all worked up now? Has there been another wire?"

"No," Addison said, "but his wife, Lorraine Ferrell,

saw Edgar Ferrell's car on the street early this afternoon."

Mason cocked a quizzical eyebrow.

"She was shopping at the time. She tried to follow it, but she couldn't. She says there was a cute red-headed trick driving the car. And she's absolutely furious."

"Is she certain about the car?"

"Absolutely certain, says she not only recognized the car but she took a quick look at the license number and saw that it was the same."

"What did she do?" Mason asked.

"Tried to get a taxicab and tried to follow the car, but the car had rounded the corner and got away from her."

Mason pursed his lips thoughtfully for a moment, then said, "Well, Addison, if your partner wants to have a love nest, I don't see that there's anything in particular you can do about it."

Addison started popping his knuckles.

"Is there?" Mason asked.

"Yes," Addison said shortly.

"What?"

"I'm in a devil of a position, Mason, a hell of a quandary!"

"How come?"

"If Edgar is using that old ranch house as a love nest, I want to catch him at it."

"Why?"

"Because then Lorraine will be in a position to get a divorce. And I'll be in a position to make Edgar sell out."

"Well," Mason said, "I'm no more clairvoyant than you are, Addison."

"I want you to go out there with me tonight. I want your advice. If Edgar is there, we'll have a showdown. I want you as a witness. I'll have my checkbook along."

"You keep referring to Ferrell as your partner. I thought the business was a corporation."

"Unfortunately it is now. It used to be a partnership. Ferrell's father and I organized the business together. Shortly before Frank Ferrell's death, we incorporated the business. We each took forty per cent of the stock."

"What happened to the other twenty per cent?"

"We gave the old-time employees a chance to buy it, just people we could trust. With a few exceptions, they never attend meetings, sign proxies as a matter of form. They collect the dividends on the stock. That's all they want. If they leave our employ, they have to sell us the stock.

"Well, Edgar inherited his father's stock, and he's been a pain in the neck ever since."

"Young Ferrell has none of the endearing qualities of his father?"

"As far as I know," Addison said, "Frank Giles Ferrell made only one mistake in his life. That mistake is named Edgar, and that boy is a mistake all the way through. Frank never had much of a formal education. He'd had to work hard. He'd worked up from the bottom. That had been his salvation, that hard work. Edgar was an only child, and Frank decided that Edgar was never going to have to work the way he had.

"It's the same old story. Edgar had an automobile as soon as he was old enough to drive one. He had a college education, and an indulgent parent impressed upon Edgar that he was never going to have to exert himself unduly."

"Why did you let him get in the business with you?"

"When Frank died, the stock was left to the boy. He didn't want to sell it at any price. That's where I made my big mistake. I thought that if he came into the business and had to dig in and work, be in the office regular hours and all that, it wouldn't be long before he was tired of it and then would want money for his stock."

"It hasn't worked that way?"

"It definitely hasn't worked that way. In the first place, he doesn't come into the office regularly, and when he does, he simply messes around with the figures, mixes into things that he knows nothing about, and gets the help . . . What's the use discussing it, Mason? It drives me nuts! It's a highly unsatisfactory arrangement."

"All right. You'd like to see Ferrell's wife divorce him?"

"For business reasons, yes."

"Are you sure there are no other reasons?"

"Don't misunderstand me, Mason. I'm a businessman. When it comes to dealing with Edgar, I'm just as cold as a fish. If Edgar bought that place as a love nest, if he's playing around with some cutie and Lorraine can catch him at it, she'll sue him for divorce. There'll be a property settlement. Get me?"

"Let's see if I do."

"In the settlement, Lorraine will get a chunk of Edgar's stock. I'll buy that stock from her at a premium. Then I'll have a controlling interest and Edgar will get the hell out of the business and stay out. He'll sit on the side lines and either sell me his stock at a reasonable value or he'll be like any other stockholder and take what dividends are paid, attend the stockholders' meetings, make his suggestions as a stockholder, and the management will either adopt those suggestions or pitch them out of the window, whichever it damn pleases."

"You dislike your partner?"

"I don't dislike him, I hate his guts!"

"But you don't hate your partner's wife?"

"Lorraine is regular," Addison said. "She's extremely attractive. Make no mistake about that, Mason. And she's levelheaded. I can do business with her. It would be nice, of course, if she could get half of Edgar's stock. But it really doesn't make too much difference how much she gets, just enough to give me the controlling interest. That's all I ask. And if Edgar is out there running a love nest, he'll know I've got the whip hand. I'll tell him we can't have a scandal touch the business and whip out my checkbook. With you there to back my play, there'll be nothing to it."

"When do we go?" Mason asked.

"Tonight, after dinner."

Mason looked at his watch.

"All right. Don't go back to your office. Don't be where *anyone* can reach you. Meet me at THE STAG at seven o'clock. Until then, keep out of touch with your office, out of touch with the police."

"The *police!*"

"That's right."

"Why the police?"

Mason said, "I pulled a fast one on your blackmailer. The way things look now, I may have been premature. Do as I say and don't ask questions."

"The police—I say, Mason, I don't like that!"

"Who does?" Mason said, getting up from his chair and moving over to the hat closet.

7

ADDISON SAID, "Slow down. It's just after you cross this next culvert. There's a road that turns to the left . . . Take it east. It's a sharp turn . . . Here it is, here. Right down to the left on that dirt road."

Mason swung the wheel of his automobile, put on the brake and eased the car down a sharp incline.

"You picked up Veronica near here?" he asked.

"She was back down the road, right by that culvert we just passed."

"All right. I just wanted to get it straight."

The dirt road dipped sharply down to the bed of the dry stream which was bridged farther down the highway by the culvert, crossed the stream on a little plank bridge, debouched onto a flat.

Addison, peering through the windshield, said, "There aren't any lights on in the place . . . I don't think he's here . . . I think Lorraine must have been mistaken. He wouldn't have passed up his vacation."

Mason said, "Since we're here, we'll at least go bang on the doors and make absolutely certain no one's home."

"What'll I say if he *should* be here?"

"Nothing. I'll do the talking."

Mason slid out from behind the wheel and walked over to the front door. Addison sat still for a few thought-

63

ful moments in the automobile, then walked over to join Mason.

The lawyer, fumbling around on the porch, said, "There's a flashlight in the glove compartment of the car. Guess I'll get that."

"Here's a knocker," Addison said.

"You use the knocker," Mason told him. "I'm going to go get the flashlight."

The lawyer walked back to the car, opened the glove compartment, took out a hand flashlight and walked back to the front door.

"Any results?" he asked.

"I almost banged the door down. No one's home."

"Well," Mason said, "it's pretty certain he's not here now. Let's take a look around."

They walked around the house. The beam of Mason's flashlight swept up and down the sides of the house, across the windows. On the lower floor, the shades were all drawn, the windows tightly locked. But on the upper floor there was a window with no shade. Mason's flashlight, shining through the window, made light on the ceiling of the room. Then suddenly the lawyer stopped, holding the flashlight steadily in one place.

"What is it?" Addison asked.

"Do you," Mason asked, "see what I see?"

Addison stepped slightly back, following the pencil of light from the flashlight.

"The glass is broken," he said.

"A neat, round hole," Mason said, "with a few cracks radiating out from it."

"Well, I'll be damned!" Addison exclaimed.

Mason moved the flashlight slightly. The light reflected back from the cracks in the window, showed him little scintillating flashes.

Addison said, "You don't suppose . . ."

"I don't know," Mason said gravely.

"But it's . . ." Addison seemed reluctant to put the thought into words.

"A bullet hole," Mason finished for him.

"We've got to get in and look around."

Mason moved the flashlight back to the ground. They

followed a path around to the back of the house. Mason pounded on the back door, tried the knob. The door was locked. He went around the house, trying the windows. They were all locked.

"I don't like this," Addison said. "The place is terribly secluded here. I feel like a burglar. Suppose someone should catch us here?"

Mason said, "I want to find out what's in that house before we make our next move. The windows seem to be all locked. There's a key in the back door. What kind of a lock on the front door? Is it a spring lock?"

"I don't know."

"Any electricity in the place?"

"Not when I looked at it. It wasn't even wired."

Mason moved around the house until finally he was back at the front door.

"Windows all bolted on the inside," he said. "Key in the back door. Whoever last left the house must have left it from the front door."

Mason tried the knob, then recoiled in surprise as the latch clicked back and the door swung open on well-oiled hinges.

There was a somewhat clammy smell from the interior of the house, an aftermath of the months during which it had been closed and uninhabited.

Mason said, "Okay, let's take a look around."

"I say!" Addison said. "Isn't this dangerous?"

"You're damn right it's dangerous. Keep your hands in your pockets. I want to see what's up in that room."

"I don't think Ferrell is going to like this—if he ever finds out about it."

Mason said, "No one likes it—and the police won't like it. Keep your hands . . ."

Addison stumbled, lurched forward, grabbed at the banister to save himself, then fell forward to brace himself on the stair threads.

"That does it," Mason said.

"Does what?"

"Fingerprints. I told you to keep your hands in your pockets."

"Bosh! Don't be melodramatic, Mason. Who's going to take my fingerprints?"

"The police," Mason said, leading the way up the stairs.

The lawyer paused in the upper corridor, said, "The room is toward the back of the house. Let's see, there are four doors to the left-hand side. I think we'll try the third door."

The beam of Mason's flashlight led the way down the corridor. He paused in front of the third door, hesitated a moment, then took a handkerchief from his pocket and held it in his hand as he turned the knob.

The door swung back. An odor of death greeted their nostrils.

The flashlight showed a sprawled figure lying on the floor, face up, one eye half closed, the other open, contemplating the ceiling of the room with a glassy stare.

Addison recoiled as sharply as though Mason had punched him in the stomach.

Mason didn't even look back over his shoulder at the sound of motion, but said, "Take a look over my shoulder. Don't touch anything. Who is it?"

Addison moved reluctantly back so that he could peer over Mason's shoulder into the room.

"It's Edgar Ferrell."

"Now you know why I wanted you to put your hands in your pockets," Mason told him.

Addison made a little whimpering noise.

Mason pulled the door of the room shut, turned and carefully retraced his steps down the corridor.

They went down the creaky staircase of the old house. Mason paused to rub his handkerchief over the knob on the inside of the door and the iron handle on the outside. Then he pulled the door shut

"After all," Addison said, "it doesn't make any difference whether we leave a print or two. We've got to notify the police that . . ."

"Let's talk that over," Mason said, leading the way to the car.

"What do you mean, we'll talk that over?" Addison demanded. "It's some sort of a crime, not to notify police when you find a body. I'm not a lawyer, but I know that much."

Mason started the car. "I said we'd talk it over."

"Well, start talking," Addison said.

Mason drove his car slowly along the narrow road, crossed the dry creek bed on the plank bridge and climbed the steep grade to the highway.

"Go on," Addison said nervously. "Start talking. But I warn you frankly, Mason, no matter what you say, I'm going to stop at the first telephone and notify the sheriff's office."

Mason said, "From the way things look, I would say Ferrell had been dead for three or four days."

"So what?" Addison asked.

"That," Mason said, "would make it about Tuesday night. Tuesday night is the logical time for the thing to have happened. Ferrell started on his vacation. For some reason or other, he didn't start out immediately on his fishing trip. He went to this house."

"Naturally," Addison said testily. "You don't need to be a lawyer or a detective to figure that one out."

Mason, having made his boulevard stop at the highway, moved out onto the pavement, said, "And you were out here Tuesday night."

"No one knows that except you and me."

"You don't intend to tell that to the police?"

"I'm not that dumb."

Mason, easing the car through the gears, said, "Remember you picked Veronica up on Tuesday night."

"Veronica has nothing whatever to do with this, and this has nothing whatever to do with Veronica."

"Let's hope so," Mason said. "Show me exactly where you picked her up, Addison."

"She was on the right-hand side of the road, right over by this culvert, the one that you're coming to."

Mason pulled the car over to the side of the road and stopped.

"Will you *please* quit horsing around and get to where we can notify the police?" Addison demanded.

Instead, Mason climbed out from behind the steering

wheel and walked over to the culvert. After a moment Addison joined him.

"I don't think that house is over two hundred yards from here in an air line," Mason said.

"What in the world are you getting at?"

"Suppose you go to the police. Your face is a mask of cherubic innocence. You're surprised and shocked to learn of the death of your partner. Police ask you routine questions. They want to know if you knew about this place. You tell them that you were looking it over, intending to purchase it, and Ferrell was along, that Ferrell must have got the idea it would make a good place for him at about the time you were looking it over."

Addison nodded.

"Then," Mason said, "the police ask you if you were ever out here after that, and then what do you do?"

Addison said, "I see no reason for telling them my private business."

"In other words, you'd tell them that you hadn't been out here since then?"

Addison nodded.

"And there," Mason said, "we come to the rub. If you say you were out here, you have some explaining to do. If you say you weren't, and the police start checking the tire marks out there in the mud and find that the treads correspond with the treads of your car and then get hold of Veronica and ask her where she was when you picked her up, they'll prove that . . ."

"That I was coming along this highway just like any other motorist," Addison said. "I'd been out a hundred miles east of here on business."

"The point is," Mason said, "there's a plank bridge across this dry wash where it runs up to the road. There's a steep grade. You came up in low gear. Sitting here at night, when it was quiet, Veronica could have heard your car from the time it left that old ranch house. She'd have heard the tires on the plank bridge, heard the grind of your motor as you came up that grade in low gear, and you, yourself, admit you were driving slow and just shifting gears when you came abreast of Veronica."

Addison said nothing.

"Now then," Mason said, "we come to another thing. When you came to my office this afternoon, you were all worked up, cracking your knuckles, pacing the floor . . ."

"Well, why wouldn't I have been? I had enough on my mind . . ."

"You're a businessman," Mason interrupted. "You're accustomed to having a lot on your mind. You have responsibility. You have decisions to make. Hardly a day goes by but what you are confronted with some problem where you'd get a terrific headache if you made a wrong decision."

"For heaven's sake, are you going to stand here talking around in circles? It's cold. I'm going to get back in the car."

"What time," Mason asked, "did Lorraine Ferrell get in touch with you and tell you she'd seen her husband's automobile?"

How can I remember all those little things—?" Addison asked.

"What time?" Mason said, his voice steady with calm persistence. "And remember Lorraine Ferrell will be asked the same question by the police."

"I don't know. Probably right after lunch."

"I thought so," Mason said.

"What do you mean?"

Mason said, "I mean that you were too worked up when you were talking with me to make your present story sound plausible. I mean that after Lorraine Ferrell told you about having seen her husband's car, you realized the problem you were up against. You didn't want to guess wrong—so you drove out here. You wouldn't have driven directly to the ranch house this time, but you parked your car down the road somewhere, climbed down that embankment, walked through the willow bushes, across the dry stream bed, under the fence, and up to where you could watch the house from the willows. You didn't see any sign of anyone moving. You became curious. You started to investigate, trying to find if Edgar Ferrell had been here. You . . ."

"No, no!" Addison said, his voice in a panic.

"You went up to the house," Mason went on calmly and inexorably. "You made certain there was no one home. You tried the door. It opened. You went in. I don't know how much looking around you did, but you found Ferrell's body. Then was when you got in a panic and came dashing to my office."

"Mason, you don't know what you're saying!"

"The hell I don't," Mason said, "and the point I'm getting at, Addison, is that if you knew that body was out there before you came to my office, you've left fingerprints all over the place. And if you've done that, you've written yourself a one-way ticket to the death cell in San Quentin Prison."

The light that came from the headlights of Mason's parked automobile was sufficient to show the dismay on Addison's face.

"Now, then," Mason said, "remember that you're talking to your lawyer," and started back for the car.

Mason opened the door on the left-hand side, got in behind the steering wheel. Addison climbed in on the other side and slumped down in the seat.

"And *now*," Mason asked, "do you still want to notify the police?"

"No," Addison said, his voice thin with terror.

Mason said, "Addison, I'm going to stick my neck out for you. I'm probably a fool for doing it, but that's the only way you're going to have a chance. We're not going to notify the police about finding the body."

"But my fingerprints, my . . ."

"Now, listen to me carefully," Mason said. "You're going to call up Lorraine Ferrell. You're going to ask her if she's heard anything more from Edgar. You're going to mention very casually that Edgar may have had a deal on involving the country home he's recently purchased, and that the reason you think so is because the agent told you Ferrell was very anxious to have the deal in such shape he could step into possession by last Tuesday morning."

Addison nodded. He was listening attentively.

"You don't think she knows anything about that deal?"

"I'm satisfied she doesn't, otherwise she'd have said something about it to me."

"Well," Mason said, "you chat on with her just as though you assumed, of course, she knew all about it."

"The minute I mention that country home," Addison said, "she'll jump down my throat, wanting to go out there."

"That's fine. You go out there with her."

"You mean go back there *again?*" Addison asked in dismay.

"That's right," Mason said. "The sooner the better."

"But then what?"

"Then you'll discover the body. And as soon as the police get done with you, you and Lorraine Ferrell go to your department store and wait for me. Tell the night watchman to keep an eye out. I'll come to the Broadway entrance and pound on the door."

"But how is all this going to change the situation?"

"When you go out with Lorraine Ferrell," Mason said, "you're going to go in that house with her and you're going to take her around the lower floors before you go upstairs. You'll be leaving fingerprints all over the place. Those will be natural, logical fingerprints, made in the presence of a witness."

"Well?" Addison asked.

Mason said dryly, "So then, when the police find your fingerprints in that house, they can't tell whether they were made at ten o'clock tonight, at eight o'clock tonight, or . . ."

"Or what?" Addison asked as Mason paused thoughtfully.

"Or last Tuesday night, when the murder was being committed," Mason said.

71

8

■

MASON PARKED HIS CAR in the parking lot next to his office building, took the elevator, started down to his office, then paused as he passed the lighted door which said *Drake Detective Agency*.

Drake's office was open twenty-four hours a day, and Drake himself usually stayed until late at night.

Mason opened the door. The night girl at the switchboard looked up, and Mason said, "Drake in?"

She nodded, gestured to Mason that he was to go in, plugged in a line under the red light on the switchboard and said, "Drake Detective Agency."

Mason walked through the latched gate, which the girl at the switchboard opened with an electric release, and down the narrow corridor to Drake's office.

Drake was talking on the phone as Mason entered.

"It was just a tip, Sergeant," Drake said into the telephone. "I can't give you the source of my tips . . . No, it didn't come from the victim. It came from information my operatives picked up . . . Hell, I *know* I'm dealing with the law, but you're dealing with a detective agency. You might just as well put me out of business as take away my sources of information. How would you like it if I asked you to tell me about your stool pigeons . . . Well, I claim it *is* the same! . . . Perry Mason? I don't know. Why don't you try his office . . . Okay, if I get in touch with him, I'll tell him you want him to call. Goodby."

Drake hung up the phone and said, "What the hell was that stuff about the forged checks, Perry?"

"Why?" Mason asked.

"That was Sergeant Holcomb calling up. They pinched

a chap named Eric Hansell late this afternoon. He was offering a forged check for two thousand dollars, signed by John R. Addison, the big department store man.

"The bank probably would have cashed the check if it hadn't been for my warning, but they looked the signature over and saw it had been traced. They tried to get in touch with Addison and he couldn't be reached, so they called the Law. The cops came out and this fellow, Hansell, gave a fuzzy story, so they took him into custody and held him for further questioning. A while ago he broke down and told them he got the check from you.

"Sergeant Holcomb always smells a rat whenever you're in a case. Mentioning the name of Perry Mason to him shoots his blood pressure up over two hundred."

"I'll give him a ring," Mason said easily. "Get hold of half a dozen operatives, Paul, and have them lined up and ready to go to work in about two hours."

"What's happening?"

Mason settled himself in a chair and said, "Well, Paul, it's rather tricky. It's like this . . ."

Drake held up a protesting palm. "Nix it, Perry. I don't want to hear it. In dealing with you, the less I know, the better off I am."

"I thought that might be a good idea myself," Mason said. "You friendly with the sheriff?"

"So-so. Why?"

"You might drop around to the sheriff's office. You're working on a case, a case involving Edgar Z. Ferrell. He's a partner of John Addison in the Treasure Chest Department Store on Broadway."

Drake's eyes narrowed. "What do I do?"

"You're working for me," Mason said. "Here's the story. Tuesday noon, Edgar Ferrell took off on a vacation. He was driving an automobile loaded with camp things, sleeping bags, fishing tackle, baggage, a gasoline stove, and a tent. The back end and the trunk were pretty well filled up. In order to get more room, he'd taken the cushion out of the rear seat and left it in his garage.

"And, this afternoon." Mason went on, "his wife, Lorraine Ferrell, saw Edgar's automobile on the street. She just saw it flash past and thinks a woman was driving it. She couldn't be certain.

"So," Mason said, his face a mask of innocence, "you're checking on the case. You want to check hospitals, you want to find out if there's been any report of an accident, or if any unidentified bodies are lying around loose. You know, Ferrell *might* have been the victim of a holdup. Someone might have taken his car, robbed Ferrell, and then conked him over the head."

"How soon?" Drake asked.

"Better get started during the next five or ten minutes," Mason said. "Give me the phone. I'll call Holcomb."

"Well," Drake said, "at least *that* will be a load off my mind. Holcomb will know I passed on his message."

Mason called police headquarters, got Sergeant Holcomb on the line, and said quite casually, "Perry Mason talking, Sergeant. I dropped in to see Paul Drake, and he tells me you want me to call you up."

Holcomb said, "Every time you get mixed into a case, Mason, there's something screwy about it."

"What's the case and what's screwy?" Mason asked.

"I have a man in my office who was caught trying to pass a forged check. He says you know all about the check."

"Are you sure the check's forged?"

"It's forged. The signature's been traced. It's the signature of John Addison, the department store man," Holcomb said.

"What does Addison say about it?"

"To date, we haven't been able to get in touch with him. The bank caught the forgery because the Drake Detective Agency had notified all banks earlier in the day to be on the lookout for forged checks signed with India ink and drawn on accounts of prominent men."

Mason winked across the desk at Paul Drake and said, "What does Drake say about it? Where did he get his tip?"

"He doesn't say," Holcomb said, "but we know that a big percentage of his business is your work. So, when this chap said you knew about the check—well, I thought we'd better investigate."

Mason said, "I'll come up and look him over and talk with you."

There was surprise in Holcomb's voice. "When?"

"Right now."

"Okay," Holcomb told him. "Hell, I thought you'd try to stall out of it."

Mason hung up the phone. Drake said, "Holcomb doesn't like the ground you walk on, Mason."

"There are some damn good cops," Mason replied. "It just happens that Holcomb doesn't come within that classification. Lieutenant Tragg of Homicide is a square shooter and a smart man. Holcomb is a moron who will frame a prisoner if he thinks the man is guilty. He actually doesn't think he's doing anything wrong. He simply thinks he's aiding the cause of justice, that there's a loophole in the evidence and it's up to him, as a good, clever cop, to plug that loophole."

"And he thinks you lead your clients right around the walls of the State prison," Drake said.

"Well, why not?"

"You argue it with Holcomb."

"There's no use arguing with that bird. He's so thick-headed, you could push a stick of dynamite right up his nostrils, set it off, and the guy wouldn't even sneeze. Well, I'll go see him."

Mason left Drake's office, got in his car, drove to police headquarters, found Sergeant Holcomb in his office, and knocked on the door.

"Come in," Holcomb called.

Mason entered the room.

Sergeant Holcomb, his heavy forehead corrugated in a frown, was chewing on a cigar. Across the battered table from him sat Eric Hansell, the insolent assurance now completely evaporated from his manner.

"Hello, Mason," Holcomb said. "Sit down."

Hansell said, "What the devil were you trying to do to me? What sort of a frame-up is this? Do you think you can . . ."

"That'll do," Holcomb interrupted. "I'll do the talking for a while, Hansell. Shut up!"

The alacrity with which Hansell silenced his protests showed the extent to which the police cracked his shell of arrogant impudence.

Sergeant Holcomb said, "Hansell was picked up trying to cash a two thousand dollar check supposedly signed by John Addison. The signature had been traced in pencil, then inked. We haven't been able to get in touch with Addison. For a while Hansell cracked smart and wouldn't tell anyone anything except what his friend, George Whittley Dundas, was going to do to the cops. We called Dundas. Dundas took a long listen on the wire, gulped a couple of times, then said that he had met an Eric Hansell, that he knew him slightly, that he had no connection with him, and considered it an outrage that Hansell would give him as reference. He said he'd only met the man once or twice in a bar."

"The damned rat!" Hansell exclaimed. "Trying to save himself . . ."

"Shut up!" Holcomb snapped.

Hansell made himself small. The coat with its padded shoulders seemed a size too big for him.

Holcomb twisted the soggy cigar around in his mouth, his manner showing only too plainly an impatient desire to tear into someone over something.

"So then what?" Mason asked.

"So then, after Dundas turned Hansell down, Hansell told a different story. He said that he went to your office, that he had some business dealings with Addison, that you gave him this check as coming from Addison."

"What business dealings with Addison?" Mason asked.

"He didn't say."

"You booked him?" Mason asked.

"Yes. A charge of forgery."

"Well," Mason said, "why not check up on his fingerprints? That's about the first thing to do, find out who the guy is. If he's going around telling fairy stories and . . ."

Hansell suddenly came up out of his chair. "You damn shyster! You . . ."

Sergeant Holcomb leaned swiftly across the desk. His hand caught Hansell on the side of the jaw, a swinging, stinging blow.

"Sit down and shut up!" Holcomb growled.

"After all," Mason went on calmly, as though there had been no interruption, "the first thing to find out is something about the man with whom we're dealing."

Holcomb studied Mason with thoughtful eyes.

"You haven't denied the guy's story yet."

"I haven't heard his story."

"I've told it to you."

Mason turned to Hansell. "You were at my office?"

"You know I was."

"And I gave you this check?"

"You know you did!"

"A check purporting to be signed by John Addison?"

"Yes."

"What was the check for?"

"You know what it was for. Do you want me to tell?"

"Of course I want you to tell," Mason said. "That's what I'm asking you the question for. If you got a check for two thousand dollars from John Addison, you certainly must have done something or planned to do something to earn it."

"Keep crowding me and I'll tell!" Hansell threatened.

"Damn it, I'm crowding you," Mason said. "What was it?"

Hansell said, "All right. I knew that Addison had retained you to . . ."

Mason interrupted with raised eyebrows. "You mean Addison was paying *you* money because you knew something about Addison and me?"

"Well, why not?"

Mason smiled and said, "A lawyer gets paid for what he knows. But if you are trying to claim that Addison paid you for something *you* knew, you're getting out of the frying pan and into the fire, young man. If you should by any chance establish your innocence on the charge of extortion!"

There was a moment's silence while that sank in.

77

"So," Mason went on, "if you're going to try to lie out of it, you'd better be careful what you say."

Sergeant Holcomb chewed on his cigar. "Damned if I don't think that's it," he said.

"What?" Mason asked.

"This guy was trying blackmail," Holcomb said. "You didn't have any way of combating it, so you trapped him so he'd get hooked on a forged check charge. Then he couldn't explain the consideration for the check without laying himself wide open to a charge of blackmail. Since he wouldn't dare to admit that, he can't say a damn thing about why he got the check."

"Any evidence to support that, Sergeant?"

"Just the way the thing looks."

Mason turned to Hansell. "Anything to that, Hansell?"

Hansell swallowed twice.

"Go on," Holcomb growled. "Answer the question!"

"No," Hansell said.

"So," Mason went on urbanely, "what *was* the consideration for the check?"

Hansell said, "I wanted someone to finance me in a business deal. I'd talked with Addison. Addison told me to see his lawyer. I outlined the business deal to Mason, and Mason said it looked good, that Addison would finance me to the tune of two thousand bucks. He gave me the check."

Mason smiled. "Just pulled the check out of a hat—just like that?"

"Out of *my* hat!" Hansell said.

Mason grinned.

Holcomb said, "For the love of Mike, Hansell, what are you trying to do, crack wise? Out of *your* hat! What the hell!"

Hansell twisted his position.

"Go on," Mason said, "tell us about the hat."

"You go to hell!"

"What about the hat?" Holcomb asked.

"Nothing. It was just a crack."

"That's your story?" Mason asked.

"Yes."

"That's all of it?"

"Yes."

"What," Mason asked suavely, "was the business deal?"

"It involved backing a manufacturer who was going to put out some stuff that Addison was going to sell in his department store."

"Who was the manufacturer?" Mason asked.

"I can't tell you."

"What was the article?"

"That's confidential."

"Did you tell me when we had the interview?"

"You know I did."

"You told Addison?"

"Yes."

Mason grinned at Sergeant Holcomb and said, "Why not look the guy up?"

Sergeant Holcomb called the identification bureau, said, "I sent in some fingerprints a couple of hours ago. What do you have on them? There's a man by the name of Hansell . . . Well, I'll hold the phone. Take a look. If you have them classified, I want to . . . Okay, I'll wait."

Holcomb shifted his eyes from Mason to Hansell, then back again, said grumblingly, "Damned if I don't think it's a fast one! It looks like a swell way of getting rid of a blackmailer to me . . ."

No one said anything for some ten seconds. Then Holcomb said into the telephone, "Okay, what is it?"

He listened intently for several seconds, then pulled a pencil and paper toward him, made notes, said, "Okay, I've got it. When was the date of the second arrest—? Okay. Thanks, Mac."

He hung up and pushed the phone to one side. He took the soggy cigar from his mouth, banged it into a spittoon, and said to Hansell, "So that's right!"

Hansell said nothing.

Sergeant Holcomb said, "You've got a hell of a record, Mr. Hansell, alias Hanover, alias Handwig."

Hansell looked down at the table.

"But," Holcomb went on, turning to glower at Mason, "it's just like I thought. It's blackmail. He hasn't done

79

any pen work in his life. Everything's been extortion and attempted extortion. There never has been any forgery. Now you want me to believe he went to a bank and tried to push a forged check for two grand through the window."

"Well, he did, didn't he?" Mason asked.

"Damned if he didn't," Holcomb admitted dubiously. "He did, for a fact."

"His bank or Addison's bank?"

"Addison's bank," Holcomb said. "The bank of which the check was drawn. Hansell had papers with him vouching for his identity, driving license, Social Security card, letter of identification from a banker. He wanted the dough."

Mason yawned. "Got a record, has he?"

"Half as long as your arm," Holcomb said. "All blackmail. Damn it, Mason, it looks to me as though you pulled a fast one on this bird and are trying to pull a fast one on us."

"How come?"

"I don't like having this guy in on this forgery business. I sounds like blackmail to me."

"Okay," Mason said, "let Hansell talk. Let him tell you what the check was for. If it's blackmail, let's nail him on that."

"I've already told you," Hansell mumbled.

"No you haven't," Mason said. "You haven't mentioned names. You haven't mentioned anything except generalities. Who is the manufacturer? Who was . . ."

"All right," Hansell blurted, "I'll come clean. I called on Mr. Addison. I told him I wanted a loan for two thousand dollars. I told him I needed the money, and Addison told me that if I'd call at Mr. Mason's office I could pick up the check."

Mason said, "Addison didn't give you the check himself?"

"No, he told me to get it through you."

Mason said smilingly, "You went to Addison and asked him for a loan and Addison told you to come to my office to get the check."

Hansell thought things over for a minute, then said,

"You let me talk with Mr. Addison on the telephone and I'll prove it."

"This story you've just told?"

"Yes."

"Then your other story was false?"

"Well . . . yes."

Mason said to Holcomb, "Well, there you are, Sergeant. He admits now that that was a lie. The way it looks to me, the guy's trying to play something smart here. He felt that if he could cash a check purporting to be signed by Addison and drawn in his favor for two thousand dollars, that he could have something on Addison. I think it's all part of a blackmailing build-up."

"That sounds crazy to me," Holcomb said.

"Well, after all," Mason told him, "this man keeps lying about the check. It's either forgery or the first step in a blackmailing setup."

Sergeant Holcomb said, "It's a hell of a way to deal with a blackmailer. I don't think I like it."

"I don't give a damn whether you like it or not," Mason said irritably. "You drag me down here on the word of a crook. The fellow has a criminal record as long as your arm. He admits now that the story he told about me giving him the check was a lie. This is where I came in."

Mason pushed back his chair.

Hansell looked up with concentrated venom in his eyes. "You're damn smart, Mr. Perry Mason," he said savagely, "and you'll regret the day you ever tried to pull a fast one like this!"

"*I'm* pulling a fast one?" Mason asked, his hand on the doorknob.

"You know you are."

"But," Mason said, "I thought you just told Sergeant Holcomb that your dealing was with Addison, that your story about me was all a fairy tale."

Hansell said nothing.

"If you want to get any statement from Addison," Mason said, "you'd better talk with Addison before this man gets a chance to talk with Addison on the phone."

"You can't do that to me!" Hansell said, half getting

up from the chair. "I'm entitled to talk with Addison on the phone. After all, it's his signature on the check."

Mason said, "I understand the signature on the check was traced."

Sergeant Holcomb said, "I don't like it."

"Even supposing your suspicions are true," Mason said, "I take it the police department isn't anxious to have blackmailers running around loose, trying to practice extortion on reputable businessmen."

"If you'd have come clean on the thing," Holcomb said, "I'd have collared this guy and given him a face massage for what he was trying to pull. The way it is now, I'm damned if I know where I stand."

Mason turned to Hansell, said in a fatherly voice, "What was it, Hansell, blackmail?"

"You go to hell!"

"Sergeant Holcomb will get the truth out of you," Mason warned. "He'll get to the bottom of it."

"I said you could go to hell."

"Okay," Mason said cheerfully, and turned back to the door.

The phone on Sergeant Holcomb's desk rang. Holcomb scooped up the receiver, said, "Yeah, hello, Holcomb talking . . . Hold on, Mason . . . Hey, Mason . . . !"

Mason, out in the corridor, turned back just before the door clicked shut, caught the knob of the door, said, "What is it, Sergeant?"

"It's something you might be interested in," Holcomb said. "Damn it, I think you are."

"What is it?" Mason asked.

"This is a call from Homicide," Holcomb said. "They knew I'd been trying to get in touch with Addison. Now, according to a report that just came in from police radio, Edgar Z. Ferrell, Addison's partner in the Treasure Chest Department Store, has been found dead in an old abandoned ranch house about twenty miles out in the country. Evidently the guy was murdered, shot by someone who lay in ambush outside the house and popped a bullet through the window."

Mason raised his eyebrows, said, "Any idea when the murder was committed?"

"Just a minute," Holcomb said.

He withdrew his hand from the mouthpiece of the telephone. said, "When was the shot fired? . . . They think Tuesday evening . . . ? Okay, stick on the line a minute, will you?"

Holcomb's broad palm once more covered the telephone. "Probably on Tuesday night."

Mason nodded sagely, looked at Hansell. "Where were you Tuesday night?" he asked.

Hansell came all the way up out of the chair. "My God, if you think you're going to frame *this* on me! You dirty two-timing, slick shyster . . . !"

"Tut, tut," Mason said, "such language, Hansell. Of course. I don't know anything about your past, but if you *have* been making a living by blackmail I'd advise you to cut it out and get into something honest for a change—provided, of course, you can clear yourself on this murder charge."

"I'm not up on no murder rap!" Hansell screamed. "I was framed into passing a phony check when I tried to make a shakedown and . . ."

Sergeant Holcomb banged the phone back on its cradle.

Mason said, "I'm very shocked to hear of Ferrell's murder. I didn't know him but I have had business dealings from time to time with John Racer Addison. I presume he'll be very much upset about it I guess I'd better get back to my office."

Sergeant Holcomb gave no indication of having heard him. He was regarding Hansell thoughtfully. "You know anything about that murder?" he asked.

Hansell almost screamed, his voice was so harsh with rage and nervousness. "For God's sake, are you going to let that damn mouthpiece not only put the words in your mouth but stick the thoughts in your mind? Are you . . . !"

Sergeant Holcomb leaned across the desk, took a long, powerful swing and slammed his fist full into Hansell's face. "I don't let blackmailers talk that way to me," he said.

Mason quietly pulled the door closed behind him as he stepped out into the corridor.

9

■

THE NIGHT WATCHMAN at the department store was waiting at the front door.

Mason showed him his business card through the heavy plate glass. The watchman nodded, opened the door, said, "Mrs. Ferrell is expecting you."

"And Mr. Addison," Mason said, smiling.

The watchman shook his head. "Mr. Addison isn't here yet. The police wanted him."

"Wanted him?" Mason asked.

"Wanted him to do something for them."

"What?"

"Well, sir, I guess you understand what's happened. It seems there's been a bit of an accident and it seems there's something about the gun that the police wanted Mr. Addison to explain. If you'll pardon me, I think Mrs. Ferrell will give you the details."

"Let's go," Mason said.

The watchman led the way through long aisles of counters covered with dust cloths, took an elevator to the fifth floor, led the way to a sumptuous suite of offices.

Lights were on in an office marked MR. ADDISON, and also in an adjoining office marked on the frosted glass MR. FERRELL.

The night watchman stepped forward, tapped perfunctorily on the door, opened it a crack and said, "Mr. Perry Mason."

"Come right in, Mr. Mason," a woman's voice answered, a voice that was well-modulated, yet resonant with rich overtones.

Mason pushed open the door and entered.

Lorraine Ferrell had been stretched out on a couch

at the far side of the room. She was throwing back a light blanket as Mason entered.

"Good morning, Mrs. Ferrell," Mason said.

She gave him a generous glimpse of flashing legs as she threw back the blanket and swung around to a sitting position. Then she pulled her skirts down, smiled up at him and said, "It's nice of you to come. I was trying to relax a bit and compose myself. Where's the watchman?"

Mason turned to look over his shoulder.

"Just getting in the elevator," he said.

"That's fine. Close the door. Come over here and sit down in that chair by the head of the couch."

She seemed perfectly at ease, thoroughly composed.

Mason closed the door, walked over to the comfortable chair she had indicated.

"These modern executives are rather good to themselves," she said. "I found the blanket in a drawer in the coat closet there. I believe my husband was accustomed to a snug little siesta after lunch. I always knew that he wasn't available on the telephone until after three o'clock."

Mason managed a somewhat noncommittal smile.

She was studying him while she was talking, appraising him carefully.

Mason, in turn, swept her with his lawyer-wise eyes, taking in the neat clothes, the large, expressive eyes, the full lips, the sweep of her neck and throat.

Abruptly, she said, "How much of a hypocrite do I have to be with you, Mr. Mason?"

"Why not be yourself?"

She laughed nervously. "You swept me with that one gaze and then turned your eyes away, as though you had me catalogued."

"A habit," Mason said, smiling, and reaching for his cigarette case.

"What's a habit?"

"That brief glance. Clients don't like to be stared at and witnesses are sometimes disconcerted by a steady, direct gaze."

"Don't you like to disconcert witnesses?"

"Only hostile witnesses, and then only in court."

"I take it I'm not to be a hostile witness."

"I hope not."

"Can you size up people in a quick glance like that?"

Mason said, "One can try."

"Successfully?"

"It depends. A lawyer who does much trial work has to make snap judgments. The clerk calls out the name of a prospective juror. That person gets up from his seat in the courtroom, walks up to take his place in the jury box. You have an opportunity to watch him for six or seven seconds. In those six or seven seconds you have to reach a snap judgment as to his character, how he's apt to react to testimony and argument, what kind of a person he is, whether he's broad-minded or liberal-minded, whether he's bigoted, good-natured or antagonistic.

"Of course, you have an opportunity to supplement that first impression by asking him a few questions, but as a rule a man has steeled himself by the time you start questioning him so his appearance is more or less of a mask. He's trying to convince you that he's intelligent and important. He knows that he's in the limelight and he has that natural tendency to put his best foot forward. He's trying to convince himself he's something of a judge. Your best opportunity to size him up is as he walks up to the jury box."

She laughed easily. "Do you want me to walk?"

Mason suddenly turned and let his eyes lock with hers. "Yes."

Apparently his monosyllabic answer somewhat disconcerted her. Then she tossed her chin up, smiled, arose from the couch and walked the length of the office, away from Mason. Her walk indicated that she was conscious of her figure, of her hips. Abruptly she turned, smiled at Mason, walked slowly toward him and sat down again.

She said, "My husband bored me to distraction."

"I gathered as much."

"I'm sorry that he had to go in such a mysterious and messy manner. As far as the conventions are concerned, I'll show the proper grief. Actually, I feel as though a

86

load had been lifted from my shoulders. Is that wicked?"

"Do you really feel that way?"

"Yes."

"Then it's much better to be frank—with me."

"I thought it would be."

"You were in love with your husband when you married him?"

She said, "Mr. Mason, I made the greatest mistake a woman can ever make. I married for money. I suppose if I'd been less—well, shall we say, less desirable—it might have been all right. But I had a good many people to choose from. I don't think I was really deeply in love with any of them, but one or two made quite an impression on me. Unfortunately, none of them had any money.

"Edgar Ferrell went about his courtship in a calm, methodical manner. There were times when he bored me terribly, but he was fair and frank. He told me that he would give me a generous allowance. He did. That was all, just an allowance, respectability and boredom.

"At the time, I had no realization of how utterly, terribly boring it would be. I wouldn't have minded if we'd fought bitterly. If he'd tried to beat me up, I might have loved him or else hated him enough to have carved his heart out. But he did neither. It was simply that steady, plodding, stolid respectability that got on my nerves so I wanted to scream.

"And then, to make matters worse, some of the other suitors who had appealed to me emotionally, but who didn't have any money, proceeded to go out in the business world and pile up some dough."

"Why didn't you divorce him?"

"In the first place, I didn't have any grounds. In the second place, if I'd tried to divorce him without grounds, I'd have had a property settlement that wouldn't have been at all satisfactory. And all the time, in his heavy, cumbersome way, he was trying to play around.

"Good Lord, Mr. Mason, if I'd only known. If I'd thought he had enough zest for life to be cheating a little bit, I probably could have whipped myself up to the point of finding something more romantic in him. But he was

87

just a stolid, steady, dependable husband, not too bright, with absolutely no imagination, a ponderous dignity, a complete lack of humor, no spontaneity."

"And so," Mason said, "being bored it was only natural for *you* to start playing around a little."

She stiffened suddenly. It might have been indignation, it might have been that she was putting herself on guard.

"Didn't you?" Mason asked casually, lighting a cigarette.

"No," she said. "I'd made my bed. I was lying in it, and in no other."

"Tempted?" Mason asked.

"Of course I was tempted. Good Lord, I'm only human. I want romance. I want to be propositioned by people who say witty things, who go about it in a clever, dashing, romantic manner. I hate the humdrum, boring routine of married life, where a husband insists on taking his wife for granted. My husband had the mind of an accountant . . . Lord, how I'd like to talk with that 'other woman' who was to have shared his country estate. I wonder if my husband tried to gambol about as a light-headed Lothario or whether the romantic approach was as sordidly commercial as his 'courtship' of me."

"Do you want a cigarette?" Mason asked.

"No, thanks."

There was silence for a moment. Then Lorraine Ferrell said, "Yes, as a wife I was true to Edgar Ferrell. As a widow I'm going to be true to myself."

"Thinking of marrying again?" Mason asked.

"Definitely not. For your private information, Mr. Mason, I have had a very large dose of matrimony. I can get along without it for a while. I have money—that is, I will have money. I'll have freedom and independence. I want to cultivate witty, articulate people. I intend to travel and—well, to be frank, I intend to arouse the instinct of pursuit in the predatory male. Then I intend to perch myself on a lofty stool and look down with amused tolerance at anyone who makes a pass at me.

"And, if I may mix a few metaphors, when some appealing knight comes tearing along on a beautiful white charger and wants to take me up in his arms and carry me off, I'm not going to resist too much if I don't feel like it."

There was a dreamy expression on her face. Her eyes, raised above Mason's head, contemplated the ceiling with a certain pleased anticipation, as though she were looking forward to the experiences she was describing. For the moment, she might have been talking to herself, utterly oblivious of the lawyer's presence.

"But," she went on, "I'm not going to marry him, unless he has a certain quality that—well, it's hard to describe, but I've found out that the big vice of all men is that when they know they can have a woman, they take her for granted. The man who can continue to court a woman after he's once possessed her is a very, very rare individual. He is priceless."

"Perhaps you won't ever find one," Mason said.

"Then I'll have more fun searching in vain then marrying one of the wrong sort."

"Youth and beauty are transient."

"All the more reason to enjoy them fully while you have them. They're no less transient when united in the holy bonds of wedlock. How did the conversation get off on this channel?"

"I was merely asking questions."

"Very personal and direct questions."

"It's something of a personal and direct matter."

"All right, let's talk about the murder for a while."

"It wasn't suicide?" Mason asked.

"Apparently not. It was murder. Police have reconstructed the crime. There was no electricity in the farmhouse. Edgar used oil lights on the lower floor. He had a gasoline lantern he used to give him light when he went to the upper floor.

"He had just filled the lantern. He went upstairs to a bedroom where he'd left his suitcases. The shades were drawn on the lower floor but there were no shades on the bedroom windows.

"He entered that room with the lantern. Someone who had been waiting down by an automobile took careful aim with a .38 calibre revolver and shot him. Reconstructing the line of the shot from the hole in the glass and the height Edgar's head must have been above the floor, police have the exact line of the shot and the place where the murderer stood, right by automobile tracks which had been left in mud. And it hasn't rained since Monday night."

"Did the gasoline lantern burn out?" Mason asked.

She frowned. "No, it must have been turned out. It was nearly full. But that's the only way it could have happened, the killing, I mean. The murderer couldn't have seen into that room either day or night unless Edgar had been standing there with the lantern lit."

"You had no idea your husband had this country place?"

"No idea in the world. When I heard about it, I was absolutely, utterly incredulous. It simply shows that even such a confirmed stick-in-the-mud as Edgar Ferrell has latent masculine instincts."

"You think it was a love nest?"

She looked at him and laughed.

"Any proof?" Mason asked.

"The police are getting proof. They've found fingerprints apparently a woman's prints, all over the place."

"Have you any idea who the woman was?"

She shook her head. "It's absolutely beyond me. I have an idea, however, it's some employee in the store. I told the police if they'd take the fingerprints of every one of the employees, I felt certain they'd find the person they want."

"What makes you think that?"

"Because I know Edgar. Edgar wouldn't have known how to go about playing around. He wouldn't have had the initiative or the verve. He'd have been as awkward as an old spavined horse trying to gambol around in pasture, come springtime. It must have been some babe here in the store who had an opportunity to make the grade by slipping past the fire lines when no one was looking."

Mason studied the tip of his cigarette. "You mean she fell in love with your husband?"

Lorraine Ferrell's laugh was rich and throaty. "Mr. Mason, please!"

"Then what did she want?"

"What do you suppose she wanted? The same thing I wanted. Money."

Mason said, "Then she wouldn't continue to be an employee in the store."

"You're right, Mr. Mason, absolutely right."

Her smile was beatific. "Then," she went on, "we can narrow our search and expedite matters. I think all the police have to do is to look for some good-looking, attractive young woman who was working here, and who quit her job."

"I believe setting a young woman up in an apartment is the accepted procedure, is it not?" Mason asked.

She said demurely, "*I* wouldn't know."

"One would hardly expect a young woman, no matter how ambitious or how well-paid, to go out and live in an old farmhouse where there were no conveniences, no electricity."

She frowned. "That's right."

Mason said, "Let's just follow that reasoning through to its logical conclusion. If no young woman would *live* there, then it must have been a meeting place."

Lorraine Ferrell's brows came together. She said, "You're being terribly logical about it, Mr. Mason, and —darn it, you're right. It looks as if it must mean an affair with a married woman, someone who could only get away on occasion, someone who didn't dare to be seen around town. That must have been it."

"So," Mason said, "we have a peculiar series of contradictory clues."

Lorraine Ferrell crossed her knees, hugged the upper knee with her clasped palms, thoughtfully regarded the pattern of the carpet, said, "You're building this thing up one step at a time. I suppose the next step will be the irate husband."

Mason took up the conversation. "Who followed his erring wife to the rural love nest, who stayed outside to watch, who saw his wife's lover standing near the window of an upstairs bedroom, and who couldn't resist the temptation to pull the trigger and then drive away.

"That left the erring wife alone in the house with a

lover who had just been shot. She did the best she could. She turned out the gasoline lantern and knew that she had to leave the place. She had only one way of leaving. That was the same way she had arrived, in Edgar Ferrell's automobile."

Lorraine Ferrell slowly, thoughtfully nodded.

"All that, of course, is predicated on one fact," Mason said.

"What?"

"That you're telling me the truth."

She didn't even look up from her contemplation of the carpet. There was no resentment, no anger in her tone. She said simply and convincingly, "I'm not much of a liar, Mr. Mason. I *have* done it once or twice, but I'm not good at it and I don't like it. I'm telling you the truth. It's easier. It's less trouble. You're a lawyer—somehow, I have an idea you'd have stripped me naked if I'd tried to hide behind a cloak of deceit. I'm telling you the truth. You're probably the only person on earth who will know that I am not a grief-stricken widow. I'm putting the cards on the table. I . . ."

Knuckles sounded on the door, then the knob turned. The door opened, and John Addison, looking haggard and worried, stood in the doorway.

"Hello, Mason. Thank God you're here!"

"What happened?" Lorraine Ferrell asked.

"Damn near everything," Addison said. "Look, I don't know my way around *this* office. Come on into my office. I keep a bottle in there. I need a shot."

Addison led the way into his own office, opened the glass door of a bookcase, pressed the catch, swung a whole shelf of books out to one side and disclosed a row of bottles, a little electric ice box.

"What do you want?" he asked.

"Scotch and soda," Lorraine Ferrell said.

Mason nodded.

Addison placed three glasses on his desk, splashed Scotch into the glasses with a shaking hand, dropped in ice cubes and cold soda.

He said, "This light gets my nanny goat. It's daylight

enough outside so this illumination seems yellow and sickly and . . ."

He walked over to the window, flung back the heavy drapes, then moved over and switched out the lights.

The sun had not yet risen, but there was enough light to show objects quite distinctly in the room.

Addison raised his glass. "Here's luck," he said, and then added, "we're going to need it."

He drained a good half of the glass.

"What happened?" Mason asked.

Addison dropped into a big swivel chair, took a cigar from a humidor on the desk, clipped off the end, lit a match and held the tip of the cigar against the flame, rotating it slowly, to get a good even light.

He shook out the match, dropped it into an ash tray and said, "Edgar Ferrell was killed with my gun."

"*Your* gun!" Lorraine exclaimed.

Addison nodded moodily.

"How come?" Mason asked, his eyes coldly cynical.

Addison kept his eyes on the tip of his cigar, consciously avoiding those of his partner's widow and his lawyer.

Mason waited patiently for Addison to answer the question.

Lorraine inhaled sharply, leaned forward as though about to say something, then caught Mason's eyes, settled back in the chair and waited.

Addison took a few puffs at his cigar, gulped down another big swallow of Scotch and soda.

"It is," he said defensively, "one of those little things that you just never think of in the ordinary course of a day's work."

He waited, and no one said anything.

"But," Addison went on, "they become damned important when a murder case crops up."

Again there was a period of silence.

"Now then," he said, looking at Mason for the first time since he had started his explanation, "you deal in murder cases, just the same as I deal in merchandise. I suppose that you will claim I should have told you this when I first talked to you. To your mind, it'll seem damn important. That's because you are trained to think in terms of murder cases. That's your business. To my mind it was simply a minor matter that had no importance whatever."

"You'd better get it off your chest," Mason said, "and quit stalling around."

"When Edgar wanted to go on this fishing trip, he wanted a revolver. He borrowed mine."

"Why didn't he buy one?"

"I'm damned if I know," Addison said bitterly, "but about three months ago, Edgar and I were out on a trip. I had my revolver along, and I wanted to do a little target work, just to keep my hand in. I don't think Edgar had ever shot a revolver before. He became interested. I showed him something about shooting, taught him quite a bit about dry shooting, and got him so he wasn't flinching. He was doing some pretty fair shooting. He was naturally tickled pink. When he wanted to go on this trip, all he could think of was my revolver."

"*You* showed him how to shoot?" Mason asked.

"That's right."

"Gave him practice on what you call dry shooting?"

"Yes."

"In other words," Mason said, "you've done a good deal of revolver shooting, is that right?"

"I was a member of a team that won first place in the Western Championship a few years ago."

"All right," Mason said, "tell us about the gun. Let's get that straight."

"Well, that's all there is to it. Edgar borrowed the gun. Police found that gun in the bed of the dry wash. They stumbled on it just by accident. I don't think they'd ever have found it in daylight, but going down there at night with their flashlights, playing around the wash, the beam of a flashlight reflected from the metal and one of the cops spotted it."

"You say it's the gun with which Edgar was killed?" Mason asked.

"That's what the police seem to think."

"How many shells in it when it was recovered?"

"There were no shells. The gun had been wiped free

94

of fingerprints and thrown away, but police say it had been fired rather recently. I'm inclined to agree with them. I always kept the barrel spotless. The gun had been discharged and hadn't been cleaned. There's powder residue in the barrel."

Mason said slowly, "That looks bad, Addison."

"How bad?" Addison asked.

"Plenty bad," Mason said.

Mrs. Ferrell said, "Surely, Mr. Mason, you don't think there's any possibility that John Addison could have . . ."

"It isn't what I think," Mason interrupted, "it's what the police are going to think, and what a jury is going to think."

There was an interval of grim silence.

Mason got to his feet. "All right, folks, I'll do the best I can. Addison, get your desk in order. They'll arrest you before noon. When they do, don't talk. *Don't - say - one - word*. Can you remember to do that?"

"My God, Mason, I'll have to explain *some* things."

"Then you'll have to explain everything."

"Well?"

"Can you do it?"

Mason's eyes bored into those of John Addison. The department store magnate squirmed in his chair.

"No," he said.

"I thought so," Mason said, and walked out, leaving Addison and Lorraine Ferrell alone in the offices.

10

■

AT EIGHT O'CLOCK Mason found
Paul Drake studying reports which had been placed on
his desk. He was holding an electric razor in his hand,
shaving himself as he read the reports. Over on the corner of his desk, dishes bore evidence of the fact that he
had had ham and eggs, toast and coffee sent in from a
nearby restaurant.

Drake looked up from his shaving, twisted his face at
such an angle that he tightened the skin along his neck,
slowly drew the head of the electric razor along his neck,
said, "Hello, Perry. How's it coming?"

"That's what I want to know," Mason said.

Drake had four or five telephones scattered around
within easy reaching distance on the desk. "Where do
you want to start?" he asked, putting down the electric
razor and splashing shaving lotion over his face. "Want
to start with Addison?"

"What about Addison?"

"Addison's in a spot, Perry. Police found a gun. They
think it's the gun that did the killing. It's a .38, and the
gun that did the killing was a .38. It had been fired recently but all the shells had been removed from the cylinder. The gun had evidently been thrown away. It lit
in some rocks. There was a wooden handle on the butt
and a bit had splintered off when it hit a rock. The police
looked around and found the splintered piece where the
gun had hit. It evidently had been thrown with considerable force, judging by the scratches on the rock where
the metal had scraped."

"Well?" Mason asked.

"They did some fast work checking the numbers. It's

Addison's gun. Apparently he's some pumpkin as a revolver shot. That gave the police a *lot* of ideas."

"You're sure a .38 did the job?"

"Pretty certain. They've measured the hole that the bullet made in the glass of the window when it went through. It's a nice, clean-cut hole, virtually nothing broken out, just the hole with a lot of radiating cracks."

"What did they do with the window?"

"Cut the glass right out of it, mounted it between sheets of transparent plastic. They're keeping it as evidence."

"They haven't recovered the fatal bullet yet?"

"Not so far as I know. The autopsy surgeon is probably working on the body about now. The bullet's somewhere in the guy's head. A wound of ingress, no exit wound."

"Anything else new?"

"I had a session with Sergeant Holcomb."

"What does he want?"

"He's all worked up about that report I made to the bank. He says Eric Hansell is a blackmailer, that he thinks the whole thing was a frame-up, to get rid of a blackmailer who was annoying a client of yours, and he thinks that client is John R. Addison."

"What did you tell him?"

"I stuck by my guns and told him I'd had a tip and had passed it on to the bank in good faith, that if there was anything doing between Addison and Hansell, I didn't know anything about it."

Mason nodded.

"Of course, now this murder case is building up," Drake warned, "you're going to run head on into that question again in a big way."

"I'm going to run into lots of questions," Mason said.

Drake said irritably, "Well, don't tell *me* anything more than I know right now. I have enough questions to answer, myself."

"You'll have more. Mrs. Laura Mae Dale is the mother of Veronica Dale. And Veronica Dale is at present working in Addison's department store on Broadway. I want to get a line on Mrs. Dale. Anything you can pick up about her daughter, Veronica, will be all to the good."

"Okay," Drake said wearily, "I've got some men reporting for duty in about fifteen minutes. I'll start them working."

"I don't want anything clumsy," Mason told him. "I don't want the heavy-footed stuff. What I want is the light touch with a clever build-up. I don't want these people to know anyone's taking an interest in them."

"Don't worry," Drake said, "I don't know how deep the water is, but I do know that the ice is damn thin. The boys I use on this case are going to be the best in the business."

"That's the stuff," Mason told him. "Now listen carefully to what I'm going to tell you, Paul, because I want you to remember exactly what I say."

"Why?"

"So you'll be able to know what I didn't say."

"Shoot."

"You'll keep this under your hat," Mason said. "Addison picked up Veronica Dale. She was hitchhiking. He brought her to the city. She impressed him as being an innocent young thing of a type that doesn't exist any more. She was posing as a synthetic creation of cherubic innocence that was in vogue in the novels of the gay nineties."

Drake said, "What time?"

"Sometime along in the evening."

"Where?"

"Oh, out east of the city," Mason said with a wave of his hand.

"Go ahead."

"Addison played the fatherly part, a very much concerned and perturbed father who was astounded at the chances the young thing was taking. Put yourself in Addison's shoes. He's amassed considerable wealth. He knows exactly where he's putting his foot down before he takes a step. He had picked up this young, apparently innocent girl who casually tossed off the remark that she was hitchhiking her way into a strange city where she

98

knew no one, had no place to stay, was virtually without funds, and was arriving well after the dinner hour."

"The big question in my mind," Drake said, "speaking as a practical detective, is how she had got that far with all that innocence intact."

"I told you she painted an impossible picture," Mason said. "Addison used his influence with the Rockaway Hotel to get her a room. He escorted her to the hotel, then tried to step out of her life."

"But didn't do so?"

"The girl was arrested on the street for vagrancy."

"On the *street?*"

"That's right."

"For the love of Mike, Perry, police don't pick girls up on the street unless they're doing one thing, and doing it damned openly."

"I know," Mason said, "but there's a chance the girl *wanted* to get arrested."

"You mean she wasn't—?"

"Perhaps she just put on the appearance," Mason interrupted.

"But why?"

Mason said, "I went to her rescue. I put up bail. I got the case dismissed."

"When?"

"The next morning."

"Then what?"

"Then her mother, Laura Mae Dale, called on me and left a phony address, by the way."

"What did she want?"

"Wanted to pay my fee."

"Did she?"

"Yes."

"How much?"

Mason grinned. "A hundred and fifty bucks."

"Bargain basement?"

"Pre-inventory sale," Mason said.

"And I suppose Addison paid another five hundred bucks."

"I told you," Mason said, "to listen very carefully to what I had to say so you'd know the things I hadn't said."

"Oh, oh," Drake observed.

"The mother," Mason said, "comes from a Midwestern town, probably within fifty miles of Indianapolis. She has a restaurant there. She's very much concerned about her daughter's adventure into the great and wicked world. The daughter doesn't have any idea the mother is here. The mother doesn't want her to know. She wants to keep an eye on what's happening, to see whether Veronica settled down, goes to work and gets a job, or whether she starts sowing a wild oat around."

"Just one oat?" Drake asked, grinning.

"Just one oat," Mason said.

The smile suddenly left Drake's face. "You plant that oat in the right soil and it might sprout into quite a crop," he said.

"A veritable golden harvest," Mason told him.

Drake suddenly sat bolt upright in the chair.

"Now," Mason went on, "I want you go to to see John Addison before police arrest him. He knows you're working for me. Get him to call Veronica in and tell her to go with you."

"Then what?"

"Take her to Della's apartment. Della will take charge from there."

"Why don't you go to see Addison yourself?" Drake asked.

Mason said, "I may not be able to regulate my own comings and goings much longer, Paul."

And he walked out while Drake was thinking that over.

100

11

MASON, entering his private office, found Lieutenant Tragg comfortably ensconced in the client's chair.

"Hello, Tragg. How did you get in here?"

"He walked in," Della Street said angrily.

Mason frowned. "I have a reception room, you know, Tragg."

"Sure, I know. And if I'd waited in the reception room, and you'd slipped in through that corridor door, Della Street *might* have given you a tip-off and you *might* have slipped right out again."

Mason said wearily, "I have a string of appointments today, so I hope you'll be brief, Lieutenant. I presume the police consider they are a special class and don't need to have themselves announced in the regular way."

"We don't like to wait in people's offices," Tragg said, grinning. "It wastes our time and gives people a sense of superiority."

"Which you don't want them to have?"

"We like to have them a little on the defensive. You know, psychology, Mason, why waste time arguing about it?"

"What do you want, Tragg?"

"I understand you had a run-in with Sergeant Holcomb."

"*I* did?" Mason asked, raising his eyebrows. "It's news to me."

"It isn't news to Holcomb."

"I don't know what Holcomb thought. I thought I was assisting him."

Tragg said, "You made Hansell mad."

"Isn't that too bad," Mason said.

"You shouldn't have done that, Mason. When Hansell got mad, he decided to come clean. He admitted the whole thing."

"Did he, indeed?"

"That's right."

"I suppose," Mason said, "Sergeant Holcomb was so anxious to get at me he promised Hansell immunity from just about everything short of murder if Hansell would give him something that would implicate me."

"I don't know what Holcomb told him," Lieutenant Tragg said. "I do know that they want to see you at Headquarters."

"Who does?"

"Several people."

"What about?"

"For one thing," Tragg said, "they want to ask you about a forgery."

"What forgery?"

"The check that Hansell presented at the bank."

"It *was* forged, wasn't it?"

"The bank says it was."

"So what?"

"Hansell says you forged it."

"That *I* forged it?"

"That's right."

"Now, isn't that something!" Mason said.

"It sure is," Tragg commented dryly.

Mason studied the police lieutenant for a moment, said, "You still with Homicide, Lieutenant?"

"That's right."

"Then how does it happen that a lieutenant of Homicide is asked to come up here and extend an official invitation for me to go to police headquarters for a forgery charge?"

"We're working on the case together," Tragg said.

"You and Holcomb?"

"That's right."

"Holcomb used to be on Homicide."

"He isn't on Homicide any longer. Sometimes he helps

out, but he's on general stuff now. Get your hat, Mason. Let's take a walk."

"Suppose I don't choose to take a walk?"

"That might be just too bad for you."

"Is that a threat?"

"You're damn right it's a threat," Tragg said. "Look, Mason, I've tried to be nice. We've got the deadwood on you on a forgery charge. You forged a check and gave it to Eric Hansell."

"You have the word of a crook."

"We have a the word of a crook for that," Tragg agreed, his voice weary, "and we have corroborating circumstances all along the line. We're going to get some more corroborating circumstances. We have enough to issue a complaint right now. You pulled a very, very slick stunt on a blackmailer, but it got mixed up in a murder case and backfired. If it hadn't been for the murder, you'd have been sitting on top of the heap. As it is, you're sitting on a keg of powder."

Mason glanced at Della Street, saw her pencil was flying over the pages of her shorthand notebook as she took down the conversation.

"What does Addison say about the check?"

"Addison's bank did the saying. The signature is forged. It isn't too good a forgery at that. And your friend Addison is in trouble up to his eyebrows."

"How come?"

"We can prove he was driving along that road which goes within a quarter of a mile of the place where the murder was committed at just about the time it was committed."

Mason kept his voice elaborately casual. "Okay, Tragg, we'll take a walk."

He picked up his hat.

"Any messages?" Della Street asked.

"Nothing," Mason said. "I'll be back shortly."

"He *may* be back shortly," Tragg corrected.

12

■

LIEUTENANT TRAGG opened the door and said to Mason, "Go on in."

The lawyer entered a big, plainly furnished room.

Sergeant Holcomb, chewing nervously on a cold cigar, sat at one end of a long oak table. Midway at the table, Eric Hansell, now once more restored to impudent assurance, was smoking a cigarette.

At the other end of the table a shorthand stenographer was taking down the conversation.

Sergeant Holcomb grinned as Mason entered the room.

Lieutenant Tragg, coming in behind Mason, pulled the door closed, said, "Take a chair, Mason."

Sergeant Holcomb said to Hansell, "Now, I want you to repeat just what you told us. Just go ahead and tell me exactly what happened. I want Mason to hear it."

Hansell said, "It was a shakedown. I'll admit that."

"Go right ahead," Holcomb said.

Hansell reached for a fresh cigarette.

Mason said, "Remember, Hansell, these people can't give you immunity. They . . ."

"Now, you keep out of this," Holcomb said threateningly. "We're handling this! When you hear the whole story you'll sing a different tune."

Hansell's green eyes flicked briefly to Mason's face. "Wise guy," he said sarcastically.

"And you," Lieutenant Tragg snapped to Hansell, "keep your trap shut except when you're spoken to, and when you're told to say something, say that and no more! Now let's cut out the comedy. Get busy. Start talking."

Hansell lit the cigarette, took a deep drag and said,

"I nose around and get bits of information. That's my business. If it's something I can't handle, I turn it over to George Whittley Dundas for his gossip column. He'll pay me peanut money. I can't make a living on that, but by having an outlet for publicity, it gives me a chance to make a better shakedown."

"We understand," Holcomb said and then added sarcastically, "of course you never made a kickback to Dundas."

Hansell was silent.

"Go on with your story," Tragg said.

Hansell said, "I keep eyes and ears open around Headquarters here, little stuff that comes in—nothing confidential, you understand. Just the sort of stuff they'd give the Press anyway.

"I got a tip that Perry Mason had been down in person getting a girl out on a vagrancy charge. It looked funny to me that a high-priced lawyer would come down and spring a broad on a vag. So I decided to investigate. Sure enough, Mason had been down and sprung her with bail money he put up from his own pocket.

"Okay, I talked with the fellow who had made the pinch. He told me his story, just the way he'd tell it to the Press anywhere. So I backtracked to the Rockaway Hotel, where the jane had had a room, and found out the room had been given her on orders of the manager of the hotel.

"I went to the manager of the hotel. I told him I wanted to know why he was playing favorites with cute little blondes. He told me to go to hell. Then I pointed out to him that the blonde baby had been picked up for vagrancy within an hour of the time she'd registered at his hotel, and that put a different light on the situation. Naturally he didn't want to have the name of the Rockaway Hotel appear in print as the residence of a cutie who had been picked up for vagrancy, and he didn't want his wife to know that he'd arranged for the room. So *he* broke down and told me *his* story. John Racer Addison had called him up and asked him as a personal favor to have a room reserved in the hotel for Veronica Dale. Addison said he'd vouch for her.

"That was swell by me. I'd been going after small fish and now I'd get some big stuff. I decided to interview Veronica Dale.

"She was pretty cagey about the Perry Mason angle, but she talked about John Addison, said he was just the nicest man. He'd picked her up hitchhiking Tuesday night and had put her in a hotel.

"Okay, I went to Addison. I cracked a whip over him. Addison was scared stiff. I gave him time to think it over and left a telephone number.

"Mason called me at that telephone number. I went up to see him. He was out. His secretary said she'd take my hat. She put it on the corner of the desk. Mason came in and talked around in circles with me. I was mad as hell. I got up to leave and there was the check for two thousand bucks in my hat, signed by John Racer Addison and made payable to me. Under the circumstances, I had no idea the thing could be questioned. I barged right in and took it to the bank myself. I never have done any pen work. I'm a blackmailer—so what?"

"All right, all right," Lieutenant Tragg said, "get back to the rest of it, about this blonde."

"I've told you about her."

Tragg glanced significantly at Sergeant Holcomb and said, "Does he know why we're interested in—?"

Holcomb shook his head.

"A little more about that blonde," Tragg said.

"Where did Addison pick this girl up?" Holcomb asked.

"Just after they'd passed Canyon Verde."

"How far from Canyon Verde?"

"Oh, ten or fifteen miles, I gather from the way she talked."

"In other words, John Racer Addison was proceeding along that road from Canyon Verde on Tuesday night."

"Sure," Hansell said. "He had to in order to pick her up. He brought her into town."

"At what time?"

"She got into the hotel around quarter to ten, and she was picked up for vagrancy about ten-thirty, I believe."

"And where is this girl now?"

"I don't know. But I'll make a bet you could find her through John Addison. When those old goats start taking a fatherly interest in a cute blonde trick who is playing the game for all the angl s—hell, don't make me laugh. Addison's hanging around her like a fly around a molasses jar and she's letting him hang. If you want to confirm the story from her, just tell Addison you want him to produce Veronica Dale, and he'll have her here."

Tragg said, "All right, Hansell. We'll give it to you straight. Don't think you're getting immunity on a black-mailing rap just because of your magnetic personality or because we're anxious to hook Perry Mason on a fast one he pulled. You're a dirty damn chiseler. You're a small-time worm and I'd personally like to take that sneering smile off your map with a bunch of fives. The only reason your yellow teeth aren't being pushed down your throat is because you've blundered into a murder. As you already know, Edgar Ferrell, Addison's partner, was murdered on Tuesday night in a house about a quarter of a mile from the Canyon Verde road. Now then, where did Addison pick this girl up? I mean, *exactly* where?"

"I can't tell you that," Hansell said, studying the tip of his cigarette thoughtfully. "Where would twenty miles from Canyon Verde put it?"

"It would put it just about opposite the place where the crime was committed," Lieutenant Tragg said.

"That's where it was."

Holcomb said, "He didn't tell it all this time. What was that you told us before, Hansell. about what the girl said about the man who picked her up?" -

"I told you. She has the opportunity to size up the cars. At night she listens for the sound of the motor and . . ."

"That's it," Holcomb said. "What about the sound of Addison's motor?"

"Oh, that," Hansell said, and then suddenly a look of shrewd, calculating caution flashed over his face.

Tragg, accustomed to dealing with men of that type, correctly interpreted that look. "Remember, Hansell," he said, "you're getting immunity only on the promise that you come one hundred per cent clean. You try holding out as much as one per cent and we'll throw the book at you for forgery, and we've got you cold on that!"

Hansell said, "I wasn't holding out anything. I was just thinking."

"Well, start talking," Tragg said. "We'll do the thinking."

"I remember now. I didn't pay any attention to it at the time. She told me she picked Addison because his car sounded expensive. She said he was coming up out of a side road. The night was still and she could hear his motor coming along the side road. Then she heard the wheels cross a plank bridge. Then the car climbed a pitch and was coming toward her and she listened to the sound of shifting gears. He had come up on the highway in low gear and had shifted into high about a hundred yards before he got abreast of her. The motor sounded smooth and well cared for, so she stood out by a culvert and turned around so the headlights would strike her face, and looked sweet and helpless."

"By a culvert," Lieutenant Tragg said.

"By a culvert."

"And Mason gave you that check?"

"Mason gave me that check. It was put in my hat."

"And Mason's secretary put the hat on the desk?"

"That's right."

Tragg said, "Okay, Mason. You've been leading with your chin for along time. I'm going to put a charge against you for forging Addison's name to a check. And I'm going to subpoena Della Street."

"On the strength of a crook's testimony?" Mason asked.

"You're damn right," Tragg said. "He's a crook but his story makes sense. You knew that if you paid him off on a blackmail, you'd never be done with it. You figured he'd have a criminal record and that if you could get him picked up for passing a forged check, we'd throw the book at him and he'd never have any opportunity to use the information he had. What's more, he couldn't ever explain because you'd have him between two horns of a dilemma. He either had to be a forger or a blackmailer. If he kept quiet, he went to jail for forgery. If he talked, he talked himself into the pen for blackmail."

Hansell looked up sneeringly. "Wise guy," he said to Mason.

"For Christ's sake, shut up!" Holcomb said irritably. The phone rang.

Holcomb walked over, picked it up, said, "Holcomb talking. Who . . . ? Yeah . . . what about it?"

Suddenly he pulled the cigar from his mouth and banged it into the spittoon. "How's that again?" he said angrily.

He screwed up his face with the intensity of his effort at concentration, then said, "Okay," and banged the receiver down on the hook so hard that it seemed as though the hook would be ripped off the telephone.

"I want to talk with you, Lieutenant," he said to Tragg.

Tragg said, "Well, let's get hold of Addison, find out about this Veronica Dale, take her out on the road and see if she can tell us exactly where the place was she was picked up."

Holcomb nodded without enthusiasm.

"On second thought," Tragg said, "I think we'll wait until night to do it. We'll take her out to Canyon Verde and let her see the road under approximately the same conditions as she saw it when she was hitchhiking."

Mason said, "Are you birds going to try to hold me? If you are, you'd better swear out a complaint and get a warrant issued."

"You just sit right there," Tragg said ominously, "and in about twenty minutes we'll have you all taken care of, Mr. Mason."

Holcomb said, "After all, Tragg, we don't want to go off half-cocked on this thing. We'd better check Hansell's story a little more."

Tragg said, "It's a typical Mason trick. I know Hansell's telling the truth. It sounds just like Mason. It's just the way Mason would play it. He was trying to protect his client, and when Mason starts protecting a client, he doesn't give a damn what he does. He protects his client's interests. He was putting Hansell into such a spot the guy couldn't talk, couldn't blackmail, and couldn't even come back."

"Well, let's talk it over a little," Holcomb said, and, catching Tragg's eye, closed his own eye in a warning wink.

Mason pushed back his chair. "Don't think I'm going to stick around here while you have a debating society. I'll be at my office."

"We'll serve a warrant on you and take you to the can in handcuffs," Tragg warned.

"Go ahead," Mason said. "Call the newspaper photographers and get some publicity, if you want."

"That's *exactly* what we'll do," Tragg told him.

"That's fine," Mason said, and stalked out of the office.

The lawyer took a taxicab back to his own office building, walked down the corridor, unlocked the door marked PERRY MASON, PRIVATE, and said to Della Street, "Della, you're going to have to take a powder."

"What?"

"That check," Mason said. "They're really going to town. They're going to drag you in front of the Grand Jury and I don't want you to be available for a while. I . . ."

Della Street said excidedly, "Chief, didn't Sergeant Holcomb get a telephone call?"

Mason had gone over to a desk drawer, jerked it open and was hastily pulling papers from his private file. He stopped in mid-motion, looked at Della Street with sudden puzzled comprehension.

"Did he?" she asked.

"Hell, yes!"

Della Street said, "I worked as fast as I could. That was the bank telephoning that there had been a terrible mistake made in charging Eric Hansell with forgery, that while it was true the signature had been traced, John

Racer Addison had acknowledged the signature as his. He'd dashed off the check in pencil at first, and, thinking that perhaps a pencil signature wouldn't be honored by the bank, had traced it over in India ink and sent it up to this office to give to Hansell."

Mason paused for a moment, digesting the information, then dropped the papers back into the drawer, walked around the desk and took Della Street into his arms. "How did you happen to thing of that?" he asked.

He was holding her so close to him that her voice was muffled. "Elementary, my dear Watson. Everyone had been so busy with the murder case they'd forgotten that Addison had never actually denied the check. So as soon as Lieutenant Tragg had left the office, I got hold of Addison and told him to call up the bank, tell them he'd just learned Hansell had been arrested for presenting a forged check, that the check wasn't forged at all, but was perfectly genuine, that it was his signature. I told him his call would cost him two thousand dollars to a blackmailer, but if he didn't make it he'd find his lawyer in jail and the two thousand and more would be on his bill."

Mason released Della Street, went over to his desk, sat down in the chair and threw back his head and laughed.

"Did I do all right?" she asked.

"All right?" Mason said. "You did perfect! Only, you violated half a dozen sections of the Penal Code."

"So what?"

"They'll sure as hell arrest you if they ever find out about that call."

She said, "Okay. Let them try to find out. I knew I was taking a chance, but a gal who won't take a chance once in a while is a stick. And besides, I've got the smartest lawyer in the city on my side."

"The lawyer," Mason said, "would be a stuffed shirt without his secretary. Gosh, Della! No wonder Holcomb looked as if he'd swallowed too much tobacco juice! Has your salary been raised lately?"

"Yes."

"Well, raise it again," Mason said. "You're getting better and better. And now you've got another job. Go to your apartment. Wait there, Paul will bring Veronica Dale there. Find some place to keep her under cover. I'll be out as soon as I can get away, but it may be late.

"Get started, Della, and let's hope we're lucky. We're going to need lots of luck."

13

■

PERRY MASON TAPPED gently on the door of Della Street's apartment.

She opened the door a small crack, saw who it was, then beckoned him in and quietly closed the door behind him.

"Everything okay?" he asked.

"She's down in Apartment 13-B."

"Making any trouble?"

"Sweet as a lamb."

"You held her here for a while?"

"Yes. But only for a while. I was afraid they'd be looking for her here. I had another visitor, too."

"Who?"

"Lorraine Ferrell."

"What?" Mason asked.

She nodded.

"How come?" Mason asked.

"She was looking for you. She couldn't get any satisfaction at the office, so she came here. That was when I was expecting Veronica and Drake's man, so I got rid of her quick. She's jittery, wants to see you, says it's terribly important. Chief, I'll tell you something about that woman. She's in love with John Addison."

"No!"

"Definitely."

"She didn't show it when I talked with her and Addison."

"You mean you didn't see it. It takes a woman to see things like that."

"Hang it, Della, that complicates things. If she knew about Veronica, she might be jealous."

"I think she does and I think she is."

"What about John Addison?" Mason asked. "Would he be in love with Lorraine?"

"I don't know about him," she said, "but I can tell you definitely that woman is in love with him."

Mason sat on the corner of the table, swinging one foot, his forehead creased into a frown. "That could complicate matters. What about Veronica?"

"She's just the same as ever. Addison told her he wanted her to go with Drake's man and she followed along like a sweet little lamb. No questions, just obedience. She came here and I told her I was getting an apartment for her and that when I did she was to stay inside that apartment without communicating with anyone."

"Give her any reason?"

"I didn't have to. She was completely docile. Chief, a woman *couldn't* be that green."

"Does she think it's connected with the murder case?"

"Apparently she doesn't think, period," Della Street said. "Now that isn't right. A girl with looks like that has had people make passes at her. She must know what it's all about. If a wealthy department store owner picks her up and gives her a ride, gets her a room in a hotel, then gets her a job, and then suddenly takes her off the job and sends her out to an apartment where she's supposed to be secluded and mysterious—hang it, Chief, even a young, innocent girl would rebel at that."

"No signs of rebellion?"

"Just sweet innocence," Della Street said, "a synthetic, round-eyed innocence."

"They got her out of the Rockaway Hotel all right?"

"Yes. Apparently police hadn't started checking on her. Drake's men made certain the place wasn't being

113

watched, then had her go in and pay her bill, take her one little bag and check out."

"She hasn't acquired any more baggage?"

"Apparently not. Most women under the circumstances would have had Addison okay a charge account and picked up some clothes. This girl looks like a seasoned traveler to me. What she can do with the few things she has in that little suitcase is absolutely astounding. Of course, her stuff is light stuff that packs well. Chief, I tell you there's something phony about that girl."

"Well," Mason said, "I'll go take a good look at her, and I mean a good look. Apartment 13-B?"

"That's right."

"How long can we have it?"

"A week. The girl who leases it is in Salt Lake. I phoned her and explained something of the circumstances. I told her I simply had to have an apartment for a single girl and that we'd pay her twenty dollars a day and make good any damage. She jumped at it."

"Okay," Mason said. "I'll go see how Veronica's getting along in her new quarters. You don't think she has any idea she's being put out of circulation because of that murder case?"

"I don't know what she thinks," Della Street said. "I claim it's an act. A girl couldn't be that dumb!"

"That innocent?"

"That dumb."

"Perhaps they don't have fatherly wolves in the little town where she was raised."

"They have movies. They have magazines. They have radios. And while they may not have wolves who live in such nice dens, you can bet they have wolves."

Mason said, "Well, I'll go take a look at the little lamb."

"The *willing* little lamb, if you ask me," Della Street said, "just wandering around outside of the fold, bleating helplessly, looking in sidelong anticipation out of its sweet little eyes for the wolf. Gosh but I'm catty! I can't help it."

Mason smiled. "I'll take a look."

114

"No, just a little place where people stop in. We had a regular trade with truck drivers and people who were on the road all the time. And then, of course, there were a few local people. We almost never caught a real transient. The town was so small, few people stopped there. They just kept right on going."

"You didn't tell your mother when you left where you were going?"

"No. I just took off."

"And have you notified her, now that you're located here?"

"No."

"Why not?"

"I'm afraid she—well, I don't know. I'm afraid she'd come and get me."

"How old are you?"

"Eighteen."

"You don't think your mother might be trying to follow you even without knowing where you are?"

"Heavens, no. She wouldn't have had any idea whether I'd gone north or south, east or west."

"Don't you suppose she's worrying about you?"

"I doubt it. I'm old enough to take care of myself."

"Veronica, what is your mother's name and where does she live? Where is this small town you keep talking about?"

"Her name's Laura—Laura Mae Dale, and I don't want to tell you where she lives."

"Why?"

"You'd write her. I don't want her to know where I am. She might take me back."

"Tell us just what happened before you met Mr. Addison."

"*Before* I met him?"

"That's right, immediately before."

"I had trouble."

"What sort of trouble?"

"Wolf trouble."

"How did it happen?"

"The same old way. I try to pick my cars. I size them up and listen to the sound of the motor. When you're standing by the side of the road you can hear a car's motor for a long ways. And, then, of course, you can tell a lot by the look of the car. If it has a lot of shiny finish on the front of it and looks expensive, I turn around so the people can see I want a ride. But if it's a shabby car, I turn my face the other way and keep my chin up in the air to show them I'm waiting for a bus.

"Sometimes I make a mistake. This man was one of them. I thought he was all right and got in the car with him. It was after dark then, and I couldn't really size him up. Almost as soon as I got in the car, he started making passes."

"Did you mind that?"

"As long as he kept his hands off of me, I—I rather liked it. Is that terribly wrong, Mr. Mason?"

Della Street, glancing up from her notebook, caught Mason's eye, closed her own in a slow wink.

"That depends," Mason said. "Why did you like it, Veronica?"

"It was so different from the small town sort of stuff, the way he went at it and everything. It was—well, it was clever. Then he started putting his hands on me and I wanted to scream. I just wanted to get out of the car right away."

"And what did you do?"

"I switched off the ignition, grabbed the ignition key after I'd locked the switch, and, of course, the car came to a stop. I opened the door and jumped out. He couldn't run after me and catch me, and he couldn't leave his car right there in the middle of the road and start running."

"And what did you do when you jumped out?"

"I tossed him the keys and—well, that's all. I just tossed him the keys."

"And then what?"

"Oh, he said a lot of things, but, of course, men do that when they're disappointed."

"How," Mason asked, "did you learn that much about men?"

"I . . . I've talked with people."

"And about hitchhiking, how did you know the way to handle the wolf?"

"A girl told me that. I guess/that's where I got the idea of hitchhiking, Mr. Mason. This girl was one of the few transients who stopped in at the restaurant and she got to talking with me. She wanted a place to spend the night. Gosh, Mr. Mason, she certainly had courage. She only had about two dollars and fifty cents. She'd been hitchhiking, and she intended to keep on hitchhiking. She said she'd get by somehow. I thought that a girl had to be—well, you know, a *bad* girl, in order to do things like that. But she told me that you didn't have to at all, that nearly all men were very gentlemanly and some of them would give a girl money, just to help her on her way. I asked her about the bad ones, and she told me about the trick with the ignition. She said that whenever she got in a car, the first thing she did was to notice the ignition lock, and when things got too bad she could always reach over and cut off the ignition, turn the key in the lock, bring the car to a stop, and then get out and wait for another ride."

"And that is what you did that night, just before Mr. Addison picked you up?"

"Yes."

"Can you remember the place where he picked you up?"

"Yes, right by a culvert."

"Now, tell me exactly what happened."

"Well, I got out of the car. This man was pretty mean and said a lot of things, but then he drove on. I was frightened. I didn't try to get a ride for a while. I guess I walked for a mile or so, and every time I'd hear a car coming I'd get off to the side of the road and hide in the brush. I thought it might be that man coming back."

"How long did you keep that up?"

"It must have been half to three-quarters of an hour."

"Then what?"

"Then I got tired and realized I couldn't keep on that way, so I sat down by the side of the culvert."

"How many cars did you pass up after you sat down?"

"None. Mr. Addison's was the first car that came along then."

"You listened to the sound of the motor?"

"Yes. As a matter of fact, Mr. Mason, Mr. Addison's car was down a side road somewhere. I heard it start and then it went along a road more or less parallel to the highway, and then I heard the wheels on a plank bridge, and then the car climbed up to the highway, came to a stop, and then started on again. I heard the driver shift the gears and the way the motor sounded and everything and—well, I was tired enough to have taken a chance with almost anything."

Mason glanced at Della Street. "How long were you sitting on the culvert, Veronica?"

"I don't know. Four or five minutes, perhaps. There wasn't too much traffic along that road at that hour. It's one of the main roads, but not *the* main road."

"While you were there did you hear anything that could have been a shot?"

"No shot," she said. "There was someone having trouble with an automobile. It backfired four or five times."

"Where?" Mason asked.

"Over on the side of the road. Gosh, Mr. Mason, it may had been Mr. Addison's car. I don't know. It was in that general vicinity somewhere."

"You heard it backfire?"

"Yes, five or six times."

"Describe those backfires," Mason said. "Was there one loud noise and then after quite a little while another one, and—?"

"No, they were all together, almost all at once. I remember wondering about them, because usually when you hear a whole series of backfires that way it's when a truck is coming down the hill or something like that. When a person starts a car and it misses and backfires, it is longer between the . . . between the noises."

Mason studied her face. She met his eyes with calm candor, the tranquillity of utter innocence.

"You didn't say anything about these backfires when I talked with you before."

"Good heavens, why should I, Mr. Mason? Just an old automobile backfiring."

"And they were all together?"

"Yes. The first one, and then another one, and then three or four really quick, right together."

"And that was the last of it?"

"I guess the person got his car started then."

"But that was some time before Mr. Addison showed up?"

"Oh, yes."

"How long?"

"A minute or so," she said innocently.

"Much more than a minute?"

"I don't think so. Perhaps a minute or two minutes. I guess, now that I come to think of it, it *could* have been Mr. Addison starting his car. It . . ."

Knuckles pounded on the door, then someone rattled the knob and kicked against the base of the panels.

"Come on, come on. Open up!" a man said impatiently. "Open up or we'll take the door down. This is the Law."

Mason said, "Veronica, I want you to think carefully . . ."

"What's the Law doing here?" she asked.

"About those backfires," Mason went on, "now did you . . ."

A voice from the hall said, "Please don't make so much racket. Here's a pass key."

A key clicked in the lock. Lieutenant Tragg and Sergeant Holcomb entered the room.

"Well, well, well," Tragg said, "interrupting a nice little tête-à-tête, eh?"

"Interrupting is right," Mason told him.

Holcomb said, "I think we've got him on this, Lieutenant. He's tampering with a witness for the Prosecution."

Mason smiled and said, "A witness for the Defense, gentlemen."

"You may think so," Tragg said, "but it'll be a different story when she tells the real truth. You knew we wanted to take this girl out on the road and have her point out the place where Addison picked her up."

"But not until night," Mason said.

"So what?"

"It's not night yet."

"She's a witness for the Prosecution."

Mason said wearily to Della Street, "There's no use arguing with these fellows, Della. I guess this is where we came in."

Tragg's smile was triumphant. "Wrong again, Mr. Mason. This is where you go out."

Out in the corridor, Della Street folded her notebook, then said, "Well, I guess we led with our chins on *that* one."

"I don't know," Mason said. "We have Tragg worried. He won't know just what Veronica told us, and he'll know that we have it down in shorthand."

"He'll ask her to tell him what she told us."

"He still won't know. And by the time he gets done asking questions, he'll have her a little rattled, unless she's the most practiced liar in seventeen states."

"As far as I'm concerned," Della Street said bitterly, "you can make it *eighteen* states."

"That bad?" Mason asked.

Della Street jabbed the elevator button viciously. "All that business about backfiring," she said, "that *really* puts Addison on the spot."

"It sure does," Mason admitted. "Of course, in a way, Addison put himself on the spot."

They entered the elevator, rode up two floors and walked down to Della Street's apartment.

Della pushed her key in the door, twisted back on the key and, when nothing happened, said, "What do you suppose is wrong with my lock? I . . ." She rattled the key again. "It won't turn," she said.

Mason tried the key, said, "Gosh, Della, it feels like it's unlocked." He turned the knob and the door opened.

"Well, I'll be darned," Della Street said. "I guess I left without snapping the spring lock on. I'd left it on the catch so you could get in, in case I had to just call to you to open the door."

"I think you did. I don't remember seeing you take the catch off the lock."

"Well, I *should* have. I always do."

"It's hard to recall little matters of routine," Mason said, "but I'm pretty sure you didn't. However, that's a minor matter. The thing we're up against now is trying to give Addison a break. Things look pretty black. His car was out there, probably at the exact time the murder was being committed. The man was killed with his gun. A witness will put him on the spot about the time the shots were fired. And now we have a witness who will testify that the shots were all fired in rapid succession. You can see the way the police will build up that theory. Addison, a crack shot, stands out by his automobile. Ferrell is in the upstairs room. Addison takes an arm rest on the door of the automobile or perhaps crouches down and takes a rest on the top of the hood. He takes a careful bead and pulls the trigger, sends one shot crashing through the window glass and into Ferrell's brain. Then he calmly turns, empties his gun, breaks open the cylinder, pulls out the shells, puts them in his pocket and throws the gun away."

"What was the idea in taking out the shells?" Della Street asked.

"Apparently the person who committed the murder," Mason said, *"thought* that if the police couldn't get hold of the bullets that were in the gun and prove that the lead alloy in the fatal bullet was the same as the shells remaining in the gun, they couldn't definitely prove what gun committed the murder."

"But it's such a peculiar thing for a man to throw a gun away at the scene of the crime, particularly when police could check up the numbers of the gun and find out who owned it."

Mason said, "You have to remember that, as Addison pointed out, the gun probably wouldn't have been found if the police hadn't been messing around there at night and the beam of the flashlights hadn't reflected from the

123

blued steel. Addison seemed rather surprised that the gun had been found. It had dropped down behind some stream-worn boulders, a couple of feet in diameter, and could only have been seen from just the one direction. It was fortunate that that police flashlight managed to pick it up—or unfortunate, depending on how you happen to look at it."

"*You* don't think Addison killed him?"

Mason said, "Addison isn't the type. He's impulsive, irritable and nervous. But he's accustomed to weighing consequences."

Mason settled himself in the conventional overstuffed chair with its cloth-covered cushions, was reaching for a cigarette when the telephone rang.

Della Street answered it, said, "Yes . . . hello . . . oh, hello, Paul . . . yes, he's here."

She handed Mason the phone and said, "Drake wants to talk with you."

Mason, holding the telephone and the receiver with one hand, groped for a match with the other, lit his cigarette and said in the general direction of the mouthpiece, "Yes, hello, Paul."

Drake said, "Perry, get out from under on Veronica. The police are on their way out to shake Della down. They have a hunch . . ."

"Your tip's too late, Paul. They've been here," Mason said.

"Find anything?"

"Yes, Veronica."

"Ouch! She'll talk."

"She talks all right. Holcomb and Tragg gathered her in . . ."

"They're all steamed up over something, Perry. They may be on a hot trail and Holcomb wouldn't be above framing you. Keep your nose clean."

"I will," Mason told him, and hung up.

Della Street took the telephone from his hand, put it back on the sideboard.

Mason said, "Paul Drake had an idea, Della. He said Holcomb might try to frame me. Whether someone opened your door with a pass key, or whether you left the place unlocked, the answer could be the same. Let's look around."

"You surely don't think they . . ."

"Could have planted a dictograph," Mason finished. "Let's look."

He started peering behind pictures, looking over the walls, moving cushions. Della joined him in the search.

"Can't find a thing," Mason said at length. "I still can't figure it." He turned over the cushion of the big overstuffed chair.

"Oh, oh!" he exclaimed.

She rushed toward him. "What is it?"

In the space beneath the cushion, six empty .38 calibre cartridges were clustered in a little nest.

"What are those?" Della Street asked.

"Those," Mason said, "represent planted evidence, Della."

"Did Sergeant Holcomb plant them there?"

"Unless Veronica sat in this chair and ditched them— or Lorraine Ferrell. You say she called on you?"

"Yes, but just for a few moments."

"Was she near this chair?"

"Yes. She sat there for a few seconds, not long."

"And Veronica sat here?"

"Yes."

Mason frowned thoughtfully.

"What do we do?" Della asked.

"If it's a trap we should ring up police headquarters and report finding those cartridges. That will put Sergeant Holcomb in his place. If it isn't a trap, and someone has left the evidence here, we'll have to try to get rid of it without being caught."

"And if we get caught disposing of the evidence?"

"Then we're hooked."

"How do you know whether it's a trap or not?"

"That's the rub. I sure wish I knew whether you had locked that door before we went down to Apartment 13-B."

"I do, too."

"You could simply have neglected to lock it?"

"Yes."

"I rather think you did neglect to lock it," Mason said. "I am quite certain we simply pulled the door closed. We were talking at the time, and I don't remember you snapping the release button on that lock."

"What'll happen if you ring the police and tell them you found these empty shells here in the apartment?" Della Street asked.

Mason said, "It will crucify our client, Della. If I *had* been trying to conceal evidence, I wouldn't have been dumb enough to have put it in your apartment. But the newspaper readers won't figure it that way. Headlines will go screaming across the front pages, *Addison's lawyer surrenders evidence! Police find empty cartridges in apartment of Mason's secretary!*"

Della Street made a little shuddering motion, said, "Gosh, Chief, I can just see those headlines, now that you mention them."

Mason said, "And if it *is* a police trap and I try to take the evidence out of this apartment and police catch me . . . Got any good powerful elastic up here, Della?"

"Yes, some thick bands that we have for holding transcripts together. I brought some of them from the office."

"Let's have a couple."

"What are you going to do?"

"If it should be a trap," Mason said, "I'm going to try to get us out of it. Also bring some string, Della, if you will, please."

Mason moved a dining-room chair up to one of the windows. He opened the window, fastened the strips of elastic to two vertical bars in the back of the chair, said, "I used to be considered a pretty good shot with one of these, Della."

He cradled one of the empty cartridges in the improvised slingshot after first wiping all possible fingerprints from it. He pulled back the elastic, aimed at the far corner of a vacant lot, and let go.

The empty cartridge case whirred and glittered

through the air, but carried it neatly into the adjoining lot.

Mason subjected the remaining five cartridges to the same treatment, then dismantled his slingshot, and closed the window.

14

MASON, pacing the floor of his office, said to Paul Drake, "Hang it, Paul, that woman must be *somewhere*. And for my money, she holds an important missing piece in the jigsaw puzzle. Incidentally, just to show you the pattern, the check she gave me on the Indianapolis bank was a phony. I telephoned the bank to get her address. She has no account there. They've never heard of a Laura Mae Dale."

"I can't find her," Drake said.

Mason resumed pacing the floor.

"What happened with Veronica?" Drake asked.

"She was just getting interesting when the party was broken up."

The telephone rang. Mason scooped it up, said, "Hello," and heard Della Street's voice saying, "I've been watching out the window, Chief. They all went away some place. Veronica had her bag with her, and she went away in a police car."

"And no one showed up to search your place?"

"Not yet."

"Okay, Della, keep me posted. I'll be here at the office for a while."

Mason hung up the telephone, said, "They've all left the apartment house out there. Veronica's with them. That's the last we'll see of that babe until they put her on the witness stand."

127

"What are you going to do with Addison?" Drake asked. "Is he going to tell his story?"

"Not until he gets on the witness stand."

"That makes it tough."

Mason nodded.

"You going to try to stall things along?"

"I'm afraid to, Paul. I can't hold Addison in line much longer. He's going to crack, one way or another. He'll either have a nervous breakdown or he'll throw caution to the winds and start talking."

"What'll happen when he starts talking?"

"He's in no position to talk, Paul."

"He didn't do it, did he?"

"No."

"Can't he tell the truth?"

"Not very well."

The telephone rang. Mason picked it up, said, "Hello . . . yes, right here."

He turned, said, "It's for you, Paul."

Drake took the telephone, said, "Hello," listened for a while, then said, "How's that . . . ? Oh yes . . . wait a minute, I'll get it . . . what's that? . . . well, I'll be damned! . . . put him on and let me talk with him . . . hello, Frank . . . how's that? . . . what's the rest of it . . .? Okay. Stick around."

Drake hung up the phone and said to Mason, "That's funny."

"What?"

"The police have another witness, a chap who lives about half a mile away from that farmhouse. He can't see the place from where he lives, but he knew generally it had been sold. And Tuesday night he heard six shots coming from the vicinity of that farmhouse. Of course, Perry, it's the same old story. At the time he heard the explosions, he thought it was a truck backfiring as it slowed up along the highway, but his wife insisted someone was shooting. So he made a note of the time."

"What time?"

"Exactly ten minutes to nine."

"Anything about the sequence of the explosions?"

"Yes, there was one shot, then another one almost im-

128

mediately, then an interval of two or three seconds, and then four more."

Mason lit a cigarette, frowningly contemplated the flame of the match before he shook it out.

"One more thing," Drake said. "There's a young woman in the department store, a sweet-looking kid, I understand, full of class and curves. Edgar Ferrell asked her to drive out to that farmhouse on Friday night. He said that if she'd come out and have a talk with him it would mean a lot to her. He promised to put her in charge of the personnel department."

"*Friday* night?" Mason exclaimed.

"That's right."

"What's her name, Paul?"

"Merna Raleigh."

Mason said, "I want to talk with her."

Drake shook his head and said, "No chance, Perry. She talked to my man and then she talked to the police. The police sewed her up like a barley sack. You couldn't get to talk with her on a bet, but my operative got her story before she told it to the police. He's writing out a report in the office. Do you want to see him?"

"You're darned right," Mason said.

Drake said, "I'll go get him. He's in my office."

He left Mason's office, walked down the corridor and returned in a few moments with a personable young man, clean-cut, efficient and one who would quite definitely appeal to women.

"Frank Summerville," Drake said. "He's my sheik. I turn him loose on cases where there are impressionable young women to interview. I had him circulating around the department store, pretending to be a customer. Just gossiping."

Drake nodded to Summerville and said, "Tell him your story, Frank."

Summerville made a characteristic dramatic gesture, running long, tapering fingers through dark, wavy hair which rippled in natural glossy waves from his forehead.

"Mr. Drake instructed me to keep moving around the department store, buying little knickknacks, asking questions, and trying to get the girls to gossip. Naturally I'd move around and pick the counters where there wasn't very much doing. I avoided the busy places."

Mason nodded.

"I'd ask discreet questions about whether Ferrell's death as reported in the papers would result in any changes, and the girl at the toilet article counter said I'd better ask that question of Merna Raleigh at the fountain pen counter—and then she gave a catty little smirk.

"So I went across the store to the fountain pen display, spotted Merna Raleigh as a cute redhead and really tried to build myself up."

"What happened?"

"I started looked at fountain pens, and I was pretty hard to please. I kept trying them out and while I was trying them out I started talking about what was happening there at the store, asking her if it was going to make any change and so forth. I hate to say so, but she had me spotted. She'd seen me at other counters, and she opened up and asked me if I was a detective.

"Ordinarily I'd have laughed at her and denied it, but something in the way she said it made me think I could strike pay dirt by telling her I was, and had the deadwood on me anyway, so I told her I was, and then she confessed that she'd been thinking this thing over and didn't know whether she should go to the police with it or not, but since I was a detective, she was going to tell me."

"And what was it?"

"She said Ferrell came to her Monday morning and seemed to be all perked up. He had always stopped by her counter and passed the time of day, and lately, as I found out afterwards, he'd been getting a little more intimate, coming around the counter and letting his hand rest on her shoulder, then slide down her back and giving her a pat on the hips."

"Go on," Mason said. "What happened?"

"He talked with her a while and asked her how she'd like to better her position, and naturally she would. She figured him as trying to be a wolf but wasn't dead sure. She was wondering just how far she'd have to go. And, as she told me very frankly, wondering herself just how far she *would* go."

"Did she like him?"

"Apparently he didn't mean too much one way or another. He was one of the bosses. She's been working for a while and knows her way around. Her mother was an old employee in the store, one of the holders of bonus stock; she died a couple of years ago and the red-head's been on her own. Think she does nicely. She was ready to string Ferrell along, I think, if he could deliver the goods."

"And just what did he promise?"

"Told her he was going to put her in charge of the personnel department at a big raise in salary and told her he wanted her to be out at his country place on Friday night, but she wasn't to breathe a word of it to anyone. She wanted to know where his country place was, and he drew her a map."

"Do you have that map?"

"No. I did have it. Merna gave it to me, but before I left I had to tell her I wasn't a police detective; that I was a private operative, and she's a smart little devil. She made me give the map back. She was going to get in touch with the police, and she didn't want to have to tell them she'd told her story to a private detective first. Under the circumstances, I figured it was better to let it go that way. But I got a darned good squint at the map. I think she's telling the truth."

"What makes you think so?"

"A lot of things. They have some paper there on which customers can try out pens, and this map was drawn on a sheet of that paper. I looked at the water mark to make certain, and the printing on it definitely was not feminine printing; it was the type of printing Ferrell would have done. He'd been an accountant, and the figures were all as neat as could be."

"What figures?"

"Distances. He gave her the speedometer distance from the department store; the number of the roads; then showed her where to turn off; even marked a place showing the plank bridge across the dry stream bed."

131

"And told her to be there Friday night?"

"That's right."

"What time?"

"He said between nine and ten."

"Didn't she think that was rather late?"

Summerville grinned and said, "Hell, you're not fooling that baby any. She's a red-headed trick who knows her way around. She figured she wasn't going to get to be manager of the personnel department without playing ball, at least a little bit.

"Ferrell was about thirty-one; she's about twenty-two. She could probably have gone for him in a big way if she thought there'd be anything in it for her. I don't think she was stuck on him at all, but he was falling for her and naturally she liked it. The other girls had noticed that Ferrell had always stopped at her counter and—well, you know, she knew he was one of the bosses, and naturally she was playing up to him."

"Darned interesting," Mason said, "but I can't figure it."

"Well, here's something that may help. The girl who's in charge of the personnel department now is Myrtle C. Northrup and she's always been a strong booster for John Addison. She worships the ground Addison walks on and thinks he's the smartest department store executive in the world. She's about forty-five; Addison's forty-eight. Apparently she's not too long on looks but she's strong on efficiency. Ferrell doesn't like her. She's been there since way back before Ferrell's time, when his dad was Addison's partner. Incidentally, she's the treasurer of the corporation."

Mason jerked bolt-upright. "The hell she is!"

"That's right, attends all the meetings. She's the biggest of the small stockholders. I guess she was pretty strong for Ferrell's dad, but she hates Junior's guts."

Mason frowned. "And Ferrell was going to tie the can to her?"

"Well, he'd promised this red-headed chick her job. But there again the babe was skeptical because she knew Ferrell couldn't fire this Northrup gal. Addison supervises most of the personnel end of the business. Ferrell makes graphs and analysis charts. Gossip is that they're a joke. He's been in there five years and has put in most of that time making charts and business forecasts and the store gossip is that no forecast has ever been right yet."

"You've been talking with a good many of the employees?"

"Uh huh. I think I've overdone it. This redhead spotted me and others may have. I've got lots of gossip and I think I'm all finished."

"What happened to the redhead?"

"She phoned the police. They eased her out of there. I don't think you'll get to talk with her."

Mason said irritably, "They don't give me any breaks. They grab the people who may know anything about it and put them out of circulation."

"Darned if they don't," Drake said.

"Anything else you want from me?" Summerville asked.

"I guess not," Mason said.

"You make out a report," Drake told him. "Make out a very complete report. Put everything in it you can think of, every little detail, no matter how small. You may think of some little thing that'll be significant."

When Summerville had left the office, Mason said, "It's late, but I'm going to take a chance." He picked up the phone, said, "Gertie, I want to talk with Miss Myrtle C. Northrup at Addison's department store. If she isn't there, find out where I can reach her."

Mason dropped the receiver into place.

Drake said to Mason, "You going to move right ahead with the request for a prompt hearing?"

Mason nodded. "Nothing else to do."

"Your man will have to tell a damn plausible story at that time; otherwise public sentiment will crystallize against him. You can't stall the thing along much longer."

"I know," Mason said.

"Does he have a story, Perry?"

"No."

"Will he have on when the trial opens?"

"No."

"When will he have one?"

"When he gets on the witness stand," Mason said.

The phone rang. Gertie's voice, sounding syrupy in its smooth cadences, said, *"Mrs.* Northrup left on her vacation yesterday. No one at the store knows where she can be reached."

"Why accent the *Mrs.?*"

"That's the way they gave it to me, Mr. Mason. I asked for Miss Northrup and the girl said Mrs. Northrup was on her vacation."

"Try to get her home number, Gertie."

"I did. I got the number. No one answers."

Mason hung up the phone, turned to Drake. "She's on vacation, probably wouldn't know anything about it, anyway."

Drake said, "It doesn't make sense, Perry. Ferrell must have been using the same old bait to string that redhead along."

Mason nodded. "But why did he want this girl out there Friday?"

Drake grinned. "Perhaps Wednesday and Thursday were already filled."

"Could have been. I'd like to talk with this redhead when the police let her get back in circulation."

"Now, I tell you what you do. According to all stories, Laura Mae Dale was running a restaurant in a town in Indiana about fifty miles from Indianapolis. Somehow I believe that story. It's part of the background Veronica gave Addison when he picked her up. The girl's accent and manner tends to bear that out. You can probably find records of restaurants on the State Board of Health reports, or city licenses, or something of the sort. Have your men get busy and start combing all these towns near Indianapolis. Locate the restaurant, find out who's in charge, and perhaps then you can find out what her address is here. And if she's gone back to her restaurant, have your men stick her on a plane and bring her out here. We can use that bad check charge if we have to. Spare no expense. I want action and I want it fast."

"Just why is she so important, Perry?" Drake asked.

"I wish I knew the answer to that one, Paul. Call it a

hunch if you want, but let's look at certain facts. Veronica is in a spot where Addison picks her up. The time is immediately after Ferrell is murdered. Her testimony will crucify Addison.

"Therefore, if there's anything phony about Veronica it may help Addison's case. Now, Veronica says she had a battle with a wolf. It sounds convincing and it accounts for her being where she was when she was. But Veronica hit town and was pinched for vagrancy within an hour of the time she moved into her hotel room.

"You can say all you want about the police being dumb, Paul, but it took *some* co-operation on Veronica's part to land in the cooler. Now, why did she want to get arrested?"

"Blackmail?" Drake asked.

"So far that's the answer. That would put her in cahoots with Eric Hansell, but if that's the picture they don't need a mother to help them frame it. Yet the mother stepped in, telling me Veronica was eighteen."

"Perhaps they intended to use the mother in case the vagrancy plan didn't work," Drake said.

"Could be. I want to talk with the mother and I want to get her before the police do. You know, Paul, the whole thing may not have been as accidental as it seems. Veronica may have been planted as bait for Addison. Hansell may have been deliberately gunning for big game . . . Get that mother for me. I want her. Check Hansell's associates, look up his record—and get *busy!*"

15

∎

NEWSPAPER REPORTERS were waiting to besiege Perry Mason as the lawyer entered Judge Keetley's courtroom.

Court was not yet in session, but because of the importance of the trial, the room was jammed with spectators.

Every seat was occupied and an overflow ring of the curious stretched in a semi-circle around the walls, standing shoulder to shoulder.

Judge Paul M. Keetley entered the courtroom.

A bailiff pounded with his gavel and announced that court was in session.

Judge Keetley settled himself behind the bench, looked over the crowded courtroom, glanced down at the burly figure of Hamilton Burger, the district attorney, then over at Perry Mason.

A bailiff opened a door and escorted John Addison into the room. He looked as though he hadn't slept since police had discovered Ferrell's body.

As the department store millionaire walked stiffly and self-consciously over to the table where Mason was seated, the courtroom buzzed with a sudden sibilance of whispered comment.

The bailiff banged with his gavel.

Mason dropped a casual hand on Addison's shoulder, smiled, said in a low voice, "Smile, damn you!"

Addison tried a twisted grin.

"That's better," Mason said.

"Case of the People versus Addison," Judge Keetley called. "This is the time heretofore fixed for the preliminary hearing. Are you ready, gentlemen?"

"Ready for the Prosecution," Hamilton Burger announced, his manner that of barrel-chested belligerency.

"Ready for the defendant, Your Honor," Mason said.

Hamilton Burger turned to call his first witness.

Mason took advantage of that dramatic moment. "Your Honor," he said, "we have issued subpoenas for Veronica Dale. I understand that she is being held incommunicado by the police and it has therefore been impossible for us to have this subpoena served. In view of the fact that this person is a material witness for the Defense, we deem it only fair that the Court instruct the police this witness must be produced at this hearing or that we be given a continuance until the witness *can* be produced."

Hamilton Burger looked at Mason with something of

a sneer. "She'll be here," he said. "Don't worry. And her testimony will be on behalf of the Prosecution."

Carl B. Knight, the assistant prosecutor and one of Burger's most aggressive young deputies, smiled approvingly at Burger and whispered something which caused Burger's grim mouth to soften into a slight smile. Burger settled his thick torso back into the swivel chair at the counsel table.

Judge Keetley said, "I take it, Mr. Mason, that you are not going to make any showing as to what this witness will testify to but will content yourself with the assurance of the Prosecution that this witness will be here and your request for a continuance is withdrawn?"

"Yes, Your Honor."

Judge Keetley nodded, said to Hamilton Burger, "Call your first witness, Mr. District Attorney."

"Charles W. Neffs," Burger called.

Charles Neffs proved to be a deputy sheriff who had, he testified, been on duty on the night of the eleventh instant. On that evening, shortly before midnight, a call had been received from the defendant, John Racer Addison, stating that Addison, in company with Lorraine Ferrell, the widow of Edgar Z. Ferrell, was at a certain designated service station; that they had discovered the dead body of Edgar Ferrell and had proceeded to the nearest telephone.

"What did you do?" Hamilton Burger asked.

"I went to the place where . . ."

"Alone?" Hamilton Burger interrupted.

"No, sir. I took another deputy with me and there was a private detective, a Paul Drake, who was in my office at the time and who had been asking questions . . ."

"Just a moment," Mason interrupted. "Any conversation between Paul Drake and this witness, which took place without the hearing of the defendant, certainly is not binding on the defendant."

"That's right," Judge Keetley ruled.

"Your Honor, I think the situation is a little peculiar here," Hamilton Burger said, "inasmuch as I think it can be proven that Paul Drake was, in fact, from a legal standpoint, the agent of the defendant."

"Can you prove it?" Mason asked.

"I can present facts from which it can be deduced."

"Can you *prove* it?" Mason repeated.

Judge Keetley rapped on the bench. "There is no need for heated argument between counsel," he said. "The Court made its ruling. The ruling will stand. The witness will not be permitted to testify as to any conversation with any third person outside of the presence of the defendant unless it can *first* be established there was some connection between such person and the defendant. Proceed with your testimony, Mr. Neffs."

Neffs said, "I went out to the place where Addison and Mrs. Ferrell were waiting. It was a service station about a mile and a half from an old farmhouse. In this farmhouse . . ."

"Just a moment," Hamilton Burger interrupted. "I think we can have a map introduced at this point so we can clarify the situation. Here is a map which I will ask you to examine and see if you can tell on this map exactly where you went. I take it, Mr. Mason, you will stipulate that this map may be used at this time, subject to the fact that I promise to connect it up later by showing that it is an accurate map drawn to scale, and showing the section of this country which it purports to portray."

"So stipulated," Mason said.

Neffs said, "Yes, I can identify the course we took very readily from this map. I went down this highway, which I will mark with a pencil line, to the point which I will mark on this map by a numeral one with a circle drawn around it."

"That was the service station?" Burger asked.

"That was the service station where Mr. Addison and Mrs. Ferrell were waiting," Neffs said.

"Then what happened?"

"Then I picked up Mrs. Ferrell and Mr. Addison. They directed me to the house where they had discovered the body of Edgar Ferrell."

"I show you a series of photographs," Burger said, "and ask you if you can identify those photographs."

"Yes, sir. These show the house where the body was discovered. They show it from various points of the compass. The body was discovered in this room near the Southwest corner of the house, as shown on this photograph."

"Did you take these photographs?"

"No, but I was present when they were taken."

"Have you examined them?"

"I have."

"What do they show, generally?"

"They show the conditions I found existing in and around that farmhouse. They show the surroundings, the rooms, the terrain, just as I saw it when I arrived."

"Let's have all those photographs marked for identification, and introduced in evidence," Burger said.

"And the room where the body was discovered, as shown in the photograph, can be marked with a circle," Mason said. "We consent to letting the photographs go in evidence."

"The window of that bedroom is shown in the photographs," Burger supplemented.

There was a moment's delay while the photographs were being marked, and then Burger went on with his examination. "What did you find, Mr. Neffs?"

"I entered the house with these people. I warned them to touch nothing. They advised me, however, they had already left quite a few fingerprints on various objects. I ascended the stairs to this bedroom and, on opening the door, I found a body lying on the floor."

"Can you describe the position of that body?"

"I had a camera in the car. I took a photograph of the body on the floor."

"Will you produce that photograph, please?"

Neffs produced the photograph and it was marked as an exhibit and received in evidence.

"Did you notice anything else in the room?"

"I did. Yes, sir, quite a few things."

"What were they?"

"There was a gasoline lantern which had been shut off by turning the knob which controls the supply valve so that the gasoline was shut off. That lantern was almost full. There was a bullet hole in the window and I . . ."

"The words 'bullet hole' indicated a conculsion of the witness, Your Honor," Mason said.

Judge Keetley nodded his head.

Hamilton Burger said irritably, "All right, all right. If Counsel wants to be technical, we'll strike out the word 'bullet' and leave just a hole in the window. What sort of a hole was it, Mr. Neffs?"

Neffs smiled and said, "A round hole, Mr. Burger, *almost exactly the size of a .38 calibre bullet.*"

Spectators in the courtroom laughed appreciatively and were silenced by the judge.

"You have photographs of that hole in the window?"

"I have. Yes, sir, I have photographs of that entire window."

Neffs produced these photographs and they were introduced in evidence.

"Also," Neffs went on, "I removed the glass from that window and placed it between two sheets of transparent plastic."

"Why did you do that?"

"Because, when the bullet went through the window, it had cracked the glass and I was afraid sections of the glass might fall out at any time, thereby destroying the evidence, since the hole would no longer be visible as a round hole."

Burger nodded to one of the bailiffs who tiptoed from the room, returned shortly with a wooden box only a few inches deep but about two feet square.

Burger took this box up to the witness stand, pulled out a sheet of glass cemented between two thick sheets of plastic.

"Is this the glass?" he asked.

"Yes, sir. That is the glass."

"Now, can you tell the Court just what you did in preserving the evidence?"

"Yes, sir. I secured a glass cutter and carefully cut a section from the windowpane, taking care to cut back so far from the cracked glass that there was no possiblility of a fracture. I had first cemented this sheet of plastic over the glass to hold it in place. When I lifted it out, I cemented another sheet over the other side, thus preserving the glass as evidence."

"Did Mr. Addison or Mrs. Ferrell make any statements to you at the time?"

"Yes."

"What were they?"

"I object to any statements made by Mrs. Ferrell which were not made in the presence of the defendant," Mason said. "I have no objection to anything the defendant may have said or to anything which was said in the presence of the defendant."

"Very well," Burger said, "what did Addison say and what was said in the presence of Addison?"

"Addison said he knew where the place was because he'd looked at it three weeks ago when it had been offered for sale; that he hadn't been out there since that date, but when Mrs. Ferrell talked with him and told him she was worried about her husband, he asked her if she had considered the possibility her husband might be at his country place. He said that she had told him she didn't know anything at all about her husband having purchased a country place."

"Exactly," Burger said. "Now, let's go back for a moment. I want to have one thing absolutely straight so there can be no possibility of a misunderstanding. Did the defendant, John Racer Addison, tell you at that time and at that place and in the presence of yourself and Mrs. Ferrell that he had not been out to that house before, save for a single time some three weeks ago when he had looked at the place when it was offered for sale?"

"Yes, sir, he did."

"Now, did you notice any tracks around the outside of that place?"

"Yes, sir."

"What sort of tracks?"

"Automobile tire tracks."

"Can you describe them to us?"

"I have photographs which I can introduce."

"These photographs were taken by you?"

"Yes, sir."

"Produce them, please."

The witness produced photographs of tire marks and they were duly marked and received in evidence.

"Now, then," Burger said, "directing your attention to this photograph, to tire marks A, B, C and D, what do they show?"

"They show where an automobile had turned around shortly after a rain. Those tracks were made in mud and at the time of the murder. The sun had baked the mud."

"And because the car was turning, the tracks of all four tires were evident at this particular point?"

"Yes, sir."

"Do you know when it had last rained?"

"Yes, sir. On the evening of the eighth and the morning of the ninth."

"That was Monday night and early Tuesday morning?"

"Yes, sir. It quit raining about four o'clock Tuesday morning."

"And at the time you went out to this house, in the company of the defendant and Mrs. Ferrell, what was the condition of the ground?"

"At this particular point and at that time the ground was quite dry."

"Were there any automobile tracks evident, other than those shown in the photograph?"

"Yes, sir. There were other automobile tracks, but these tracks lettered A, B, C and D were made by tires that were almost new, therefore they show more distinctly than do the others. Also those four tracks at the point marked on the photograph passed over a strip of clay-like mud where very distinct tracks were left."

"So, these tracks which are lettered A, B, C and D must have been made some time previously, while the ground was soft."

"Yes, sir, I would say within twenty-four hours of the time the rain ceased."

"Now, then," Hamilton Burger said triumphantly, "I notice that these four tires show very distinctive and individual tire patterns. In other words, the tires apparently were almost new and the treads in this soft, wet soil left almost a perfect imprint of each of the tires."

"Yes, sir."

"Now, did you have occasion to examine the automobile of the defendant?"

"I did, yes sir."

"When?"

"On the afternoon of the twelfth."

"And what did you find?"

"I prepared a soft substance which would yield imprints of tire tracks. I then ran the automobile over this substance, turning the steering wheel so that the wheels would leave individual patterns; in other words, so it would be possible to duplicate the turning radius of the automobile which had made the tracks A, B, C and D shown in this photograph."

"And what did you find?"

"I have here a photograph of that plastic material after the tracks were made."

"And what did those tracks show? I think it will be permissible for you to state generally, as an expert in such matters."

"The tracks showed absolutely identical tire patterns. There could not be any doubt of it."

"You have those photographs here?"

"Yes, sir."

"Produce them."

The photographs were produced and received in evidence. It was quite apparent that Judge Keetley was greatly impressed by the indisputable evidence of the identity of the tires.

"You noticed the makes of tires on the defendant's automobile?"

"I did. Yes, sir. As can be seen by the tread patterns, tires A and D were of the same pattern, and tires B and C were also of identical make and tread. Each one left a distinctive tire pattern."

"You may inquire," Hamilton Burger said.

Mason indicated the sheet of glass which had been removed from the window. "You removed this glass personally?" he asked.

"Yes, sir."

"And it is now in exactly the same condition as it was when you first saw it there in the window?"

"Yes, sir. Except for the fact that it has been removed. There are, therefore, the marks made by the cutter around the outside . . ."

"I understand that," Mason said. "I'm referring only to this bullet hole and the cracks radiating out from that bullet hole."

"Yes, sir."

"Those cracks radiate for a distance of some two or three inches?"

"Yes, sir."

"Following a fairly uniform pattern?"

"Yes, sir."

"By the way," Mason said, "which side of this glass was the inside, the side toward the room?"

The witness smiled and shook his head and said, "I couldn't tell you, Mr. Mason."

"You didn't deem it necessary to so indicate on the glass at the time you removed it?"

"No, sir. One side of a glass windowpane is identical with the other side."

"Except that one's inside," Mason said, "and one's out."

Hamilton Burger, with a tone of ponderous dignity, said, "Oh, if the Court please, this is hardly legitimate cross-examination. 'One side of the glass is inside and one side is out.' What difference does it make? It's a question of tweedledum and tweedledee."

"What happened to the rest of the glass that was in that windowpane?" Mason asked.

The witness glanced dubiously at Hamilton Burger.

"I think I can answer that question," Burger said. "The pane was taken out. The glass that remained was used for tests in the police laboratory."

"What sort of tests?"

".38 calibre bullets were fired through it," Hamilton Burger said, "for the purpose of measuring the diameter of the hole. I think the witness saw these tests."

"Did you?" Mason asked.

"Yes."

144

"And," Hamilton Burger said triumphantly, "the measurements of the holes left by the bullets as they went through the glass were exactly identical to the measurements of the hole in this glass which has been introduced in evidence. The cracking patterns were almost exactly identical."

"Are you going to introduce those in evidence?" Mason asked.

"I see no reason for doing so," Hamilton Burger said. "In fact, I believe the pane of glass was destroyed after the measurements were taken. However, there were some photographs taken of these holes in the glass, and I believe some attempt was made to save some of the glass. I think the witness knows about that."

Neffs said, "The glass could not be saved. The holes were too close to the edge of the glass, and when an attempt was made to cut out more of the windowpane, the cracks in the glass ran the rest of the way through the sash, and the glass was fractured."

"That's all," Mason said. "No further questions."

Burger, seemingly surprised at the brevity of the cross-examination, called his next witness, a fingerprint expert who had carefully gone over the house for evidences of fingerprints.

This witness testified to finding numerus prints of Lorraine Ferrell, of the defendant, John Racer Addison, and, in addition to that, latent prints which had not as yet been identified, prints, however, which he believed to be those made by two different, and as yet unidentified women.

On cross-examination, Mason saw that photographs of all of these latent prints, which were so plain as to make identification and comparison possible, were introduced in evidence.

Burger's next witness was Frank Parma, who, it seemed, was also a deputy sheriff.

"You arrived at the Ferrell country house on the morning of the twelfth?" Burger asked.

"Yes, sir."

"At about what time?"

"At about one o'clock in the morning."

"And you made some special investigation there?"

"I did, yes, sir."

"And, in the course of that investigation, did you find an object?"

"I did, yes, sir."

"What was it?"

"A .38 calibre Smith and Wesson revolver number S-64805."

"Can you describe it?"

"It was a .38 calibre double-action Smith and Wesson revolver with a six-inch barrel. While it was a .38 calibre revolver, it was on a .44 frame and was a heavy gun."

"Where did you find it?"

"If I may refer to the map," the witness said, picking up one of the maps that had been introduced in evidence, "I found it at a distance of approximately eighty-seven feet from the base of the house, at a point immediately opposite the window of the room where the body was found. The distance was eighty-seven feet and two inches from the base of the house at the nearest point. The revolver was lying among the rocks in the dry stream bed at that point. There were some willow bushes immediately adjacent to it, and the revolver was well concealed between these small stream-rounded boulders, boulders which were, I would say, on an average of two inches to twenty-four inches in diameter."

"You have photographs of the gun in the position in which it was lying?"

"I have, yes, sir, and I also have a photograph of a rock next to it, showing where the gun had struck and glanced when it had apparently been thrown from . . ."

"Never mind where it was thrown *from*," Burger interrupted. "Just tell what you know, not what you surmise."

"Yes, sir, the revolver had struck this boulder and then had glanced a distance of some two feet. There were the marks of blued-steel on the rock and a few wood fibers. The gun had a wooden handle, and a small corner of that wooden handle had been broken off. It was found at the base of the rock. The revolver itself was some eighteen inches away."

"Did you make any identifying marks on that revolver?"

"I did, yes, sir."

"What was it?"

"I marked my initials in pencil on a part of the wood stock, after the gun had been tested for fingerprints."

"Were any found?"

"No, sir, there were no latent prints on the gun."

"None whatever?"

"None. The gun had been wiped clean."

Burger opened a small handbag which his assistant handed him, took out a gun and passed it to the witness.

"That is the gun," the witness said after examining it.

"Now, did you do anything about tracing the ownership of that gun?"

"I did, yes, sir. I got access to the records and found that that gun had been sold to John Racer Addison approximately eleven months earlier."

"You thereupon exhibited the gun to the defendant?"

"I did."

"And what happened then?"

"The defendant identified the gun and admitted that it was his. He then made the statement for the first time that he had loaned Edgar Ferrell this gun to take with him on his fishing trip."

"What was the condition of the revolver when you found it, with reference to shells in the gun?"

"The gun was empty."

"What was the condition of the barrel?"

"The barrel had a distinct powder residue and a distinct trace of fresh powder."

"Cross-examine," Burger said.

"No questions," Mason announced.

"Call Dr. Parker C. Loretto," Burger said.

Dr. Loretto took the stand, qualified himself as a physician and surgeon, mentioned that he had been with the county for some time as an autopsy surgeon, that he was connected with the coroner's office, that he had performed an autopsy on the body of Edgar Z. Ferrell.

"What was the cause of death?" Burger asked.

"A gunshot wound which entered on the left side of

the head, slightly back of the ear, had an upward course, ranging toward the front part of the head, and had lodged against the far wall of the skull on the right side.

"That is, of course, expressing it in layman's language so that it can be readily understood," Doctor Loretto added, after a moment.

"Did the bullet penetrate the brain?"

"It did. There was considerable damage to the brain tissue and extensive cerebral hemorrhage."

"This wound was the cause of death?"

"It was, yes, sir."

"How long would you say the person lived after sustaining this wound?"

"No appreciable time. Consciousness and motion ceased instantly and death followed within a matter of seconds."

"Then the person didn't move after receiving this wound?"

"No. The person didn't move. But the body changed position, in that it fell to the floor. There was no *voluntary* motion."

"Did you recover the fatal bullet?"

"I did, yes, sir."

"And what was the condition of that bullet?"

"Flattened out on the point, but the base was undamaged."

"What do you mean by that?"

"I mean the base of the bullet retained its original cylindrical shape, and the marks of the rifling of the weapon which had fired it were plainly apparent."

"Did you mark that bullet in some way so that it could be identified?"

"I did, yes, sir."

"What mark did you make?"

"I etched my initials on the base of the bullet."

"I will show you a bullet and ask you if that is the bullet concerning which you have testified."

Burger lumbered forward, dramatically opened a small sealed envelope, shook a lead slug into the outstretched hand of the doctor.

Dr. Loretto examined the bullet gravely, turned it

over between his thumb and forefinger and said, "That is the bullet."

"And what did you do with it?"

"I delivered that bullet to George Malden of the department of ballistics of the sheriff's office."

"That's all," Burger snapped to Mason. "Inquire. Cross-examine."

"No questions," Mason said.

"Call George Malden," Burger said.

George Malden was a chunky, competent man with a dry, husky voice. He was short of stature, partially bald, and he walked deliberately to the witness stand, where he was sworn, took his seat, gave his name and address to the reporter and looked expectantly at Hamilton Burger.

"Your occupation, sir?"

"I am a deputy sheriff."

"How long have you been a deputy?"

"Twenty-three years."

"During that time have you specialized in any particular branch of crime detection?"

"I have."

"And what is that?"

"The science of ballistics and the science of fingerprinting."

"What experience have you had in the science of ballistics?"

"I have studied most of the standard textbooks on the subject. I have attended lectures in police school, and I have had better than fourteen years actual firsthand experience."

"I show you the bullet which Dr. Loretto has just identified as the fatal bullet and which was received in evidence as such, and ask you to examine this bullet and state whether you have ever seen it before."

"I have, yes, sir."

"What is that bullet?"

"That bullet is a .38 calibre lead bullet. It is made by the Peters Company and it has been fired from a .38 calibre revolver."

"I call your attention to certain grooves and indentations near the base of the bullet, and ask you what they are."

"Those are the marks of the barrel of the gun that discharged the bullet."

"Is there any way of identifying the gun from which this bullet was fired?"

"There is, yes, sir."

"Please describe it briefly to the Court."

Malden turned to the judge. "Every gun barrel," he said, "has certain distinctive marks of identification which are placed there by the manufacturer, for instance, the number of grooves, their shapes and dimensions. In addition to that, each rifle barrel has certain peculiarities of its own, minor imperfections in the metal which, in turn, leave telltale scratches on a bullet which is fired from the barrel with the terrific force of the compressed gases behind it. These marks are as highly individualized as the ridges and whorls on the finger tip of an individual."

"Did you make some attempt to examine this bullet and identify the weapon from which it had been fired?"

"I did, yes, sir."

"What did you do?"

"I took the .38 calibre Smith and Wesson revolver which has been introduced in evidence, loaded it with Peters shells containing bullets exactly identical to this fatal bullet in weight and dimension. I fired several shells into boxes containing loose cotton. I then recovered those shells and placed them in a comparison microscope.

"A comparison microscope is a microscope consisting of two separate microscopes so coordinated that objects may be placed in each microscope and rotated on revolving tables so that the images which are superimposed may be compared. Obviously, if the two images assume points of identity, they fuse into one image.

"In this way, I was able to place the fatal bullet and one of the test bullets in such a position that every mark and groove, every scratch, completely coincided.

"I have here photographs showing the base of the fatal bullet and the tip of the test bullet, placed one above the other and so placed that the scratches and marks on the bullets absolutely coincide. In other words, each scratch and groove seems continuous. Yet the photograph shows two bullets. You can see a transverse line of demarcation, marking the fatal bullet on the lower part, the test bullet on the upper part. Yet, so perfectly do those lines coincide that it would seem to be a photograph of only one bullet. That, incidentally, is the standard way of showing identity and similarity of barrel scratches and groove markings."

Malden produced the photographs, handed them to Burger, who submitted them to Mason and then asked that they be introduced in evidence.

"Any objection?" Judge Keetley asked.

"None, Your Honor."

"They will then be received in evidence and marked with appropriate exhibit numbers."

"Cross-examine," Burger said.

Mason rose to cross-examine.

"You said that you were a fingerprint expert?"

"Yes, sir."

"Then you doubtless examined the premises for latent fingerprints?"

"I did, yes, sir."

"And did you find the fingerprints of the defendant, John Racer Addison?"

"I did, yes, sir."

Hamilton Burger smiled complacently.

"And the fingerprints of Lorraine Ferrell, the widow of the decedent?"

"Yes, sir."

"Now, did you find other latent fingerprints?"

"Naturally."

"You found those of the decedent?"

"Yes, sir."

"And you did, did you not, find fingerprints which you took to be the fingerprints of a woman?"

"Yes, sir, I think there are the latents of *two* other women."

"And for the purposes of identification, have you made any attempt to arrange a set of those fingerprints?"

The witness glanced dubiously at Hamilton Burger,

said, "I have tried to get some of those fingerprints assembled in an order which *might* facilitate an identification in the event the persons who made those fingerprints are located by the police."

"Where are those fingerprints?"

"Oh, Your Honor," Hamilton Burger said, "I object to this testimony. Let Counsel hire his own detective if he wants to."

"Yes," Mason said, "now that the fingerprints have been completely obliterated from the premises, I would be free to search in vain."

"It's not up to the police to turn over evidence to the attorney for the Defense," Burger snapped irritably.

"Why not?"

"Because you'd twist it and distort it and try to use it to get your client off."

"If the police have fingerprint evidence we're entitled to it."

"You're not entitled to such evidence as the police have."

"You've qualified this man as a fingerprint expert. I am entitled to cross-examine him on anything he may have in his possession, for the purpose of testing his qualifications."

"You're not trying to test his qualifications. You're on a fishing expedition."

Mason grinned. "Well, the bait I am using happens to be legal."

"Your Honor, I object," Hamilton Burger said. "It is not proper cross-examination."

Judge Keetley said, "The only theory upon which the Court would support a demand for the surrender of fingerprints would be on the ground that cross-examination is permissible as to the qualifications of this witness as a fingerprint expert. However, while he stated he was an expert on fingerprints and ballistics, his testimony on direct examination went only to the subject of ballistics. Therefore, the question of his qualifications as a fingerprint expert has no bearing upon this testimony."

"Except that it might go to impeach his credibility," Mason pointed out.

"I will permit you to ask questions as to what he did and what he found, but I don't think I will broaden the scope of the inquiry at the present time to permit you to call upon this witness for the production of fingerprints. After all, the other witness has put photographs of those latents in the evidence."

"But this witness tried to *arrange* those prints, Your Honor."

"So he did. I would be inclined to give you more latitude if it were not for the fact you already have photographs of those prints."

"Very well," Mason said, "I accept the Court's ruling. That concludes my cross-examination."

"Your next witness?" Judge Keetley said to Hamilton Burger.

Hamilton Burger glanced at the courtroom clock. "It is drawing toward the time for adjournment."

"We still have some fifteen minutes left," Judge Keetley said.

"Very well," Burger said. "Call Eric Hansell to the stand."

Eric Hansell, ushered into the courtroom by a bailiff, came forward, was sworn, and, obviously ill at ease, gave his name and address.

"Are you acquainted with the defendant, John Racer Addison?" Burger asked.

"Yes, sir."

"Did you have occasion to talk with him on or about the eleventh of the month?"

"Yes, sir."

"What was said?"

Hansell shifted his position uneasily.

"Go ahead," Burger snapped. "Tell what happened at that conversation."

"Time, place, persons present?" Mason asked.

"Where was this conversation?" Burger asked.

"At his office in the department store."

"Who was present?"

"Just Addison and me."

"All right, what happened?"

"Well," Hansell said, "I was trying to get some information to pass on as a tip to a friend who was running a column in a newspaper. I asked Mr. Addison about his picking up a young girl out on the highway Tuesday night and getting her a room in a hotel. Addison told me to see his lawyer."

"Did he name the lawyer?"

"Yes, sir. Mr. Perry Mason."

"And did you see Mr. Mason?"

"Yes, sir."

"When?"

"That same day."

"Where?"

"At his office."

"And what did Mr. Mason say to you at that time?"

"Mr. Mason told me his client didn't want any publicity and gave me a two thousand dollar check which Mr. Addison had signed."

"Do you want this Court to understand that Mr. Addison gave you two thousand dollars in order to keep you from disclosing that he had been out on that section of the highway on Tuesday night?"

"Yes, sir."

Hamilton Burger's grin was one of extreme self-satisfaction as he tossed the bombshell into Mason's lap. "Cross-examine," he said, and then added sarcastically, "If you want to."

Mason said calmly, "In other words, you went to see Mr. Addison for the purpose of collecting blackmail, didn't you?"

The witness met Mason's eyes. His manner was insolent. "Yes," he said, "and if your client hadn't been trying to cover up, why would he have paid me the two thousand bucks?"

"Cover up what?" Mason asked.

"You ought to know."

"I don't. I'm asking you."

"Cover up the fact that he'd been playing around with a blonde cutie and that he'd been out on that road the night of the murder."

"Which fact do you think he was paying you two thousand dollars to cover up?"

"Probably both."

"That's what you *thought?*"

"Yes."

"Then you *knew* about the murder when you started blackmailing him?"

Hansell suddenly averted his eyes.

"Did you?" Mason persisted.

"No!"

"Then why did you say you thought he was paying you the two thousand dollars to cover up the fact that he was out on that road the night of the murder?"

"That's what I think now."

"But not what you thought then?"

"No."

"At that time you didn't know anything about the murder?"

"Certainly not."

"You were trying to blackmail him simply because he had befriended a young woman?"

"He got her a room in a hotel," Hansell said, his eyes once more back on Mason's.

"And you made a bargain with the district attorney's office by which you'd be granted immunity for the extortion in return for testifying in this case?"

"I haven't reached any bargain at all."

"But you do have that understanding?"

"Well, I . . ."

"We'll stipulate that he does," Hamilton Burger said. "Extortion is a mild crime compared with murder. The State is willing to overlook minor infractions of the law in order to get these men whose wealth, position and power give them the idea they can violate the laws of God and man with complete immunity."

"A nice speech," Mason said, "but the fact remains that Hansell is being promised immunity."

"Yes," Burger snapped.

Mason turned to Hansell. "Why didn't you say so?"

"You asked me if I'd made a bargain with the Prosecution. I hadn't. It was an agreement. It isn't any bargain."

"Not for you?"

"No."

"Is it for the Prosecution?"

"I don't know."

"You're rather technical in splitting hairs, aren't you, Mr. Hansell? You were quite willing to state that you had not made any *bargain* with the district attorney, when you knew all the time that you had made an *agreement?*"

Hansell didn't answer the question.

Mason waited until Hansell raised his eyes once more.

"Ever been convicted of felony?" Mason asked.

Hansell dropped his eyes again.

"Come on," Mason said, "answer the question. Have you ever been convicted of a felony?"

"Yes."

"What was it?"

"Blackmail."

"More than once?"

"Yes."

"All right," Mason said, "how many times have you been convicted?"

"Four."

"Now then," Mason said, "you had a woman accomplice with whom you worked in those cases, didn't you?"

"Objected to as incompetent, irrelevant and immaterial and not proper cross-examination," Hamilton Burger said. "Counsel is given the right under the law to inquire into this man's past only for one specific purpose, and that is to impeach his veracity by showing that he has been convicted of a felony. After that he cannot elaborate by throwing a lot of details and he can't besmirch the witness's reputation by dragging out all of the points involved in those other crimes. The law gives Counsel one privilege and one privilege only, and that is to ask whether a man has ever been convicted of a felony and that only for the purpose of impeaching his testimony."

"Isn't that your understanding of the law, Mr. Mason?" Judge Keetley asked.

Mason made a little gesture of deference to the Court. "The purpose of my inquiry, Your Honor, was not to besmirch the reputation of this witness, but to find out who the feminine accomplice was that he used in connection with his other blackmailing schemes and see if the fingerprints of that feminine accomplice do not match the unidentified fingerprints of the mysterious woman found in the murder house."

And Mason sat down, smiling at the prosecutor.

There was a buzzing of sound from the back of the courtroom, a sound which Judge Keetley silenced with his gavel.

"Well," Judge Keetley said, "I don't feel that the question is in order. It could only tend to discredit the witness by showing collateral matters. I doubt if it is proper cross-examination.

"However, it is the time for adjournment and Court will adjourn until tomorrow morning at ten o'clock. I will rule on the objection at that time. I am inclined to sustain it, however.

"Court adjourned."

16

∎

AFTER JUDGE KEETLEY had left the bench spectators formed in little groups, discussing the case. Newsmen crowded forward, tried to speak with Hamilton Burger, but he brushed them to one side and hurriedly left the courtroom.

Mason, urbanely smiling, stood waiting to receive the reporters.

"Come, come, gentlemen," Mason said, "I can't be expected to give away my entire case. The facts speak for themselves. You have seen the calibre of the Prosecution's case, a case founded on the testimony of admitted blackmailer's. There are the fingerprints of at least one mysterious woman in this murder house. There may be the prints of still another woman. Who are these women? Does the Prosecution know? Apparently not. Is the Prosecution willing to try and find out? You, gentlemen, will have to answer that question for yourselves."

Paul Drake, pushing his way through the crowd, grabbed Mason's arm, said in a hoarse whisper, "Perry, we've got a break for you."

"What?"

"We've located the woman you wanted."

"You mean Hansell's partner?"

"No, Laura Mae Dale. Veronica's mother."

"Now," Mason said triumphantly, "we're getting somewhere!"

Drake said, "My men found her in her restaurant in a little town in Indiana. She jumped at a chance to come out here by plane. Of course, my men put it on rather thick, that her daughter needed her and all that."

Mason nodded.

"Anyhow, they grabbed a plane and are here. I didn't want to interrupt you at the trial."

Mason raised his voice. "Oh, Addison," he called, "just a minute. Bailiff, hold Mr. Addison for a minute, will you?"

The deputy sheriff who had been taking Addison back to jail paused at the door leading to the private corridor in which prisoners were transported back and forth to the courtroom.

Mason, hurrying over, gripped Addison by the arm, pulled him to one side, whispered, "It's okay, Addison, we're beginning to get somewhere. At last we've got the breaks."

"What is it?" Addison asked hopefully.

"I can't tell you tonight, but have a good night's sleep. I think things are going to start coming our way in the morning."

Mason thanked the deputy sheriff for waiting, hurried back to Paul Drake and said, "Okay, Paul, let's get away from here. Now I want to get Della and her notebook and I want to get a written statement from this woman. I want her to repeat what she told me in my office, and I want to get her fingerprints and check them with the prints the police found in that house. Where is she?"

"I have her in a hotel here."

"Any chance she'll take a powder?"

"She can't," Drake said. "I have two of my men on the job. I've told her we're trying to get Veronica for her. Of course, that's a stall and I hate to pull a line like that, but we have to keep her sewed up, at least for a while, and that's the only way to do it."

Mason grinned, "Well, at least we can *try*. We'll contact Hamilton Burger and tell him Veronica's mother is staying with us and wants to see Veronica, and ask him if the daughter can come up to visit us."

"Burger will blow his top," Drake said.

"Of course," Mason told him. "Then after a while he'll get to thinking things over and realize that he passed up a bet. He'll ring up and insist upon talking to Mrs. Dale so he can tell her that if she'll come to *his* office he'll have Veronica there to meet her."

"You don't think he'll think of that the first time?"

"Not the first time," Mason said. "He'll be too mad. Where do you have her, Paul?"

Drake said, "I took a chance. I got her in the Rockaway Hotel. You see, her daughter was registered there and then checked out. It all ties in with the line I'm handing her about finding Veronica for her."

"You don't need to hand that woman any line," Mason said. "She's a smart cookie and if she isn't part of a blackmailing ring I'm a damn poor guesser. Let's go give her the works."

Mason caught Della Street's eye. "Be sure you have plenty of notebooks and pencils, Della. We're going to take a statement from Laura Mae Dale. I'll tell you the details later. Let's go."

The three of them pushed through the exit door into the private corridor, caught the elevator and, in Drake's car, rushed to the Rockaway Hotel.

"Room 612," Drake said.

They went up and tapped on the door.

A man opened the door a half inch, said in a hoarse, belligerent voice, "What do *you* want?" Then, recognizing Paul Drake, opened the door and said, "Okay, boss, come on in."

Drake stood to one side. Della Street entered the room, followed by Perry Mason. Drake brought up the rear.

The room they entered was the parlor of a two-room suite. The two detectives who were guarding the place were heavily muscled men who were thoroughly capable of taking care of themselves in any emergency.

"Where is she?" Paul Drake asked, looking around the room.

One of the men grinned, said, "She's in the adjoining bedroom, lying down, resting. She isn't even registered at the hotel, and, as far as anyone could tell from snooping around, that room isn't even rented. The two of us are up in this room discussing a business deal, in case anyone asks questions."

Drake, instantly suspicious, said, "How do you know she's still there? How do you know she can't get out through the other door or down the fire escape, or . . ."

"Keep your shirt on," the spokesman for the two detectives said. "The door's locked and we have the key. There's a DO NOT DISTURB sign on the corridor side of the door. There isn't any fire escape. She's in there, all right. You want to talk with her?"

Drake nodded.

"We'll get her."

"Just a minute," Mason said. "I think it'll be a little better if you simply announce there are visitors to see her and we three go in. It will make the party a little easier to handle than if she comes in here."

"Okay."

The man who seemed to be in charge nodded to the other, who tapped on a door to a communicating room and said, "You have some visitors, Mrs. Dale."

The door opened. They heard a woman's voice raised in a question. Then Drake's operative said, "Oh, don't worry about dressing up. They're home folks. They'll only stay a minute. Here they are."

He flung the door open and nodded.

Della Street, entering the room first, suddenly stopped, looked questioningly back at Mason, then, catching her-

160

self moved calmly on in as though nothing had happened.

Mason, prepared to see the woman who had entered his office and told him about her daughter, fought to keep his surprise from showing on his face as he saw a slender, work-worn woman in the late forties who smiled shyly at Della Street and said, "Hello, are you bringing me information about my daughter?"

Mason, stepping forward, said, "My name is Mason. This is Paul Drake, a detective. We're going to try and locate your daughter for you. As it happens, she's a witness. I'm going to call the people who are holding her and see if they'll let her come here."

Drake, somewhat nonplussed, said, "I thought you two knew each other. Haven't you been in Mr. Mason's office?"

She smiled and shook her head. "Heavens to Betsy, I just this minute got into this town! I'm terribly anxious to see Veronica. I haven't seen her for over a year. She sent me a post card from the Rockaway Hotel here, so I thought I'd come and . . ."

"You haven't seen her for over a year?" Mason asked.

"That's right."

"Where do you live?"

"It's a little town in Indiana. You wouldn't recognize the name. I have a little restaurant and lunch counter there, nothing pretentious, just eight or ten tables and this lunch counter. It's all nice, clean, home-cooked food."

"You're Veronica's mother?" Mason asked. "You're not someone who has been run in as a ringer?"

"What do you mean 'run in as a ringer,' Mr. Mason?"

"Nothing. Skip it. Tell us about Veronica."

"What do you want to know about her?"

"How old is she, for one thing."

Mrs. Dale frowned, said, "She's eighteen, going on nineteen . . . no, wait a minute, the girl's—why, bless me, the girl's twenty. My heavens, how time flies!"

"And you haven't seen her for over a year?"

"Right around a year. Perhaps a little over. Do you know if she's all right, Mr. Mason? I've been really worried about her. Something about this last time she left . . ."

"She's left you before?"

"Heavens, yes, she's a regular little vagabond. I suppose I've been expecting too much of her. The town is pretty small. There aren't many young folks in it. I guess Veronica gets pretty lonely when she's there; but she's such a help to me in the restaurant, waiting on tables, and she's always so cheerful and sunny. The customers like her and—well, when I had Veronica there just wasn't any help problem at all."

"When was the first time she left?"

"Let me see, that's been three or four years ago."

"What did she do?"

"She just up and left, and I didn't hear from her for two or three months. I was terribly worried. I even notified the police. Then she showed up. She'd just been hitchhiking around. She said she'd had her fling and seen the country and now she was ready to settle down and work. Well, she did, but not for long. It wasn't over three or four months before the old wanderlust got to gripping her again, and the first thing I knew she'd taken off."

"Alone?"

"Alone," Mrs. Dale said. "Don't misunderstand me about that. Veronica's a *good* girl. She may have had a ride with someone when she started out, but that's all it was, just a ride."

"You're sure?"

"Of course I'm sure. I tell you, Veronica is a good girl that way. She's just restless, just a wanderer at heart. She can't stay in one place.

"I don't know as a body can blame her. Her father before her was that same way, always restless, always running around from one place to another, looking for some place where he could do what he called 'carving out a career.'

"Almost as soon as Veronica was born he went traipsing off to find some Land of Opportunity. He never found it. He kept me broke financing his travels, but always he'd have the same reassuring line of talk.

"Sakes alive, that man could make you thrill all over

when he talked to you. He was full of golden dreams. Sometimes he'd tell me about business opportunities he'd just missed by not being there just a little mite sooner. Seemed like he missed a chance to be a millionaire a couple of times—just missed it by a day or two. He was killed in an automobile accident when Veronica was five."

"And how long since Veronica left on this last trip?"

"Something over a year. I'd get postal cards from her at different parts of the country. I never had any chance to write to her. She was always on the move. Sometimes it'd be three or four months before I'd get a card from her, and when I did get one she'd just tell me the places she'd been. She didn't write any news, just a list of the places she'd been through. Seems like that's all she's interested in, just travel."

"Has Veronica ever had any trouble on her travels?"

"Not a speck, Mr. Mason. She's a wonder when it comes to handling people. She can look them right in the eye and make them feel lower than the dirt under her feet. And I don't know for the life of me how she does it. It's just the way she can get that baby stare in her blue eyes.

"And then again when she feels like kidding along she can be the life of the party. But most of the time she likes to sit back and be quiet like. And you never saw anything like the way she can get what she wants out of people. All she has to do is just crook her finger and people fall all over themselves doing just what that girl wants."

Mrs. Dale beamed with pride.

"Does she ever get pressed for money and wire you for help?" Mason asked.

"Bless you no! That girl's the best little financier. How she does it, I don't know, but every time I see her, she's well-dressed and she has plenty of money. She actually buys me presents every time she comes home. And travel! Mr. Mason, you'd be surprised the places that girl has been. I guess she's been almost every place in the United States and once she went right on down to Mexico City.

"My, but I'm dying to see her!"

"You may have to wait until tomorrow to see her. She's busy with some things now."

"That's Veronica. She's always busy as a bee. No grass ever grows under *her* feet."

Mason said, "I'd like to have some proof that you're Veronica's real mother, just to keep the record straight. Could you furnish any?"

"Why, Mr. Mason, *of course* I'm Veronica's mother."

"I understand, but can you prove it? I may have to show some evidence as to who you are."

"Well, I've my driving license and—the card Veronica sent me, and pictures of her."

She opened her purse, handed Mason a driver's license, some snapshots, and a post card.

Mason studied them for a moment, then went to the telephone and called Hamilton Burger's office.

When a secretary answered the telephone, Mason said, "I know it's after office hours, but I felt that Mr. Burger might have gone to his office after court. This is Perry Mason talking. I'd like to speak with him."

"Just a moment. He's here. He's just leaving for home."

Mason heard the girl's voice say, "Mr. Mason wants to talk with you," then, "just a moment Mr. Mason, he's coming on the other phone."

There was the sound of pounding steps audible through the receiver, then Burger's deep, booming voice growled over the telephone, "What is it, Mason?"

Mason said, "I have a favor to ask of you."

"You're in a rather disadvantageous position to seek favors. What do you want?"

"Veronica Dale's mother is here with me and she wants very much to see her daughter. Could you arrange it so that we could call on Veronica sometime tonight and . . ."

"Very definitely not," Burger interrupted. "Veronica Dale is a State's witness. If you want to talk with her, talk with her on the witness stand. I'm sorry, Mason, but that's final. I have neither the time nor the inclination to discuss the matter. It's late, and I'm headed for home. Good-by!"

The phone banged up at the other end of the line.

Mason grinned, slipped the receiver into place and winked at Paul Drake.

"How is Veronica?" Mrs. Dale asked.

"Doing just fine," Mason said, "but it's just as I anticipated. You may not be able to see her until tomorrow. Della, if Hamilton Burger should start calling for me rather frantically, be sure to tell him that I'm out and you don't know where I can be reached."

17

AS COURT RECONVENED the next morning, Hamilton Burger, a smile on his face, arose and said, "If the Court please, Eric Hansell was on the stand and, as Court adjourned, the question had arisen over Counsel's questioning of Hansell concerning female accomplices."

Judge Keetley nodded. "The Court will sustain your objection, Mr. Burger. The law gives the Defense the right to impeach this witness by showing he has been convicted of one or more felonies. That does not permit Counsel to introduce evidence of specific details for the purpose of stultifying the witness.

"That is the Court's ruling. Mr. Hansell will take the witness stand. Proceed with your cross-examination, Mr. Mason."

"In this present case," Mason asked Hansell, "how did you get the information which enabled you to approach Addison, as you claim you did?"

"*You* gave it to me by rushing down to the jail to furnish bail for Veronica Dale."

"And just how did that give you any lead to Mr. Addison, the defendant in the case?" Mason asked.

"Well, sir, I hang around the press room at police

headquarters quite a bit. I know some of the boys there, and, through arrangements with a friend of mine, I have certain courtesies. I pass the boys a tip once in a while and I'm always ready to help out. They give me tips. None of them, of course, knew what I was doing. They all thought I was free lancing information for a columnist friend of mine. And that's what I did do most of the time.

"Well, when the word got around that you had come tearing down there to defend some babe that was charged with vagrancy, it didn't mean much to the other fellows, but that's the sort of stuff that's right down my alley. I started looking around. I found out the girl was registered at the Rockaway Hotel and that the charges against her had been dismissed.

"I still didn't have anything to go on, but I went up to the Rockaway Hotel and told them I was representing the Press and wanted to know about the case, and the clerk, who had been pretty well filled up with being questioned up one side and down the other, told me he'd given the police all the information he had; that the jane had come in to get a room; that the manager of the hotel had telephoned to see that she got one.

"I went to the manager of the hotel. I told him I was representing a columnist, and we wanted to know how come that this cutie rated his personal attention. I spread it on pretty thick that we had a tip she was his dish, and he got in a panic and let the cat out of the bag before he thought what he was doing. He said that Addison had telephoned in to see about getting a room for her.

"Well, so far I hadn't got anything except a run-around, but I went up to Addison, and I hadn't been talking with him ten seconds before I knew I'd struck pay dirt. So then I—well, you know, I put the heat on him."

"You told Mr. Addison you were working for some columnist?"

"Well, something to that effect."

"Who was the columnist?"

"I don't want to tell that. As a matter of fact, I was running a bluff there, and I don't think it's fair to . . ."

"Neither do I, Your Honor," Hamilton Burger said, getting to his feet. "After all, this gets back purely to a collateral matter, a conversation this man had with John Addison, the defendant in this case. I hold no brief for this witness. He is a blackmailer. I will use every bit of power my office possesses to see that his nefarious activities are brought to a halt. But, in the meantime, it happens that because of his activities, a murder case is being brought to a solution. We have here a defendant so anxious to avoid having it disclosed that he was out in the vicinity of the house where the murder was committed that he paid two thousand dollars to keep his activities from being published in a gossip column."

"Of course," Judge Keetley said, "that's only incidental and depending upon your interpretation of the evidence, Mr. District Attorney. It is quite possible that the defendant was willing to pay money because of some relationship with a young woman who may have been a minor and . . ."

"We expect to clear all that up by our next witness," Hamilton Burger said. "And when Your Honor sees that witness, the Court will realize how preposterous it is to even think for one moment that anything could have transpired which would give Addison any grounds for being blackmailed. No, Your Honor, the alacrity with which this defendant tried to purchase the silence of this witness is due entirely to fear on the part of the defendant that he would be placed in the vicinity of this murder at the time it was being committed."

"Let me ask one question of the witness," Judge Keetley said. "Mr. Hansell, was there actually any relationship between you and the columnist whom you mentioned?"

"Only to this extent," Hansell said, "that from time to time I'd pass on tips to him and he'd give me a little dough once in a while and a few favors. Tickets and passes here and there, and things of that sort. You see, in my business I have to have some sort of a publishing outlet to threaten people with, but this man didn't have the faintest idea of what I was doing and thought I was just a friend who was passing on tips."

"Under the circumstances," Judge Keetley said, "I see no reason for bringing this man's name into disrepute. After all, we have here a witness who is quite possibly giving evidence of considerable value in clearing up a murder case, but that does not constitute any justification for his reprehensible activities. The Court feels that it would be an imposition upon justice to permit this witness to sully the good name of any reputable newsman; moreover, the Court is very frank to state that in the event there is any substantial conflict in the evidence, the word of this witness will be accepted by the Court only so far as it is corroborated by other evidence."

"That's all," Mason said.

"No further questions," Hamilton Burger announced.

"I take it," Hamilton Burger said, "there is no question on the part of Counsel but what the defendant in this case actually paid this witness two thousand dollars."

"None whatever," Mason said cheerfully.

"That eliminates the necessity of introducing the check in evidence," Hamilton Burger said.

Judge Keetley, leaning forward from the bench, said, "Mr. District Attorney, it occurs to me that while the question of whether a witness should be given immunity is entirely within your discretion, the witness in question shows a smug complacency, a complete lack of repentance, a flippant disregard for all ethical considerations."

"I think, if the Court please," Burger said, flushing slightly, "there are certain matters in the background which Counsel *could* have brought out on cross-examination had he desired, which would account for the attitude of the witness. There is a certain personal element of antagonism in the case between Counsel and this witness, due to things—well, things which I cannot with propriety comment on at the moment. But I can assure Your Honor that the action of my office in granting this witness immunity from the charge of extortion was taken with considerable reluctance and only after a very searching investigation."

"Very well," Judge Keetley said, "I merely wanted to call your attention to the fact that the demeanor of this witness on the stand does not impress me at all favorably. Call your next witness."

"Veronica Dale," Hamilton Burger said.

A matron opened the door of the witness room, brought Veronica Dale into court.

She was attired in neat-fitting cream-colored tailored suit, which, matching her blonde beauty, gave her a virginal appearance of innocence, an angelic beauty which struck the crowded courtroom with terrific impact.

The witness apparently knew exactly the part she was to play, and, from the moment she entered the courtroom, registered as a beautifully sweet young woman. Courtroom attachés whispered that any attempt on the part of Perry Mason to cross-examine her at length would be disastrous in that it would alienate the sympathy of spectators and judge alike.

Hamilton Burger set the stage for her act by arising, his manner plainly indicating that he considered it a shame such an unspoiled child should be forced to enter the sordid atmosphere of a murder trial.

"What's your name?" he asked, deferentially.

Veronica Dale lowered her lids, said primly and in a voice that was barely audible, "Veronica Dale."

"How old are you, Veronica?"

Her voice this time was hardly more than a whisper, "Just eighteen."

"Hand the witness the microphone," Judge Keetley said.

A bailiff handed the microphone to Veronica Dale.

"Use that to talk into," Judge Keetley said. "Try and talk as loud as you can."

"Yes, sir," Veronica Dale said submissively.

"Now, where do you live, Veronica?"

"Well, I don't exactly have any residence," she said. "My mother lives in a small town in Indiana. I left home to try and find some way of bettering myself. I had just come here to this city when—when all of these things happened to me."

She blinked back tears.

"I understand," Burger said sympathetically, his manner showing that he intended to use every effort at his disposal to shield the unsullied innocence of this child. "Now, I'll try to make this as easy on you as I can and make my examination just as short as possible. I hope we can spare you any great ordeal, Veronica."

And Hamilton Burger glanced singificantly at Perry Mason, as though warning the lawyer to keep his cross-examination equally short.

The spectators were leaning forward, listening intently, afraid they might miss some word.

Judge Keetley was also absorbed in listening, his eyes showing keen and serious interest.

"Now, Veronica," Hamilton Burger said, "you're acquainted with the defendant in this case, John Racer Addison, aren't you?"

"Yes."

"When did you first meet him?"

"On the night of the ninth."

"Where?"

"He gave me a ride."

"I understand, but just where were you, Veronica, when he gave you a ride?"

"I was sitting beside a culvert."

"Now, Veronica, since you have talked with me, you have been taken out by the sheriff's office along the road where you met the defendant?"

"Yes," she said, almost in a whisper.

"Speak up, Veronica, so we can hear you. And did you point out that culvert to the sheriff?"

"Yes, sir."

"And was a photograph taken of that culvert in your presence?"

"Yes, sir."

"Your Honor," Mason said, "Counsel is leading this witness, putting the words in her mouth. His entire examination is viciously leading."

Burger glowered at Mason. "If the Court please, we have here a young woman from a small town, a frightened young child. I say to you that it is a shame this young woman should be sucked into the atmosphere of crime. It is monstrous that a murderer should have been at liberty to give her a ride . . ."

"The Court understands," Judge Keetley interrupted, "but try and refrain from leading the witness."

"Very well, Your Honor."

Berger glared at Mason, then turned to Veronica. "Now, I show you a photograph and ask you if you recognize the place shown in that photograph."

Hamilton Burger passed a copy of the photograph to Mason, said, "That is a print I have made for you, Counselor. It shows a section of the road which I will presently locate on a map. The picture is taken facing west. Now, Veronica, I hand you that picture and ask you if you identiy it."

"Yes, sir."

"What is it?"

"It's the culvert where I was waiting when Mr. Addison came along in his car. I was sitting right here on that little cement projection, and then when I heard the car coming I stood up."

"Yes. Now where did this car come from, if you know?"

"It came from a side road, down here, over at this part of the picture."

"Did you *see* the car?"

"Not the car, but I could catch glimpses of the lights and I could hear the motor. The night was calm and still."

"And what happened?"

"This car motor sounded very plainly as it went along a dirt road that was screened with willows, a road that's back here."

"Now, Veronica, I'm going to show you a map, a map of the house where the body of Mr. Edgar Z. Ferrell was found and showing some of the surrounding terrain. This is a map which has been previously introduced in evidence. Now, can you orient yourself on that map?"

"Orient myself?" she asked.

"Get yourself located, show just where you were, just where the culvert is."

"Oh, yes," she said, studying the map, and then, with the swift alacrity of one who has been well coached and who has thoroughly familiarized herself with the map in

171

question, said, "I was sitting right here. That's where the culvert is."

"I will mark that spot with the figure number one in a circle," Hamilton Burger said, making a mark on the map. "Now, Veronica, can you tell us where that car came from?"

"Yes, it came along this road over here."

"Indicating two parallel lines on the map which bear the legend ROAD CONNECTING FERRELL COUNTRY PLACE WITH MAIN HIGHWAY," Hamilton Burger said. "Now, go right ahead, Veronica, and tell us what happened."

"Well, the car came along this road, going rather slowly. It sounded like it was in low gear, or perhaps second gear, and then it came crawling up this steep bank up to the highway."

"Did you see it?"

"No, I couldn't see it at that time. I could hear it. That steep climb up to the highway is about—oh, perhaps, a little over a quarter of a mile from the culvert where I was sitting."

"And then what?"

"I'm sure the car came up this steep bank to the road in low gear. Then it went into second gear and about the time it was shifting into high, I showed myself in front of the headlights."

"Now let's go back a moment, Veronica. *Before* you heard this motor, did you hear any other sounds?"

"Yes."

"What were they?"

"Shots."

"How many shots, Veronica?"

"Six."

"Can you describe them?"

"Well, I thought it was a motor backfiring at the time, but now I've had a chance to think it over, I know they were shots. I heard one and then in about a second another, and then after a second or two I heard four more fired very rapidly."

"Now *when* did you hear these shots, Veronica?"

"Just a minute or two before the car started."

"As much as five minutes?"

"I don't think so. Maybe two or three minutes, just a little while."

"Would you know what time this was?"

"Not exactly. I think it was just about nine o'clock, probably a few minutes before."

"Very well. Now you heard the shots. You heard the car start. You heard it come to the road. You saw it approaching you."

"Yes, sir."

"Did you try to thumb a ride?"

"No, I made no motion whatever, but I did look at the headlights so that the man who was driving the car could—well, you know, get a good look at me."

"And what happened?"

"The car wasn't going very fast. It was just getting into high gear, and just after it passed me, it stopped and then started to back up."

"And then what?"

"Then Mr. Addison asked me if I wanted a ride."

"Now, you are referring to Mr. John Racer Addison, the defendant in this case, the gentleman sitting on Mr. Mason's left?"

"Yes, sir."

Burger, his voice oozing with sympathy, said, "Now, Veronica, I know it's not a pleasant subject, but will you please go ahead and tell us exactly what happened. Tell us everything."

"Well," she said, "Mr. Addison stopped and backed up. He asked me if I wanted a ride. I'd been sizing him up all the time."

"What do you mean by that?"

"Well, I'd sized up the sound of his motor. I knew it was a big expensive car from its purring. Then I had a chance to look at his silhouette as he drove by. There was enough light from the dash light in the car, so I got a pretty good idea of him. He looked like a substantial businessman, not the type I'd been having trouble with the last thirty or forty miles."

"So what did you do?"

"I smiled at him and thanked him and told him I'd

173

like to ride to the city if he was going that far. He said he was and I got in."

"And you talked?"

"Yes, we talked." She smiled and said, "That's one obligation a young woman hitchhiker owes to people who pick her up. If they want to talk, she talks. If they don't want to talk, she keeps quiet."

"And Mr. Addison wanted to talk?"

She smiled and said, "I think he wanted to hear me talk."

"So what did you do?"

"I talked. I told him about myself and told him I was coming to the city to—well, sort of look around, to seek my fortune."

"And told him you had left home?"

"Yes."

"And what did Mr. Addison do?"

Veronica raised her eyes and her voice. "I want one thing definitely understood. Mr. Addison was a perfect gentleman, a *perfect* gentleman."

"Yes, I understand," Burger said, "but tell me just what transpired. What took place?"

"Well, he asked me if I had any place to stay and I told him no, and he asked me about how much money I had and I tried to avoid that question but he kept being very insistent, and when it turned out I only had a small amount of money and didn't know just where I was going to stay when I got to town, he gave me a little fatherly advice. He told me that a girl couldn't do those things in a big city, that it was different from a country town, and then he said he was going to get me a place to stay."

"And what did he do?"

"He stopped the car at a service station and went in and did some telephoning, and when he came out he said it was all fixed, that I had a room in a hotel, and that it was all paid for."

"And then what?"

"Then when he came to the city, he drove me to the Rockaway Hotel and saw that I registered, and the clerk said a room was already engaged for me, and that's all I know about that."

"Now, you saw Mr. Addison again?"

"Yes."

"When?"

"On the afternoon of the tenth I went to see him at his department store."

"At his request?"

"Yes."

"What happened?"

"He sent me down to the personnel manager with a card and—well, I was given a job and started work at once."

"And did you at any time know any of the sordid details of this blackmail?"

"No, sir, never."

Burger turned to Mason. "I suppose," he said reproachfully, "you will wish to cross-examine this young woman?"

"I most certainly do," Mason said, getting to his feet.

Burger said, wearily, "The law gives you that right. Go ahead."

"Your mother is living?" Mason asked.

"Yes."

"And you were living with your mother?"

"Yes."

"And went away from the family domicile?"

"The family domicile," she said, smiling faintly, "was a restaurant. I waited on tables. It was in a pitifully small town. There were no opportunities. One never met anyone except a few awkward, shy young men who lacked the courage and initiative to get up and get out."

"And so you left?"

"Yes."

"And hitchhiked out here?"

"Yes."

"That's interesting," Mason said. "Now, Miss Dale, how long did it take you to hitchhike here?"

"What do you mean?"

"You are young and personable and attractive and, I take it, you don't have to wait long for a ride."

Veronica Dale began to show panic in her eyes.

"Well, no."

"So how long did it take you from the time you left your home to get out here?"

"Not very long."

"As much as a week?"

"I . . . well, perhaps. Yes, I guess so."

"Then you were at home with your mother in this restaurant up to a week before you first met Mr. Addison?"

There was a long silence.

"Can't you answer that?"

"Oh, if the Court please!" Hamilton Burger said, getting to his feet, his manner that of a fatherly protector for the girl and, as far as the Court was concerned, an advocate whose patience was entirely exhausted. "I object to that. Let Counsel confine himself to the approximate vicinity of the crime and the approximate time of the crime. Surely, this young woman has been crucified enough. Simply because she happened to be where she saw the defendant in the vicinity of the crime at about the time of the crime was committed is no reason she should be pilloried by a remorseless and desperate counsel."

"Neither remorseless nor desperate, Your Honor," Mason said cheerfully. "I'd like to find out something about how the young lady happened to be in the place at the time she mentioned. Since this all hinges on the time element, I'd like to check on it."

"I think the question is within the permissible bounds of cross-examination," Judge Keetley ruled, "but it does seem to the Court, Mr. Mason, that the cross-examination of this young woman should not go too far afield."

Again there was silence.

"Answer the question," Judge Keetley said.

"May I have a glass of water?" Veronica Dale asked in a low voice.

"Certainly," Mason said.

But it was Hamilton Burger who sprang to his feet and came rushing toward the witness stand. "Now, Veronica," he said, "don't overtax yourself."

"What's the matter with her?" Mason asked. "Is there something wrong with her?"

176

"What do you mean?" Burger roared at him. "That is entirely on a par with your insinuations, your dastardly . . ."

"She seems to me to be a healthy young woman, some twenty years old," Mason said. "She certainly should be able to answer a question as to what time she left home. The way you're coddling her, I'm beginning to think there's something wrong with her."

"Well, there isn't!" Burger shouted.

Mason took advantage of Burger's sputtering rage to pour a glass of water and hand it to Veronica Dale. "Go ahead Miss Dale," he said suavely, "take all the time you want, drinking the water, and then when you have finished with the water, just tell the Court what time you left home, just when it was you left that resturant and your mother."

"Twenty years old!" Burger stormed. "This girl is a child, a young, unsophisticated, unspoiled young woman of eighteen—barely eighteen, at whom you are consistently throwing mud, simply because . . ."

"That will do, gentlemen," Judge Keetley said. "The examination will proceed in an orderly fashion, and Counsel will refrain from personalities."

Judge Keetley looked from under bushy eyebrows at Veronica Dale slowly sipping water from the glass Mason handed her. The trace of a frown appeared upon his forehead.

"Are you finished with the water?" Mason asked.

"No."

"Are you feeling better?" Burger inquired solicitously.

"Just a little faint," she said.

Mason extended a hand for the glass, but Veronica Dale ignored the hand, continuing to sip the water, slowly and thoughtfully.

"Have you thought of the answer yet?" Mason said.

She looked up at him, then abruptly started to cry.

Mason gently took the glass of water from her fingers, walked over to the table where he had been seated, placed the water glass on the table, sat down and waited.

Burger moved forward, placed a fatherly hand on the girl's shoulder. "There, there, Veronica," he said, "It's almost over. The Court is going to protect you. Judge Keetley isn't going to let him make any more of those dastardly insinuations. If the Court please, this unwarranted, despicable insinuation, this accusation that there was something wrong with this young woman, has upset her, and justifiably so. I feel that every man in this courtroom felt his blood boil when Counsel . . ."

"Please refrain from personalities, Mr. District Attorney." Judge Keetley said, his keen eyes resting speculatively on Veronica Dale's face.

Mason settled back in the swivel chair at the counsel table, clasped his hands behind his head and waited.

There was something in the calm, silent waiting which did more to place Veronica Dale's actions in their true perspective than any amount of remonstration with her would have done.

"Your Honor," Hamilton Burger said after a while, "I am going to renew my objection, and I think that the cross-examination of this witness should terminate. Counsel himself is responsible for the upset condition of this witness. He has only himself to thank if his insinuation . . ."

"Let her alone. She's thinking," Mason said, grinning.

Judge Keetley said, a tone of firm finality in his voice, "The Court sees no reason why the witness can't answer that question."

"It is not that question, Your Honor," Burger protested. "It is the manner of this cross-examination, the insinuations as to this young woman's pregnancy."

"He merely asked if there was anything wrong with her condition," Judge Keetley said, "and as far as the Court is concerned, it would appear that you brought that on yourself by a display of undue solicitude. How old is this young woman? Have you checked her age?"

"She is barely eighteen, Your Honor, a young woman . . ."

"She's twenty," Mason said.

"How old *are* you?" Judge Keetley asked Veronica. She looked up at him and then again had recourse to tears.

Judge Keetley settled back in his chair, his manner

somewhat similar to that of Perry Mason. "Very well," he said, "let's wait until she can answer that question."

"Do you feel as though you could go on answering questions, Veronica?" Hamilton Burger asked.

"No!" she said promptly.

"She answered that question all right," Judge Keetley said, "Now try answering this one. How old are you, young lady?"

She glanced desperately around the courtroom.

"How old?" Judge Keetley asked.

Burger looked at the Judge with a certain amount of exasperation.

"I think you can go back and sit down, Mr. District Attorney. I don't think she's going to fall off the witness stand. How old are you, Miss Dale?"

She waited a full five seconds before she answered the question. "Twenty," she said.

"Humph," Judge Keetley snapped, and then with a sharp edge to his voice, said, "When did you leave your home, when did you last see your mother, how long did it take you to get out here? Now, tell us just exactly how long you've been hitchhiking on the road."

"I . . . I can't tell. I didn't keep account of the time."

"How long since you've last seen your mother?"

"I . . ."

"Your Honor," Hamilton Burger said, "if I may interpose one more suggestion . . ."

"Well, interpose it briefly," Judge Keetley snapped.

"I am given to understand that this girl's mother is here in the city, that she is in the custody of Mr. Perry Mason, and that Mr. Perry Mason for reasons best known to himself does not have the mother in court this morning. Therefore, it seems to me that at this time Mr. Mason should be instructed to let this young woman have the comfort of her mother's presence."

Mason said, "I rang you up last night, you'll remember, Counselor, and suggested that *you* let Miss Dale and her mother have a friendly reunion, and you scoffed at the suggestion."

"Nevertheless," Burger said, "and while I resent Counsel's statement that I scoffed at the suggestion, I feel

179

that this young woman should have an opportunity to see her mother. Last night I was taken unawares, at a time when I was in a hurry to get home, by Counsel's offer that I should surrender Veronica Dale to him so that she could see her mother. I naturally refused. Later on, after thinking things over, I decided that if Mr. Mason would send Mrs. Dale to me, I would personally escort her to her daughter. I spent some time vainly trying to reach Mr. Mason. I had the hotel registers searched in vain. I fell, however, that Counsel shrewdly timed his suggestion so as to court a refusal. I feel that his deliberately keeping this young woman from her mother is in keeping with the tactics he has used . . ."

Judge Kettley's gavel banged sharply. "Kindly refrain from these personalities, Mr. Burger."

"That's all right. Let him go, Your Honor," Mason said. "He really doesn't mean them. He's trying to give this witness time to think. She had her answers all ready, but now that she's learned I have her mother here, she's had to change her story."

"She should see her mother," Burger shouted.

"She'll have an opportunity to see her mother when she answers a few questions," Judge Keetley said irritably. "After all, here's a healthy, husky woman, twenty years of age. She certainly can answer a simple question without having to sip her way through a full glass of water and then have the district attorney pat her solicitously on the shoulder. And she can answer questions without waiting until her mother is brought to hold her hand. I want to know when she left that restaurant, when she last saw her mother, and I propose to find out!"

There was an awkward silence.

"How long was it?" Judge Keetley asked, his voice utterly devoid of sympathy.

"About a year," Veronica Dale said.

Mason was on his feet. "And so," he said, "you wanted us to think it had only been a matter of a week?"

"I . . . I was confused."

"Are you confused now?"

"Yes."

"You understand my questions?"

180

"I understand them now. Yes."

"You left home about a year ago?"

"Yes."

"You haven't seen your mother since?"

"No."

"When were you twenty?"

"I . . . about three months ago."

"Where have you been for the last year? Have you been on the road all the time coming here?"

"No."

"Where have you been?"

"Various places."

"Oh, Your Honor," Hamilton Burger said, "surely the whereabouts of this young woman for the past *year,* what she has done and where she has been, don't enter into any legitimate scope of cross-examination. Her direct examination was limited to an interval of approximately one hour, during which she met the defendant at a spot on the road near where the defendant had just finished killing his partner. Naturally, the defendant doesn't like to have that brought out, and I have no objection to any cross-examination as to anything within reasonable limits—a day, two days, a week—but to go back for a year and attempt to besmirch this young woman's reputation is carrying cross-examination too far."

"Under ordinary circumstances, I would agree with you," Judge Keetley said, "but the manner of this witness certainly indicates that she is trying to cover something up."

"What if she is? She may have left home for various reasons. She certainly doesn't want to blab out her heart's secrets in this crowded courtroom, and I don't think any Court should make her. Counsel has no right to discredit the witness by collateral evidence, whether he introduces it from other people or drags it from the mouth of the witness herself."

"He doesn't want her heart's secrets," Judge Keetley said. "He merely wants to know why it took her a year to hitchhike here from Indiana. The Court wants to know that, too. However, if the district attorney persists in his objection, I am afraid asking this witness in detail where she has been and what she has done during the last twelve months may be a little remote as to the time element."

"We insist on our objection, as a protection to the privacy of this young girl," Burger said.

"Very well," Judge Keetley ruled, "the Court will very reluctantly sustain the objection as to anything as remote as a *year* ago. You are entitled to show just what happened within a reasonable time limit, Mr. Mason, and certainly the Court is going to permit you the most searching cross-examination as to what occurred in the immediate time bracket covered by the testimony of this witness and within a reasonable interval preceding such time."

"Very well, Your Honor," Mason said, "Now, you had been hitchhiking in a westerly direction, Miss Dale, when you got out to wait at this culvert?"

"Yes."

"And what happened? Why did you get out at that particular point?"

"I left the car in which I was riding voluntarily," she said. "I resented the pawing intimacies of the man who was driving the car and who was trying to take advantage of me."

"So what did you do?"

She answered readily enough now in a firm voice, "I protected myself in the only way a girl has under circumstances of that sort. I leaned forward and switched off the ignition and pulled out the car keys. I opened the car door—naturally, with a dead motor, the car slowed to a stop. I jumped out and flung the keys at the man."

"Rather a neat trick," Mason said. "How did you learn it, Veronica?"

"I'd done it before."

"Many times?"

"Your Honor," Hamilton Burger said, "here we go again, right back to this girl's past, trying to besmirch her reputation . . ."

"Objection sustained," Judge Keetley snapped. "Confine your examination to a reasonable time interval before she is alleged to have seen Mr. Addison."

"Very well, Your honor," Mason said.

"So you switched off the motor and got out of the car."

"Yes."

"Was there any attempt to stop you?"

"Yes. He tried to grab me and paw me and take certain liberties with me, but, of course, he was more or less busy steering the automobile, and then he put on the brake so he could have both hands free, and that was when I jumped out of the car and threw the car keys onto the floorboard."

"What did he do then?"

"He got out and started to chase me, then realized the position in which that put him, cursed me, called me all sorts of names, got back in the car and groped around until he found the car keys. By that time I was off in the brush at the side of the road."

"It was dark?"

"Yes, of course."

"How long had you been struggling with this wolf?"

"For some little time. I remember that I intended to get out at this little town, Canyon Verde, but I thought I could stick it out. He was only making passes at me then."

"And he became amorously violent shortly after you passed Canyon Verde?"

"Yes."

"As an experienced hitchhiker," Mason said, "you appreciate the danger of picking up with anyone who happens to come along?"

"I am very discriminating," she said. "Before I let anyone give me a ride, I size things up."

"And when the right sort of a car comes along, you give the driver the eye?"

"I let him see that I would be interested in accepting a ride. I don't do anything crude, such as trying to thumb my way."

"So you sized up this man with whom you were riding?"

"Well, I tried to, but, of course, you can't size up a man when he's coming toward you at fifty miles an hour and . . ."

"But you sized up thē car?"

"Yes."

"Then you got in the car and rode in it?"

"Yes."

"What kind of a car was it?" Mason asked. "What make? Quick, what make?"

"A Lincoln sedan."

"A sedan?"

"Yes, a Lincoln sedan."

"New?"

"A late model, yes. It looked new."

"What was the license number?"

"I don't know."

"You mean you didn't notice the license number either before you got in or after you got out?"

"Well, I . . . I think I did, but I can't remember."

Mason said, "As a matter of fact, don't you make a habit of writing down the license numbers of automobiles in which you have been given a ride?"

"I . . ."

"Do you or don't you?"

"I have on occasion."

"In a notebook?"

"Yes."

"Do you have that notebook in that purse with you right there?"

"I . . ."

"Do you or don't you?" Mason said.

"Oh, Your Honor," Hamilton Burger said, "this browbeating. This . . ."

"Sit down, Mr. District Attorney!" Judge Keetley snapped. "Don't interrupt the cross-examination. The Court wants to know whether the witness has such a book as much as Counsel does. It's entirely relevant. Do you have that book in your purse, Miss Dale?"

"I . . . I have a notebook, yes."

"And you took down the license number of the automobile driven by John Racer Addison?"

"Yes," she said.

"Why did you do that?"

"It's a matter of precaution, in case there should be any trouble."

"When did you take down the license number of Addison's automobile? Before you got in or after you got out?"

She smiled and said, "It would be difficult to take down the license number of an automobile before you got in, Mr. Mason. That would be rather obvious."

"So, naturally, you do it when you get out."

"Yes."

"Then *why* do you do it?"

"Well, it's nice to know with whom one has been riding, in case there should be complications."

"What sort of complications?"

"Well, in case the man has got rough."

"You take down the license numbers of the men who try to get rough?"

"Yes, it's a matter of protection."

"For whom?"

"Well, I . . . I want to know."

"Mr. Addison didn't get rough."

"No."

"Yet you took down his license number."

"Yes."

"Let me see that notebook."

She once more looked around the courtroom like a trapped animal, then rather reluctantly opened her purse and took out a small leather notebook which held a small lead pencil in a loop in the cover.

"Let me see that book too," Hamilton Burger said. "Let's take a look at it."

"Certainly," Mason said.

Burger bent over him as they looked through page after page of automobile license numbers. Opposite many of these numbers were a name and address, and there were dates subdividing the licenses and the daily groups.

Mason said, "So, on the day that you wrote down the license number of John Addison's automobile you had had about twenty other numbers written down. Is that right?"

"I haven't counted them."

"Count them now," Mason said.

He handed her the notebook. She counted and said, "Yes, twenty-two."

"You'd had twenty-two rides that day?"

"Yes."

"And had taken the precaution of taking down the numbers of all of the men?"

"Yes."

"*All* of the *men?*"

"Yes."

"Weren't any of the drivers women?"

She hesitated.

"Any women?" Mason asked.

"No."

"Where's the license number of this wolf who tried to paw you and forced you to jump out of the automobile?"

"I didn't say he forced me to jump out of the automobile. I did that of my own free will."

"That's right. What's the license number of the automobile?"

"It isn't there."

"But you have stated that you took down the license numbers of every automobile . . ."

"Well, that one I failed to take down. I was excited."

"You take down these numbers as a precaution, in case anything happens?"

"Yes."

"What could happen after you get out of the car?"

"Why . . . well, I don't know. It's just a habit, that's all. I like to know the people with whom I've been riding."

"Oh, all right, all right," Hamilton Burger interpolated. "The young woman has done a lot of hitchhiking. She's restless. She goes from place to place. She accepts rides from men. So what? That doesn't prevent the fact from being clearly established that she saw John Racer Addison approximately at the scene of the crime at approximately the time it was committed. And, Your Honor, after all this grueling cross-examination, these damnable nasty insinuations, I know, and Your Honor knows, that she *did* ride in John Addison's automobile and that he was out there at that house on that Tuesday night. And John Racer Addison *isn't going to deny it!*"

"We'll take up the rest of the case in its logical sequence," Judge Keetley said. "Let me see that notebook."

He took the notebook, thumbed through the pages, frowned down at Veronica Dale, said, "Where are you employed?"

"I'm working—that is, I was working in the department store until police took me."

"Before that, where were you working?"

"I haven't been working for some little time, that is, at regular jobs."

"Well," Judge Keetley said, "I think we have a picture here. It's not a picture that I like, but I see no reason for going into it any further. Even is this young woman had a complete lack of moral character, that would not be a ground for a stultifying attack on her testimony. I think the cross-examination has probably covered the ground rather thoroughly."

"Except," Mason said, "that I want to know how it happens she was at this particular culvert at the time she claims the defendant picked her up."

"She's told you how she happened to be there," Hamilton Burger said.

"But her testimony doesn't check," Mason said, "she hasn't any license number indicating how she got there."

"Well, she's told her story, and told it several times," Judge Keetley said.

"One or two more questions," Mason said. "Let's take these numbers that you have written down prior to your ride with John Addison. Now, the Addison license number is the last license number for that day. That's because he was the last person with whom you rode?"

"Yes."

"And you admit that you do not have the license number of the person with whom you rode immediately prior to the license number of John Addison?"

"No."

"But the one that you have just before that," Mason said, "let's have a look at this license number—45S533.

187

Do you remember that car?"

"No," she said, "not distinctly."

Suddenly Addison was struggling to his feet.

Mason motioned him back. "Sit down," he said.

But Addison, his face showing startled surprise blurted out, "That's the license number of Edgar Ferrell's automobile!"

"What?" Mason exclaimed.

"That's right," Addison said doggedly. "That's the license number of Edgar Ferrell's automobile."

Hamilton Burger was frantically pawing through notes in his files. "There must be some mistake," he said.

"Look at the witness's face if you think there's a mistake," Mason said. "And then, if you want really to do something, take the fingerprints of this young woman and compare them with the fingerprints of the mysterious woman who had been in Ferrell's country house immediately before the murder."

And Mason dramatically walked back to his chair and sat down.

The courtroom was a pandemonium of noise. Judge Keetley and the bailiff tried in vain for several seconds to get silence, then Judge Keetley said, "I'll have silence in this courtroom! If the spectators can't preserve decorum, they will be ejected. Now, let's proceed with this case in an orderly manner."

"Your Honor," Burger asked, "may I ask for a short recess?"

"No!" Judge Keetley snapped. "Proceed with your cross-examination, Mr. Mason."

"Your Honor, before I proceed with this cross-examination I want the fingerprints of this witness taken."

"You have no right to make any such aspersion," Burger said. "That's simply a grandstand and . . ."

"If you think it's a grandstand," Mason interpolated, "take a look at the latent fingerprints on this water glass which the witness hold in her hand. There's a fingerprint which I think you will find corresponds exactly with one of the fingerprints your own witness has testified to finding in that house. Now, let's have the other prints taken."

"Let's have the other prints taken," Judge Keetley

said. "Where's that fingerprint witness? Come forward and let's get this thing straightened out."

George Malden came forward, carrying a small box which contained his fingerprint outfit.

Veronica Dale gave him her hand. With a face as expressionless as that of a wax doll, she let him take rolled impressions of her fingers. Malden then retired to Hamilton Burger's table, where he compared the prints with those of the latents. During all of this time, Veronica Dale obviously was thinking, but her face retained its childlike expression of complete innocence. There was not so much as a furrow in her forehead.

Hamilton Burger cleared his throat twice, rose ponderously, said, "They're the same, Your Honor," and sat down.

"Now," Mason said, "suppose you tell us what you were doing in the house where that murder was committed, Veronica? You have already, by your own testimony, established the fact that you were in the vicinity at the time of the murder."

Judge Keetley leaned forward, said, "Take the microphone, young lady, and answer that question."

Veronica Dale said with complete assurance, "I was in the house for only a few minutes."

"Who took you there?" Mason asked.

"Mr. Ferrell."

"That's better. Now let's get it straight," Mason said. "How did you meet Mr. Ferrell?"

She said, "I . . . I was working a racket with my hitchhiking."

"What's the racket?" Mason asked.

She said, "I make my living that way. I go out on the roads and let people pick me up. At first I go away from the city, and then I turn around and come back to the city. I only ride with older men in good cars. I tell all of these men about an unhappy home life and about how I have gone out in the world to seek my fortune. I'm careful to tell them all that I'm eighteen."

"What's the idea?"

"Invariably they are nice. I pick the good cars. They ask me how much money I have, and I tell them only a

189

few cents. They nearly always give me money. It's never less than five dollars; sometimes it's as much as fifty."

"Now we're getting somewhere," Mason said. "What about your ride with Mr. Ferrell?"

She said, "I had been riding with a very nice gentleman. He had given me ten dollars. I knew he wouldn't give me any more. I told him that I wanted to get out at the service station and get myself made as presentable as possible before I entered the city. He was reluctant to let me go, but I kept insisting, and told him not to wait."

"You were coming toward the city then?"

"Yes."

"And what happened?"

"While I was at the service station, Mr. Ferrell drove up. He was going in the other direction, but—well, directions really didn't mean anything to me because what I wanted was the contact."

"So you sized Mr. Ferrell up and gave him what you call 'the eye'?"

"I looked, I suppose, rather demure and helpless."

"Then what happened?"

"Mr. Ferrell asked me if I wanted a ride, asked me in which direction I was going."

"So then what happened?"

"I rode with him. While I was riding, I sized up the car. It was loaded, as though for a long trip. I got acquainted with Mr. Ferrell and told him my stock story."

"And he gave you money?"

She said, "I think he was going to give me money. He told me he had to go out to his country house for a little while; that he was going to meet some people there and that after that he was going back to the city and that if I'd go back with him he'd see I was all fixed up with a place to stay and with a job."

"And what happened then?"

She said, "I drove out to this house with him. He kept telling me that I was perfectly safe with him and not to be nervous. He stopped the car and asked me if I wanted to come in. I told him I did, because it was cold in the car. I walked around behind the car and got the license

190

number, just as I always do. I made an excuse to get something out of my purse and wrote down the license number. Then I went into the house with him."

"And then what happened?"

"He lit a gasoline lantern and also lit a fire in a wood stove. He apologized for the shape the house was in and said it was just a hide-out he'd picked because he was working on a business deal that was so secret no one could have an inkling of what it was. And then he became rather embarrassed and suggested that when his visitors came I should keep very much out of sight because he didn't want these persons to have any false ideas about our relationship."

"What happened after that?"

"A car turned into the driveway. Mr. Ferrell said, "Here comes my party now. If you'll wait out in the kitchen, my dear . . . I hope you won't be too uncomfortable. It won't be long and then I'll take you to the city and see that you have a place to stay and a job.""

"So what did you do?"

"I started for the kitchen. Mr. Ferrell peeked out of the window to look at the car, and then all of a sudden he came running out to the kitchen, his face white as a sheet."

"And then what?"

"He said, 'My heavens, it's my wife! I didn't know she knew anything about this place. Get out! Get out through the back door. Get out there into the fields. Get out where she can't find you. For God's sake, hurry!' "

"And what happened?"

She said, "I didn't know what to do. He unlocked the back door, opened it and almost pushed me out into the night."

"So what did you do?"

She said, "I started to run, keeping the house between me and the automobile. It was dark, and I stumbled and fell over things, and then quit that blind panic of running, and started to walk. Then I suddenly remembered the little overnight bag that I always carry with me. I'd left it in Mr. Ferrell's automobile. I was afraid that his wife might search the automobile and find my bag."

"And you were afraid that would make trouble for Mr. Ferrell?" Mason asked.

"I was afraid it would make trouble for *me!* I had all of my clothes and things in there. I've practiced packing so I can really carry a lot of things in a small space."

"So what did you do?"

"So while she was in the house I simply doubled back around her car, went over to Mr. Ferrell's car, quietly opened the door and took out my little overnight bag. It was, of course, on top of everything—and believe me there was a lot of stuff piled in that automobile, a lot of camping stuff, it looked like—a sleeping bag, and duffel bags, and things like that."

"All right. You took out the overnight bag. Then what did you do?"

"Then," she said, "I started putting distance between me and that house. It wasn't any part of my business to get mixed up in any domestic discord and I certainly didn't intend to be named as a corespondent in anyone's divorce suit."

"Which direction did you go?"

She gave a wry little smile and said, "I don't even know that, myself. I started out to make a detour and circle back to the road. I wandered along for a ways and then blundered into a barbed wire fence. I managed to crawl under that fence and then the next thing I knew, I was in a lot of bushes, willow bushes, I guess they were. I wandered around and proceeded to get myself good and lost."

"Then what?"

"Then," she said, "I got in a panic. I guess I ran a little, I don't know. I got all disheveled and finally came to my senses and took stock of the situation. I decided that I'd wait until some car came along the highway. I thought I could hear that."

"Could you? Did you?"

"Yes, I waited five minutes or so then I heard a car along the highway. It wasn't anywhere near where I thought the highway should have been. I thought the highway was ahead of me, but this car was off to the left and behind me. I could tell from the sound the car was making that it was speeding along a highway, so I started to work my way over in that direction."

"Then what happened?"

"By that time I realized I had made a little fool of myself and I took time to work my way carefully when I came to more willow bushes. It had been raining the night before and there were patches where the going was pretty soggy. I tried to avoid them and keep to the higher ground. I found that I was in sort of a stream bed and by keeping to the rounded gravel, I kept out of the mud. Every once in a while there were cars going by on the highway, so I kept my directions all right. Then I knew I was getting close to the highway and realized I must look pretty bad. So I stopped on some high ground and slipped off my skirt. I opened my overnight bag, took out a clothes brush and gave the skirt a good brushing. Then I brushed my shoes. My stockings had become pretty badly snagged. I got a fresh pair out of the bag and put them on there in the dark. Then I made up my face as best I could and put on a little lipstick, and felt I'd made myself presentable."

"Then what?"

"Then, working very, very cautiously so that I wouldn't snag my stockings or get into any more brush, I went up to the highway and sat down. I had only been there a few minutes when I heard this car start up from what I thought at the time was a ranch house. I had absolutely no idea that I was so close to the house where I had left Mr. Ferrell. I must have walked around in a big circle. I realize now that Mr. Addison's car actually had started from that house, but I most certainly didn't realize it at the time."

"What about the shots?"

"Honestly, when I heard those I thought it was a truck backfiring."

"When did you hear them?"

"That was—oh, I don't know, ten minutes or so before I got up to the highway."

"Didn't you tell me you heard them just before you got to the highway?"

"Well, that was just before, wasn't it?"

193

"As much as ten minutes?"

"Perhaps."

"Didn't you tell me that . . ."

She said desperately, "All right, I tried to protect myself as much as I could. I wanted to give myself as much of an alibi as possible. I certainly didn't want anyone to think that I could have been anywhere around that house when the shots were fired, so I may have shaded the time a little bit."

"Quite a little bit?"

"Well, perhaps."

"You don't know how long Mr. Addison's car had been there at Ferrell's house before you heard it drive out?"

"No."

"And when you heard it moving along the dirt road, crossing the plank bridge and coming up the hill to the highway, you thought it was coming from an entirely different house?"

"Mr. Mason, I'll be frank with you. I thought I was at least a mile from the place where Mr. Ferrell had left me."

"As a matter of fact," Mason said, "throughout this entire episode, your first and only thought was of yourself, isn't that right?"

She let her eyes widen slightly. "Why, of course. Who else was I supposed to think of?"

"And this story that you have concocted for us about the passionate wolf in the Lincoln sedan was a complete fabrication?"

"Yes."

"Actually, you have the license numbers of everyone with whom you took a ride on that day? Be careful now, young lady, because we can check up on every minute of your time."

"Yes," she said, "you can check those license numbers. They'll all remember me."

"How much money did you make that day?"

"About eighty dollars."

"Was that an average day?"

"I do pretty well. Most of the time I make at least that much."

"That's all," Mason said, "I have no further questions."

"And I have none," Hamilton Burger said.

Judge Keetley said, "I think, under the circumstances, the Court will take a recess until tomorrow morning at ten o'clock. In the meantime I want every phase of this young woman's story checked, and I suggest that the district attorney's office and the police make a further investigation for the purpose of finding out what actually happened there at the scene of the crime, and I suggest that this witness has most certainly been guilty of perjury."

"Yes, Your Honor," Hamilton Burger said, very much chastened.

"Court is adjourned," Judge Keetley said.

Della Street came up to grab Mason's arm. "Oh, Chief," she said, "you were wonderful! Simply wonderful!"

Paul Drake's grinning countenance said, "Nice going, Perry."

"It's a nice start," Mason admitted, "and a lucky break. Thanks to the fact I had her mother's story as an ace in the hole, I was able to ask as my first questions ones that appeared innocent and routine, but were actually the ones she couldn't answer. If I'd tried the other questions first I'd have had the whole courtroom, including the judge, on my neck the minute I tried to sweat the truth out of her."

"What do we do now?" Drake asked.

"Now," Mason said, "we really go to work. And to start it off, Paul, you take that list of license numbers, have your men get in touch with the car owners, and see how many of them were being blackmailed by Eric Hansell."

PERRY MASON, pacing back and
forth restlessly across his office, from time to time tossed
comments over his shoulder.

Della Street, seated at her secretarial desk, doodling
idly with a pencil, making assortments of various curli-
cues, kept her eyes on the point of her pencil, her mind
following Mason's utterances.

Paul Drake, having slid around sidewise in the big
leather chair, his knees dangling over one overstuffed arm,
the other supporting the small of his back, from time to
time interposed a comment.

Mason said almost irritably, "The damn case presents
a complete, utter impossibility." He walked back and
forth four or five more times across the office, then went
on, "Look at the evidence! Someone stood outside and
shot through the window at Ferrell, hit him first shot,
then whirled around and emptied the gun, apparently
shooting into the air. Then he took the cartridges out of
the chamber of the gun and threw the gun out into the
river bed. It doesn't make sense."

"Why not?" Drake asked. "The guy was dead."

"How did the murderer know he was dead?"

"He'd taken a careful bead, shot him in the head,
and saw him fall down."

"He might have grazed him," Mason said. "I'm telling
you, Paul, it takes a darn good shot to stand down on the
ground and shoot up through a window and be absolutely certain of a head shot. And then the man must have
entered the house, walked up to the room, turned out the
light, then gone down and driven away. Now, a man
wouldn't have done that."

"Why not?"

"Because, if he *had* taken a shot at Edgar Ferrell and was then going into the house, he'd have kept the gun with him. He'd have been holding it in readiness in case Ferrell had been only wounded and was preparing to put up a fight."

"Well, how do you know he didn't?"

"Because the evidence shows that the shots were all fired in rapid succession, not in a uniform rhythm but, nevertheless, all within a space of a few seconds. That's why the shots sounded like a truck backfiring as it came along the road."

Drake said, "A really good shot, a really expert shot . . ."

"And that narrows it right down to my client, John Racer Addison," Mason said.

"Hell," Drake muttered. "Perhaps the guy's guilty."

Mason said nothing, kept on pacing the floor.

Suddenly he whirled. "We're all making the most asinine of all fundamental errors!"

"What's that, Chief?" Della Street asked.

"We're looking at the thing from the standpoint of the Prosecution. The Prosecution reconstructed the crime and we're falling right in with their reconstruction. Let's go back to first principles. Let me see those photographic exhibits, Della."

Della Street brought out the photographic exhibits.

"Now go over to my library on forensic medicine and criminology and get me LeMoyne Snyder's *Homicide Investigation;* get *Legal Medicine and Toxicology* by Gonzales, Vance and Helpern; and get me *Modern Criminal Investigation* by Soderman and O'Connell."

Della Street brought the books to Mason's desk. Mason sat down and thumbed through the pages, pausing occasionally to drum with his finger tips on his desk.

"I thought so," he said at length.

"What?" Drake asked.

"I remember their stuff on bullet holes through glass—now, then, let's do the thing I should have done right at the start. Let's begin at the beginning instead of the place where the police tell us to begin."

"Where's that?" Drake asked.

"That bullet," Mason said, "how do we *know* that it was fired by someone who stood out by the place where the automobile tracks ended and was fired throught the window, killing Ferrell?"

"How do we know it!" Drake said. "Because the evidence shows it, that's why. You have the bullet hole in the glass lined up with the wound in Ferrell's head, and the line points unmistakably to a place where a man would have been standing if he'd got out of that automobile."

Mason said, "That's evidence, all right, Paul. It's the same sort of evidence that goes back to the old story of the New England pie maker who baked a lot of mince pies and a lot of other pies. She wanted to keep the pies straight so she cut the initials, *TM,* in the pie crust of the mince, meaning ' *'Tis Mince,'* and *TM* in the crust of the other pies, meaning ' *'Tain't Mince.'* "

Drake straightened up in the chair. "What the heck are you getting at?"

Mason, studying the pictures of the glass windowpane, said, "Humph!"

"What is it?" Drake asked.

"Take a look here at Soderman and O'Connell on page 217," Mason said. "Incidentally, Paul, there's a darn fine book. You take these three books and you can come pretty close to covering the whole field of forensic criminology. Now, here on page 217 is a diagram showing glass fractures from bullet impact, illustrating the *direction* of the bullet. Now, remember that the officers, having cut out the glass to preserve it in court, didn't take any steps to mark which side was the inside and which side was the outside of the pane, and when I asked them about it I received some sarcastic comment to the effect that one side of a pane of glass was about the same as another side. That's all very true, but one side was *in* and the other side was *out,* and that's the significant difference."

"Now, look at this photograph showing the body on the floor. That was taken before the pane of glass had been cut."

"But you can't see anything there, no details," Drake said.

"You can see details that show a pattern of little cracks. Now, compare this photograph—there you are, Paul. See, this side *has* to be on the inside, otherwise that curve would have been pointed the other way."

Drake nodded.

"But," Mason said, "notice these pit marks, notice this type of cleavage, then compare them with that diagram in Soderman and O'Connell's book. Paul, just as sure as you're born, that bullet was fired from the *inside* of the room. It went through the glass and ended up where the automobile was standing on the ground below."

Drake came up out of his chair with a bound. "Let me see those pictures, Perry."

Drake and Della Street gathered around Mason, looking over his shoulder, studying the pictures."

Drake gave a long, low whistle.

Della Street said, "But, Chief, it's all there in black and white. This *has* to be the inside of the window. You've got it!"

"All right," Mason said, *"what* have I got?"

Drake and Della Street exchanged glances.

Mason pushed back his chair, began walking slowly back and forth across the office floor. Finally he paused, turned to the other two and said, "All right, we've established that the bullet which went through that glass was fired from the inside of the room. If we assume that bullet was fired by Ferrell, we find ourselves again faced with an impossible situation."

"I don't see why," Drake said. "Ferrell was in that room. He looked out and saw someone standing by the automobile and that person was someone he was deathly afraid of. He was willing to shoot to kill."

Mason nodded glumly, said, "I follow you in all that, Paul, but then what? The claim of the Prosecution is that Ferrell was standing there in that lighted room, with the gasoline lantern back of him, furnishing plenty of illumination for the murderer to pull the trigger. The murderer could see in, but Ferrell couldn't see out.

"Now, then, under our reconstruction of the case, we are forced to face an entirely different set of facts. If we follow that theory to its logical conclusion, the light must have been turned off, not by the murderer, but by Edgar Ferrell himself. He couldn't have seen well enough to shoot *out* of the room unless the light had been off."

"Okay," Drake said, "it all fits in, Perry. Ferrell turned the light off."

"Then what happened?" Mason said.

"Ferrell saw the man outside and fired a shot."

"And then," Mason said glumly, "the man must have got inside and killed Ferrell with Ferrell's gun, then four other shots must have been fired within a space of a few seconds. Now, how do you figure that one out?"

Drake scratched the hair on his temples, glanced sheepishly at Della Street and said, "I don't."

Mason said, "Well, there has to be an answer, and I've got to have it by the time court opens tomorrow."

19

■

MASON, Della Street, and Paul Drake pushed their way through the crowd which overflowed Judge Keetley's courtroom and milled about the corridor of the hall of justice.

Newspaper reporters crowded around them, begging for a statement. Mason merely grinned, said, "Wait until court opens, boys."

One of the newsmen, pushing his way through to Mason's side, said in a low voice, "Here's a tip for you, Counselor. Hamilton Burger is going to ask for a continuance."

"Thanks," Mason said.

They pushed on through the crowd. Drake said in a low voice to Mason, "Will you give them a continuance, Perry?"

"I can't, Paul," Mason said. "I've got a bear by the tail. I don't dare to let go. I don't dare to slack up, and somehow, some way, I've got to keep myself in such a position that the audience thinks *I'm* dragging the *bear*."

There was comparative order in the courtroom, and Mason was able to move down the corridor, through the gate in the rail at the bar, and into his position at the counsel table.

Hamilton Burger, who had been sitting over at the Prosecution table, arose nervously, came over to Mason, said, "I suppose you'll want a continuance, Mason."

"Not in the least," Mason said confidently.

Burger was visibly disappointed. Finally he said, "Well, of course, the Court may feel there should be a more complete investigation."

"It's your trial," Mason said.

Burger was still standing somewhat uncertainly behind Mason when Judge Keetley entered the courtroom. Counsel and spectators dutifully stood. The bailiff called court to order, and a deputy sheriff brought John Addison into the court.

Burger started speaking almost immediately.

"Your Honor," he said grandiloquently, "it is always the desire of the prosecutor to be fair. I think that I would be remiss in my duties if I did not call the Court's attention to the fact that it is necessary for the police and the Prosecution to re-evaluate the evidence. In justice to the defendant, I want to take time to examine that evidence more carefully."

"You wish a continuance?" Judge Keetley asked.

"Yes, Your Honor."

"For how long?"

"At least one week."

Judge Keetley looked at Mason.

Mason smiled, and shook his head. "Your Honor," he said, "the defendant objects. This is the time heretofore

201

fixed for the preliminary examination of this defendant. If the Prosecution had sufficient evidence to warrant the Court in binding the defendant over, no new evidence which adds to that can change the situation. If the new evidence refutes the position of the Prosecution, my client is entitled to vindication. I want the case to go on.

"I call the Court's attention to the sections of the Penal Code providing that the examination must be completed at one session unless the magistrate, for good cause shown by affidavit, postpones it. The postponement cannot be for more than two days at each time, nor more than six days in all, unless by consent or on motion of the defendant.

"If I may have the privilege of reopening my cross-examination of one or two of the Prosecution's witnesses, I will consent to a continuance for one week."

"That seems a reasonable condition," Judge Keetley said. "What witnesses do you wish to cross-examine, Mr. Mason?"

"I will first cross-examine the witness, Eric Hansell."

"Come forward, Mr. Hansell."

"Who? Me?" Hansell asked, surprised.

"Yes, you," Mason said.

"Come forward, Mr. Hansell," Judge Keetley repeated.

His manner showing apprehension, Hansell slowly walked toward the witness chair. As he went past Mason, the lawyer said under his breath, "Wise guy!"

Hansell turned, glared at Mason, then took the witness stand.

"Now, then," Mason said, "suppose you tell us a little more about your blackmailing technique, Mr. Hansell. Isn't it a fact that in this case you used a feminine accomplice, a woman who posed as the mother of Veronica Dale, a woman who could assist you in putting on pressure for a financial settlement?"

"Definitely not!" Hansell said.

"And you," Mason went on, "used such an accomplice in this case to take the part of Laura Mae Dale?"

"Definitely not."

Mason said, "Hansell, a preliminary check-up of the

list of license numbers which were in Veronica Dale's small notebook shows that the owners of these cars all had picked up Veronica Dale, had given her a ride, and had given her, for the most part, some money."

"I can't help that," Hansell sneered. "If these old goats want to fall for a broad and give her dough, you can't hold me responsible for it."

"And some of the cases," Mason said, "those where Veronica had been able to maneuver the car owners into a compromising position, had been paying blackmail, and the person to whom they had been paying was a redhead named Eric Hansell. What have you to say to that?"

Hamilton Burger was on his feet. "Your Honor, I object. This is not proper cross-examination. I hold no brief for this man, but certainly these other crimes . . ."

"I'm going to overrule the objection," Judge Keetley said. "Let him answer the question, and when he does, Mr. Burger, may I call your attention to the fact that he has not been given immunity for these other acts of blackmail, if it should appear there were such acts of blackmail. And I don't think your office should try to keep whitewashing him. Now then, the Court's going to rule that this question calls for a part of the *res gestae*. Answer the question, Mr. Hansell."

Hansell squirmed on the witness stand. "I want to see a lawyer," he said.

"Answer the question," Mason told him.

"I can't. I'm not going to."

"Upon what grounds do you refuse?" Judge Keetley asked.

"On the grounds that it would incriminate me."

Judge Keetley nodded to Hamilton Burger. "Now, Mr. District Attorney," he said, "you've been very diligent in working up certain aspects of this case. Suppose you instruct the police to go to work with equal diligence and work out these cases against this blackmailer."

"Yes, Your Honor," Hamilton Burger said sheepishly.

Mason said, "Hansell, you worked hand in glove with Veronica on a commission basis, didn't you?"

203

"I refuse to answer."

"And Veronica arranged to get herself arrested for vagrancy so that Addison would have his own attorney get her out and thereby lay himself open to blackmail?"

"I refuse to answer, on the ground that that will incriminate me."

"You've already been given immunity in that case," Mason said. "Therefore you need fear no prosecution and can claim no privilege."

"All right. That's the answer. I worked it out that way, yes."

"Then you rang in another woman as Veronica's mother?"

"Mr. Mason, I'm telling you straight, I don't know anything about that woman who posed as Veronica's mother. Veronica and I worked the game between us, and the two of us were all we needed. We didn't need . . . say, wait a minute, I'm talking too much."

"You certainly are," Mason said dryly.

There was a moment of tense, dramatic silence.

Mason's smile was contemptuous. "That's all. I have no further questions. I have now concluded my cross-examination and am willing to consent to a one week's continuance."

Judge Keetley glanced at Hamilton Burger. "Do you have any questions on redirect of this witness?"

"None, Your Honor."

Eric Hansell pulled a handkerchief from his pocket, mopped his perspiring forehead, cleared his throat nervously, then, in place of returning the handkerchief to his pocket, sat on the wintess chair twisting the handkerchief around and around his fingers, pulling it tight, then twisting it again.

Suddenly the realization of what he was doing came to him and he guiltily thrust the handkerchief into his pocket.

Mason stood calmly contemptuous, sardonically watching Hansell's hands.

Judge Keetley broke the silence.

"The case," he announced, "will be continued for one

week. The defendant is remanded to custody and Court is adjourned."

His banging gavel was the signal for the release of a babble of conversation in the courtroom.

Mason picked up Paul Drake and Della Street, moved out into the corridor.

Drake said, "You certainly gave Hansell something to think about."

Mason nodded.

"Did he do it?"

"I don't think so," Mason said. "I simply had to use him as a red herring to keep the district attorney from knowing what I really have in mind."

"And what's that?"

"We'll talk that over in the car," Mason said.

Driving back to the office in Mason's car, Paul Drake said, "You certainly have Hamilton Burger about half crazy, Perry. He started out with what looked like a dead open-and-shut case and now he's running around in circles. And what's driving him crazy is that right now he hasn't the faintest idea who killed Edgar Ferrell."

Mason said, "I *think* I know who killed him, Paul."

"Who?"

Mason said, "Let's look at the evidence. In the first place, Ferrell wanted that house for something. What?"

"A love nest," Drake said. "The cute little redhead at the fountain pen and automatic pencil counter . . ."

"Would have turned up her pretty little nose at a dump like that," Mason interrupted. "But let's look at the significance of certain dates we have heretofore passed up."

"What dates?"

Mason said, "Ferrell left on his vacation. He told his partner he was going trout fishing up in the Northwest, and he told his red-headed friend at the fountain pen counter he was planning on putting across a big business deal and was going to make his headquarters in a country place."

"That's right," Drake said.

Mason said, "Several things complicated the case,

205

Paul, so that the issues weren't clear for a time. But now they're becoming clarified."

"How come?"

Mason said, "Lorraine Ferrell must have gone out to that house on the night of the murder. She must have gone in. She must have found evidences that Veronica Dale had been there. She and her husband must have had something of a row."

"But police didn't find *her* fingerprints there," Drake said.

"Oh, yes, they did," Mason said. "They found her prints all over the place, just as they found Addison's because she had gone out there with Addison when they discovered the body . . ."

"That's right," Drake interrupted. "I'd forgotten about that."

"And the police," Mason said, "have no way of knowing when those fingerprints were made, whether they were made the night the body was discovered or the night the murder was committed."

Again Drake nodded.

"Now, then," Mason said, "we come to another peculiar phase of the case. Out in Della Street's apartment we found six empty cartridge cases. I'm satisfied they were the empty cartridge cases from the murder gun. For some reason the murderer had taken those away from the scene of the crime. I thought for a while it might have been a police plant, but it wasn't. Someone else must have planted the evidence."

"Who?"

Mason said, "It narrows down to two people. Veronica Dale was in the apartment and had an opportunity to plant the evidence, and so did Lorraine Ferrell. Veronica Dale had a much better and more favorable opportunity than Lorraine."

"Then one or the other of them must be guilty, Perry, and the way it looks now, it's probably Mrs. Ferrell."

"She was very anxious to see me for a while," Mason said, "and then suddenly she changed her mind. I think she was about to confess to me that she had gone out there the night of the murder. Then I think she changed her mind. And, of course, that business about just happening to see her husband's car on the street was sheer poppycock. She knew he wasn't on a vacation. She knew he'd bought that house. She'd had a bitter fight with him. She wanted Addison to investigate, find out what was happening and report to her. That would give her a corroborating witness and would make Addison partisan to her side of the case. That's probably one of the reasons she didn't tell him about her visit to her husband's country place the night of the quarrel. Another reason may well have been that she heard the sound of shots. Remember, the way the time element has to work out, she must either have met that other car coming down the driveway, or must have seen it turn in just as she was driving out. It's not too remote a guess to surmise she stopped her own car when she got to the highway and listened, may even have walked part way back. Anyhow, she wanted Addison to be her stalking horse. So she rang up Addison with this cock-and-bull story about the red-headed chick in the automobile. Incidentally, Paul, Della says Mrs. Ferrell's in love with John Addison.

"Could be, all right," Drake said.

"I know she's in love with him," Della Street said quietly. "I watched her eyes when she talked about him. I watched the expression of her face. I listened to the tone of her voice when she mentioned his name."

"Then she must be in pretty much of a stew with Addison in all this mess," Drake said.

"She is," Mason commented briefly.

"What about the dates, Perry?"

"Anything strike you as particularly significant about the dates taken for vacations in this case, Paul?"

"I don't get what you're driving at, Perry. Of course, it was a peculiar time for Ferrell to take a vacation to go on a fishing trip. Say, wait a minute, Perry! My gosh, this isn't trout fishing season!"

"Exactly," Mason said.

"Well, I'll be damned," Drake commented.

"Furthermore," Mason went on, "the vacation was to

be of two weeks' duration. Ferrell was to get back in time for one particularly important piece of business."

"What's that?" Drake asked. "I missed it."

It was Della Street who explained. "The annual stockholders' meeting."

Mason nodded, said, "Now notice something else rather peculiar. I ring up the department store and try to talk with the manager of the personnal department who is, incidentally, the treasurer of the corporation, Myrtle C. Northrup. What happens? I'm advised that she too has gone on her vacation. Rather a peculiar time to take vacations, don't you think?"

"What the heck!" Drake said. "What's going on here?"

Mason said, "Ferrell and Addison hated each other. They both owned an equal amount of stock. There were a few blocks of stock which had been distributed among the faithful employees of the store. Those employees ordinarily would never have taken sides. In fact, it was part of the policy of the heads of the company to refrain from discussing any matters of policy at the stockholders' meetings. The directors handled all of those, and Myrtle Northrup was the only person present at those directors' meetings. The other stockholders gave her their proxies."

"Say, what are you getting at?" Drake asked.

"I don't rightly know myself," Mason told him. "I'm simply calling your attention to significant facts. Now, then," Mason went on, "of all the people in this case, there's one phony, one person who took desperate chances in order to get something she wanted."

"Who?"

"The woman, whoever she was, who called on me in my office and said she was Laura Mae Dale, Veronica's mother."

"Who do you suppose she was?"

Mason said, "Let's look at it this way, Paul. Where do you suppose she got the information?"

"What information?"

"She knew that Veronica's mother was named Laura Mae Dale. She knew that the mother ran a restaurant in a small suburb of Indianapolis. She didn't know Veronica's correct age. She knew Veronica had a job at the department store and at what salary. Now, where could she have secured that much accurate information and yet had her erroneous information about the girl's age?"

"I don't know," Drake said.

"It must have been from Veronica herself," Della Street said.

Mason nodded.

Mason drove in silence for a few blocks, and both Della Street and Paul Drake were engrossed in their own thoughts as they tried to dovetail the facts Mason had presented into some logical pattern.

"But why on earth did this woman come to us with that story?" Della Street asked. "She must have known she was going to get exposed later on. She must have realized she was taking chances."

"All right," Mason said, "why *did* she come to us?"

"I don't get it. Unless she was mixed up with Eric Hansell the way you intimated."

"When I asked those questions," Mason said, "I wanted to look at Hansell's face. His face told me more than his answers. He's scared stiff, but he is, I think, frightened of something else. Probably, he has such a long list of blackmail on which there have been no prosecutions, he's afraid of that coming out."

Drake said, "Well, one thing's certain. Hansell and Veronica were standing in together with a blackmail racket. An examination of those license numbers, coupled with interviews from some fifty-two of the cars' owners, showed that nearly all of them made some substantial donation to Veronica, and one or two of them, who had put themselves in a position which might have been considered as compromising, paid blackmail. In every instance, Hansell walked in and collected."

"And, of course, made some settlement with Veronica," Mason said. "After all, you know Veronica *tried* to get arrested for vagrancy that night the police picked her up."

"Well, then," Drake said, "this other woman, this fake mother, is a part of the blackmailing ring. She . . ."

"But why did they need her?"

Drake grinned and said, "Be your age, Perry. They wanted a *mother* who could show righteous indignation, talk about the blasted good name of her daughter and then be willing to settle for a cash consideration."

"But they didn't need her in this case, and the other cases show there was no mother angle involved. Veronica let them pick her up, get fatherly; then Hansell showed up with the newspaper angle. In fact these men hadn't really done anything to Veronica. They wouldn't have been moved by any outraged-mother act. No, there's no slightest evidence to show this outfit had any accomplice. Just Hansell and Veronica working together, hitchhiking, making touches on a hard luck story and then, in proper cases, the blackmailing shakedown."

"What does that add up to, Perry?"

"That woman," Mason said, "came to me because she wanted something."

"Naturally."

"And," Mason went on, "the best way to determine what a person wants is by surveying what he gets."

"What did this woman get?"

"She got a receipt," Mason said, "showing that she had paid me one hundred and fifty dollars in full settlement for all charges in the case of the People versus Veronica Dale."

"And she paid you one hundred and fifty dollars?" Drake asked.

"No. She gave me a check for that amount. The check was no good. Yet she either wanted me to have that check or else she wanted the receipt—or both. Notice also, Paul, that the check was a single blank check with the name of the bank to be filled in. It had been torn from a pad of similar checks. Those are the sort of blank checks big firms have for the convenience of out-of-town customers who haven't their check books with them. This woman had torn a single check from such a pad."

Drake said, "You're going too fast for me, Perry. Why would she have done that? She must have known you wouldn't do anything more than accept the check for collection."

"She did it because she wanted me to have the check."

"Why, Perry?"

Mason said, "We've acted so far on the premise she was part of the blackmailing setup. That premise won't hold water. Let's try the other angle. Suppose she was trying to give me a defense to the blackmail. Suppose she wanted me to be able to say to Hansell, 'You're nuts. Addison didn't pay my fee. Veronica's mother did. There's the check to prove it.'"

Drake whistled.

Mason went on, "Now consider this. We have Ferrell taking a two weeks' vacation just before the stockholders' meeting to put across a super secret deal. We have Myrtle Northrup, the treasurer of the company, taking a similar vacation. Both vacations are at a very unusual time for vacations."

"But the Northrup woman hates Ferrell's guts and is loyal to Addison."

Mason merely nodded.

"And Ferrell had promised this red-headed chick to give her Myrtle Northrup's job, which certainly means that he was going to fire Myrtle Northrup."

"Or promote her," Mason said dryly, "so her job would be vacant."

Drake started thinking that over. Mason swung the wheel of the car.

"Hey," Drake said, "where are you going, Perry?"

Mason said, "We are about to call on Myrtle C. Northrup, Paul. And when we do, I think we'll find out something."

20

■

THE BRIGHT MORNING sunlight gilded the tall white buildings in the apartment house district.

Mason, bringing the car to a stop, said, "Okay, Paul, this is the place. Have your notebook ready, Della."

Mason led the way to the doorway of an apartment house, glanced at his wrist watch, said, "I'm afraid this is going to call for a pass key, Paul."

Drake grumblingly produced a small ring of pass keys.

"I wish you'd use more conventional methods, Perry."

"It's just the outer door of an apartment house," Mason said. "No one's going to say anything about that. It isn't as though you were getting into a private apartment."

Drake grudgingly tried his keys. The third one snapped back the lock.

"What's the number?" Drake asked as they walked down a corridor.

"Third floor," Mason said. "321."

The elevator rattled up to the third floor. Mason found Apartment 321, jabbed the button.

The door opened. An aroma of coffee and bacon greeted their nostrils. A woman, clad in a house coat, holding a morning newspaper in her hand, said, "I'm sorry I . . ."

What else she was going to say was cut off in a gasp of consternation.

Mason pushed the door open, said, "Come on in," and entered the apartment.

The trio filed in. Paul Drake and Della Street followed Mason. Drake kicked the door shut.

Della Street, moving unobtrusively, slipped over to the table where an electric coffee percolator was bubbling, seated herself by an electric toaster, opened her shorthand notebook and unscrewed the cap from the pen.

Mason said, "Perhaps I'd better introduce you folks. This is Paul Drake, head of the Drake Detective Agency, and this, Paul, is Myrtle C. Northrup, holder of a small block of stock in the corporation that owns the department store on Broadway. The last time I saw her, she was masquerading as the mother of Veronica Dale —and I think Mrs. Northrup is going to tell us just what happened out there at Ferrell's country place the night he was killed. I think it'll be better for you, Mrs. Northrup."

The woman, her face a sickly yellow beneath her make-up, moved slowly backwards, as though hoping that by some magic a hole would open in the wall and enable her to disappear.

Mason said, "I guess you thought that I wouldn't find you, Mrs. Northrup. After all, you left rather a broad trail. As the person who was in charge of the personnel department, you have given Veronica Dale a job at Mr. Addison's request. You, therefore, knew her background as well as the salary she was to get. When you interviewed her, she had filled out a card giving her age, the name of her mother, and a few other matters which enabled you to pose as the girl's mother when you came to my office.

"You were just about the only person who could have had that combination of correct and incorrect information at that time.

"And, quite apparently, you were working with Ferrell to form a coalition of stockholders that would have enough stock to control the corporation at the stockholders' meeting on the twenty-fifth. Now, suppose you tell us what went wrong."

"I don't know what you're talking about," she said defiantly.

Mason grinned. "You won't deny that you came to

my office and said you wanted to pay Veronica Dale's bill for legal services? My secretary and my receptionist can both identify you."

"No," she said slowly, "I won't deny that."

"*Why* did you do it?"

"I . . . I had a peculiar idea that I could save Mr. Addison from being blackmailed."

"How did you know he was being blackmailed?"

"I happened to have some business which took me to Mr. Ferrell's office, and while I was in there I heard this conversation in Mr. Addison's office. I could tell someone was threatening him. I went to the door and listened. I heard this—this despicable character call him *Fatso!*"

"So then you listened to the whole thing?"

She nodded.

"And came to me to pose as Veronica Dale's mother, so I'd have a worthless check signed Laura Mae Dale, which I could show the blackmailer?"

"I thought that might help."

Mason said, "All right, you've admitted that readily enough because you realize I have witnesses who can identify you. Now, what do you have to say about going to Mr. Ferrell's house out in the country?"

"I know nothing whatever about any house in the country. I didn't go out there."

Mason grinned and said, "Witnesses say you did."

"They are mistaken."

"The witnesses, in this case," Mason said, "are fingerprints which you left out there and which police have recovered. You can't dodge the evidence of those fingerprints, Mrs. Northrup."

"*My* fingerprints?" she said in dismay.

"Sure," Mason said. "You haven't had any experience at being a crook; therefore, you forgot all about your fingerprints."

"How . . . how do they know they're mine?"

"*They* don't. *I* do. But all they have to do is to take your fingerprints and compare them with the fingerprints that were found in the house. Then you'll have to tell them why you went out there and what you did while

214

you were out there. You'd better begin by telling me."

She thought that over for a few moments, then said quietly, "I guess I'm licked."

Mason nodded.

The resistance seemed to ooze out of the woman. She said, "I guess you know it all already. I'm glad. I couldn't have stuck it out, anyway."

"I'd like to hear the details," Mason said, "particularly about the shooting."

She went to a clothes closet, opened the door, took out a heavy coat. There was a powder burn and a jagged hole in the cloth.

"Go ahead," Mason said, "you may as well make a clean breast of it."

"Believe me, Mr. Mason, I want to! I want to get it off my chest. It's been preying on my mind. I didn't get to sleep until four o'clock this morning. That's why I'm so late getting breakfast."

The lawyer's nod was sympathetic.

She said, "It's so simple, the wonder of it is someone didn't find out about it before. I knew I couldn't get away with it."

"Just tell us," Mason said, glancing at Della Street to see that she was taking down what was said.

"It started out," Myrtle Northrup said, "when I began to play the ponies. I had a system. I felt sure it was an infallible system, but it went haywire. I thought it was a temporary setback. I dipped into company funds. Ferrell was always fooling around with his charts and graphs and audits. It was simply a way he had of wasting time.

"He owned forty per cent of the stock. Addison owns forty per cent. The remaining twenty per cent is scattered around among the old time employees of the store who are in responsible positions. It's always been a matter of policy for the two heavy stockholders, or the partners, as they call themselves, to thresh out all the matters of policy between themselves and present a harmonious front at the meetings. Therefore, the stockholders' meetings have always been, more or less, a matter of formality."

She paused to take a cigarette from a package and light it with a trembling hand.

"Well," she said, "Ferrell caught me. He put it up to me. I had to sign a confession. I had to agree that I would vote my stock the way he wanted me to. And, as a matter of form, nearly all the little stockholders mail proxies to me so I can vote them at the meetings. Then through me, Ferrell started approaching the one or two who usually came to the meetings. There was a girl down at the fountain pen counter, Merna Raleigh, who had a few shares of stock. He was going to promise her a big boost and a salary raise, and there was my boy friend, Tom: Thomas P. Barrett. In order to keep from being prosecuted on my shortage, I had to agree to swing Tom into line.

"Ferrell took this house out in the country so that he would have a place to work, getting all the stock transfers and agreements and everything lined up so he could walk into the stockholders' meeting and control it."

"Isn't Merna Raleigh rather young to have been in on that stock distribution?"

"She inherited the stock from her mother. Her mother worked in the store for years."

"So what happened?" Mason asked.

She said, "On Tuesday Ferrell was supposed to leave on his vacation. He didn't go anywhere. He went out to that house and started opening up his headquarters. He had told me to be out there a little before nine Tuesday night and to have Tom with me.

"I didn't tell Tom what was in the wind. We drove out there in Tom's car. Just before we turned off the highway, we passed a car going out. That was Mrs. Ferrell, although at the time I didn't know who it was."

"Then what happened?" Mason asked.

"When we got to the house, I left Tom outside in the car. I went in to talk with Ferrell. That was the way we'd planned it. Tom didn't even know what it was all about or why he was out there. I was to sound Tom out on the road out and see how he'd feel about tagging along with us, the understanding, of course, being that when Ferrell got into control, he'd put Addison out of the managing position into a subordinate position and give Tom, Merna, and me responsible positions at a great salary increase. Also I was to get my confession of shortage back, and the shortage was to be covered up."

"And what actually happened when you went out there?" Mason asked.

"I found Ferrell in a very nervous state. He told me he'd picked up a little blonde girl named Veronica Dale, that she was running away from the humdrum life of a small town where her mother ran a restaurant. He had taken pity on her and told her that if she'd come out to the house and wait while he transacted a little business, he'd take her into the city and see she had a place to stay."

"Did he intend to do it?"

"*I* don't know," she said. "Perhaps he thought he could talk her into staying there in the house overnight. Perhaps he did intend to take her in. Ferrell was something of a wolf when the breaks came just right. I know that he was making awkward passes at Merna."

"Go ahead," Mason said. "What happened?"

"He told me that in some way his wife had found out about that country place, that she'd driven out there and unfortunately had caught Veronica there, that he'd told Veronica to duck out the back door, but his wife had seen her. His wife thought it was a love nest and was going to get a divorce with all the resulting publicity and scandal. He was afraid at the time to tell his wife the real purpose of the place because he felt she wouldn't believe him."

"So what did you do?" Mason said.

"So, he told me he'd been thinking the thing over, that the only thing to do was to go right back to town and go to his wife, that he was going to show his wife my confession, that he was going to have me go along and that I was going to tell his wife the real purpose of that place, and we'd trust to the fact that his wife would keep the thing secret. He said it was the only thing to do. He told me to go back out and tell Tom to go home and we'd start right after Tom left."

"And you did that?"

"I went to Tom and told him to go home and say nothing about having been out there. Then Mr. Ferrell went upstairs to get that confession I'd signed. He had it in his suitcase in an upstairs bedroom. He intended, of course, to use that as a prop to bolster his story to his wife. But when I saw the confession—well, I thought I should have something too. So I told him if I was going to co-operate with him the way he wanted, I wanted it understood that my confession was to be torn up and my shortage would be taken care of no matter whether the stock deal worked out or not. That made him angry. We had a lot of words and I don't know what in the world ever possessed me, but his suitcase was lying there and this gun was on top of the suitcase. He was holding the confession in his hand. I grabbed up the gun and pointed it at him and told him to give me that confession. I knew as soon as I'd done it, I'd made a terrible mistake."

"What happened?"

"He hit me, and when he hit me, the gun went off. That's the bullet that went through the window. Then he grappled with me. He bent my arm back. The folds of my coat were over my wrist and when he twisted my hand back, he twisted the finger against the trigger.

"I screamed with pain and yelled for him to stop, but he kept twisting the arm, and the gun went off. The bullet went through my coat and into his head. He fell over and I guess he died instantly. I suppose it was because the coat was over the barrel of the gun that there were no powder burns on his face.

"I was in a panic. I wanted to get rid of the gun and of the shells. I just didn't think, and then I don't know very much about such things anyway. I opened the window and fired all the rest of the bullets down into the ground. Then I took the empty shells out of the gun and put them in my pocket. I wiped the gun clean, threw it as far as I could into the darkness and then realized I was stranded with a corpse. I put the window back down, turned out the gasoline lantern and the oil lamps downstairs.

"I had to get out of there and get out fast. I thought of hitchhiking, but I didn't want to do that because I might have some trouble. I'm not young and good-looking like Veronica is. And I didn't want to leave a back trail."

"So what did you do?"

"So, I knew that Mr. Ferrell had told everyone at the store he was going up to the Northwest on his vacation. I got in his car and drove it to Las Vegas, Nevada, filed a telegram which was to be sent, and signed Ferrell's name to it. I left the car and caught a plane back. I went into the store just as though nothing had happened. I was late but no one thought anything about that because I was free to keep my own hours. I didn't have any time clock to punch.

"Late that afternoon Veronica Dale came in with a card from Mr. Addison. I knew right away that she was the hitchhiker that had been out there in the house with Mr. Ferrell, and I realized then that Addison must have been out there and must have picked up Veronica Dale. I asked her a few questions under the pretense of giving her an aptitude test, and she told me quite a bit about herself and about how she had met Mr. Addison. She was putting on an act of baby-faced innocence.

"I gave her the job, of course, and had all the information about her age and about the name of her mother. I also had those six empty shells which were burning a hole in my pocket, and I was terribly angry at the smug hypocrisy of that baby-faced little bitch."

"But you didn't do anything that day?"

"No, it wasn't until the next day. I was in Mr. Ferrell's office and the door was open just a crack. His office adjoins that of Mr. Addison. I heard Hansell giving him a blackmail shakedown, and I knew right then that blonde hussy was in with a ring of blackmailers, and they were trying to stick Mr. Addison. You know, I always admired Mr. Addison, and, Lord, how I hated to turn against him with a rat like Edgar Ferrell. I guess that was one of the reasons I went so crazy trying to get that confession back."

"Go on," Mason said.

"I have always admired Mr. Addison. I respect him.

219

I think all the employees do. I thought that if I could get over to your office quickly enough, pretend I was Veronica's mother and pay the lawyer's fees, that would give Mr. Addison a defense to the blackmail. I thought I'd come back then and tell him what I'd done."

"Go on," Mason said.

"So I dashed over there and pretended to be Veronica's mother, left you a worthless check so you could show it to the blackmailer. I thought that might confuse him, and that if Veronica thought her mother was out here—well, it might nip that little blackmail scheme of theirs. I knew you wouldn't lose anything because of the forged check and I felt neither Veronica nor the blackmailer would ever know it was a forgery."

Mason nodded.

She said, "I took the receipt that you gave me and then, all of a sudden, decided to go tell Veronica that I was wise to her, that she could lay off of Mr. Addison or face the consequences, and frighten her so she'd skip out. Then I thought that when—well, you know, when Mr. Ferrell's body was discovered, it would look as though this little blonde trick had been with him and—well, had done the job. And then I thought that she could squirm out of it with that baby-faced innocence of hers. She could get on the stand and tell a jury that he had attacked her and she had to shoot him in self-denfese."

"You did some pretty quick thinking," Mason said. "What did you do after you left my office?"

She said, "I went over to see Veronica. Veronica wasn't in the hotel as yet, because she was still working in the department store. They'd put her to work immediately in the hosiery department.

"Of course, Mr. Mason, I had those six shells. They were burning a hole in my pocket. I didn't know what to do with them. I was frightened to death. They represented evidence. Well, I went over to the hotel to wait for Veronica. And then I got a bright idea. I went up to Veronica's room and tried the door. It wasn't open but there was a chambermaid on the floor. She saw me and I told her I was Veronica's mother. I showed her the receipt that you had signed to prove it, and the maid, on the strength of that receipt, my story and a dollar tip, opened the door and let me in. I planted the shells in the bottom of Veronica's little suitcase where I didn't think she'd find them, and then I went back and waited for nature to take its course. I felt sure that the police would give Veronica a shakedown, would examine her bag, would find the empty shells, and then I thought—well, I thought that would put her on the defensive and give her something to think of and—well, that's all of it."

"And Veronica," Mason said, "played the cards close to her chin, found the shells, realized what they were, took them out and planted them in the apartment of my secretary."

"No!" Myrtle Northrup said. "Why, that two-timing little . . ."

"Save it," Mason said. "You have your own troubles to think of now."

"Darned if I haven't," she said.

Mason walked over to the telephone, picked up the receiver, and said, "Get me police headquarters, if you will, please. This is an emergency call."

Paul Drake sighed, walked over to the table and poured himself a cup of coffee from the electric percolator.

21

∎

MASON, Della Street, and Paul Drake lined up at the lunch counter in a drugstore.

"Give," Paul Drake said.

Mason poured cream in his cup of coffee, dumped in sugar and said, wearily, "It all came from falling for a plausible police theory, Paul. The facts of the case stuck out like a sore thumb, but because I thought that shot had been fired from the outside, through that window, I passed up every really significant clue. Since those clues didn't fit in with that theory of the case, I ignored them."

"What were the significant clues?"

"You know most of them," Mason said. "The woman who came to my office wasn't Veronica's mother. Yet she had information that could only have been received from Veronica, and if she wasn't Veronica's mother, she was obviously trying to save Addison. Therefore, it must, of necessity, have been some loyal employee of Addison's store. There was only one employee who would have had those facts that soon, and that was the woman who was in charge of the personnal department. And I had you rushing all around the city trying to find the woman who posed as Veronica's mother when a little real thought would have told me who and where she was.

"Then I fell for all that stuff about Ferrell leaving on a vacation just as everyone else did. But I began to feel uneasy when I heard Myrtle Northrup had left on a vacation at the same time. It wasn't until later I realized the significance of the fact that both of them were going to be away until the day of the stockholders' meeting. As a lawyer I realized the danger of Addison's position so far as control of his own company was concerned as soon as he told me of the corporate setup. He told me himself that he hated Ferrell. Therefore, it was pretty certain Ferrell knew of that feeling and hated him. I realized that if one of the partners wanted to be a little unscrupulous, resort to a little pressure, and a little bribery, it would be a relatively easy matter to get control of the stock. But because there had always been a policy of threshing everything out outside of the presence of the employees who were stockholders, apparently the idea never occurred to Addison. It occurred to Ferrell all right, and it occurred to me. But for the moment it didn't seem to tie in with the murder . . . Oh, what's the use? It was all caused because I fell for the police theory and relied on the false premise that the shot must have been fired from the outside of the house, through the window, and into Ferrell's head. It simply shows how much damage a false premise can do."

"Yes," Della Street said demurely, "look at Addison's premise about his little virgin. At that, the man was right when he first rang us up. It would have been pretty difficult for the police to make a vagrant out of a virgin."

"As difficult," Mason said grinning, "as it was for Addison to make a virgin out of a vagrant."

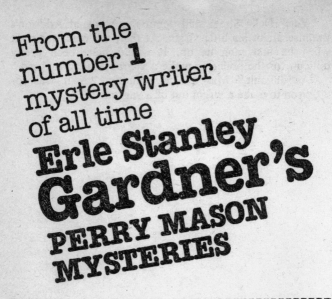